FALSE
IMPRESSIONS

FALSE IMPRESSIONS

Copyright © 2008 by Dr. Stanley Woods-Frankel, D.D.S.

Excerpt of "Death" from *Posthumous Poems of Percy Bysshe Shelley* by Percy Bysshe Shelley. Original Publication, 1824 by John and Henry L. Hunt. Copyright is Public Domain.

Cover Design Copyright © 2012 by The Zharmae Publishing Press, L.L.C.

For more information, to inquire about rights to this or other works, or to purchase copies for special educational, business, or sales promotional uses please write to:

The Zharmae Publishing Press, L.L.C.
ATTN: Marketing & Sales/Rights Mgr.
1827 West Shannon Avenue
Spokane, Washington 99205
www.zharmae.com

FIRST EDITION

Printed in the United States of America

Zharmae, the Zharmae logo, and the TZPP logo are trademarks of The Zharmae Publishing Press, L.L.C.

ISBN: 978-1-937365-04-2 (pbk.)

10 9 8 7 6 5 4 3 2 1

To Herb.

I hope you

enjoy False

Impression

Stanley Woods-Imbel

FALSE

IMPRESSIONS

STANLEY
WOODS-FRANKEL

Zharmæ

Spokane, Washington

To:

The astonishing, talented singer and poet,
Elayna Woods, my lifetime muse and
ultimate editor.

And:

To my three beautiful daughters
and their gang.

Acknowledgement

Colonel William M. Morlang, D.D.S. Diplomate of the American Board of Forensic Odontology, who got me started on my forensic journey.

Neal Riesner, D.D.S. Diplomate of the A.B.F.O., Forensic Dentistry Chief Medical Examiner, Westchester County, New York.

Vincent Furano, D.D.S. Consultant, NYPD Homicide, Missing Persons, and Arson Unit.

Jeff Burke, D.D.S. Diplomate of the A.B.F.O., Former Chief of Forensic Dentists, New York City, New York.

Howard Glazer, D.D.S. Diplomate of the A.B.F.O., Chief of Forensic Dentists at 9/11 site.

Amy Kapatkin, D.V.M., Associate Veterinarian, Bronx Zoo, New York City, New York.

Sally McPherson, Former Editor, City Island Current, and the editor who kicked my tail into gear.

Special kudos to the members of the American Society of Forensic Odontology, and to my brother and sister authors at the Mystery Writers of America.

Stanley Woods-Frankel

Anna McDermott, my Goddess of how to put the finishing touches on a novel, and the rest of the gang, Suzanne and Travis Grundy at Zharmae Publishing.

The advice I received from the forensic and veterinary experts was spot on, however, I did fudge a few times in order to enhance the story and make it a more interesting read. I take full responsibility for whatever mistakes might have been made

Stanley Woods-Frankel
New York City, New York
January, 2012

FALSE
IMPRESSIONS

Death

Death is here and death is there,

Death is busy everywhere,

All around, within, beneath,

Above is death—and we are death.

—Percy Bysshe Shelley

1

Steve Landau

A three-hundred and fifty pound Bengal tiger lay motionless on a stainless steel table, mouth agape. His orange and black coat contrasted sharply with the stark, white-tiled operating room. A Bach sonata played softly on a portable stereo. Outside, gale-force winds drove horizontal sheets of rain against the stained-glass windows, periodically overpowering the music. A blend of antiseptic and musky animal scents wafted up to the rafters of the high arched ceiling.

Steven Landau, D.D.S., in a white operating gown, leaned over the head of the unconscious cat. His gloved hand moved deftly while he performed a root canal on the tiger's prodigious canine tooth. Nancy Gill, his nurse, also in white, stood on the opposite side of the table, retracting the lip of the huge predator.

"Ready for the number forty, Nance." Landau handed her the instrument he had been manipulating.

Nancy's almond eyes widened as she passed him the largest circular file from a sterile bracket table. "I still can't get used to the size of these monsters, compared to the ones we use in the office."

"Different strokes for different folks," Steve's fingers were obscured as he moved the file up and down within the canal of the outsized tooth.

"Ready to fill?" Nancy asked.

"You bet. I wasn't sure I could complete this sucker. I was barely able to reach the apex, even with the forty. I'd hate to be at the working end of this baby when he's awake and hungry."

Nancy crinkled her freckled nose and nodded vigorously. "I still get goose-bumps when I think about last year, when Peter the wolf came out of anesthesia before we were through, and tried to huff and puff us down."

Steve chuckled.

Speaking of working, when the hell do I get my next raise?" Nancy suctioned, while Steve irrigated the canal.

"What're you talking about? I just gave you one."

"That was a year and a half ago."

"No kidding!"

"I don't kid about salaries. I swear you're getting cheaper than Jack Benny."

"Jack who?"

"You sure you're older than me? He was the comedian, who had a radio show, with a running gag about being a miser. The best one I heard on my mother's old recording was when a mugger told him, 'your money or your life.' Benny said, 'I'm thinking, I'm thinking.'" Nancy handed Steve an opened pack of cotton points.

Steve looked at her over the point of the canine. "What's a radio show?"

"There are times you sound like a nerdy deprived teen."

Steve smiled behind his surgical mask. He remembered how naïve and rabbit-shy Nancy had been when he first hired her straight out of Catholic school. She couldn't finish a complete sentence without stammering, and her eyes would practically bug out of her sockets after one of his colorful conversations with his dental lab. After the first few months of her training, Steve had feared the crimson blush that periodically spread over her heart-shaped face might become a permanent condition. Now, after ten years, she was always two steps ahead of him and could out swear a teamster stuck in

2

a traffic jam. He inserted a cotton point to dry the prepared canal. "I thought my varied practice would be enough reward," he said.

"Ha! That'll be the day." Nancy handed Steve a college plier with a cement coated number forty gutta-percha point locked at the tip. "I'm at the butt-end of a lot of jokes by all my wise-ass friends. They never know where to reach me. If I'm not in the office, I'm here in the zoo, or in court, or in jail—and then, of course, there's my favorite place, the damn morgue, where I freeze my tush off." She crossed her hands over her chest and shivered to emphasize the point, then handed Steve a heated plugger.

"Quit complaining. I bought you a down jacket, didn't I?"

"What a sport. Hey, I hope you're finishing up."

"What's the rush? Got a big date tonight?"

"Yeah, and it'll be with Tony the Tiger, if you don't get cracking. He just winked at me."

Steve quickly completed the root canal with the same material he used on human teeth, and closed the access opening with a white composite filling. He opened the door and motioned to the two attendants waiting outside.

"Okay, guys, you can take our striped friend back to his cage to sleep it off."

"Hey, Doc," Nick, the attendant in charge, said, "How come you're always playin' this kinda music whenever you do these root canals?" Nick's dialect seemed appropriate here in the Bronx Zoo, which now had a new, but seldom used name: The International Wildlife Conservation Park.

Steve peeled off his latex gloves. "Bach's our man for root canals, Surgery gets Beethoven; for gums or periodontal work, we play jazz; and we rock n' roll during emergencies."

Nick shrugged. "Anyone crazy 'nough to work on the biggest tooth of our largest cat should listen to whaddever he wants."

Steve was toweling his hands in the O.R. scrub room when Nancy stuck her head in. "The Medical Examiner's Office, line two."

Steve picked up the washroom extension. "Dr. Landau here."

"It's Barbara from the M.E.'s office. Doctor O'Brien requests your presence at a crime scene."

3

"An on-site call? What's up?"

"The Doctor told me not to discuss it with you. He wants your unbiased opinion."

"Where is he?"

"336 East 61st Street, off York, apartment 30A."

"I'm on my way."

"Problem?" Nancy placed the last of the root canal instruments into the sterilizer.

"Pack my forensic kit, Nance. I have a murder scene consult. What's it been, nine months since the last one?"

Nancy nodded. "Hope you don't expect me to go. I really do have a heavy date tonight."

"You're clear. Who's the lucky guy?"

"His name's Tony and he better be a tiger."

"What happened to Joe?"

"Went back to his wife."

"I'm not going to say I told you so."

"Look who's giving Dear Abby advice." She handed Steve his forensic bag. "Last I heard, your batting average with the opposite sex is like zero for ten."

"Ouch," Steve called from the doorway. "See you in the a.m., by the way, add twenty-five to your paycheck tomorrow." He smiled as he closed the door.

Nancy thrust her fist in the air. "Yes!"

The rain had not let up when Steve folded his six-four frame into his Porsche for the drive downtown. After plowing through a mini lake on the Bruckner Expressway he said a silent prayer for not using the Harley today. He turned onto East 61st Street, parked in between two blue and whites in front of a stony high rise, and turned the visor down to display his NYPD permit. He flashed his police ID at the doorman and took the elevator to the thirtieth floor. Tenants stood in groups, whispering in the corridor when he

4

stepped into the hallway. *Typical,* he thought, *takes a murder to get neighbors together in the Big Apple.*

Steve recognized the detective questioning a nervous, middle-aged couple in front of the door next to 30A and waved before he ducked under the yellow crime-scene tape to enter the apartment. A squat man in overalls was spraying gray powder on a kitchen counter, and then bent over to stare at the smudged surface through his thick glasses.

"O'Brien?" Steve asked.

Without lifting his head, the technician pointed to a doorway. Steve turned and a camera flash temporarily blinded him.

He blinked, and was aware his palms had become moist and his heart rate had shifted into high gear as he crossed the living room. He thought, *I've headed DMORT teams on two airline crashes, and identified hundreds of mutilated bodies. Why the hell, do I get so worked up over a murder scene?* He continued to rub his eyes and stopped at the doorway. He took a deep breath to steel himself, but still came close to giving up his lunch at the scene that greeted him.

The naked body of a woman lay sprawled on a queen-sized bed. Puddles of un-coagulated blood haloed her head. Sprayed droplets randomly filled the padded headboard. Shiny red-stained blotches covered the walls, and dripped off the mattress to form scarlet pools on the carpet. Her throat looked as if it had been ripped out. The trachea and inner muscles of her throat hung out of the gaping hole. Dark clots matted her blonde hair to form a sickening blend of crimson and ash yellow. Her contorted face was frozen in a mask of pain, and tinted in the pale blue of death.

Steve swallowed a mouthful of bile.

Dr. John O'Brien, the potbellied medical examiner, knelt between her spread legs, as if engaged in a ritual sex act. The overhead light reflected off his cue-ball-sized bald spot as he withdrew a swab from her vagina with his gloved hand and transferred it to a plastic container. When O'Brien moved away from the corpse, Steve saw why he had been called. In the center of the abdomen, where her navel should have been, was a gaping, elliptical hole. The edges of the wound seemed consistent with a human bite. The oozing crater mesmerized Steve. He was barely aware of the technicians and detectives in the room.

"So, what's up, Doc?" one of the detectives asked the medical examiner.

"The perpetrator was either royally pissed off, wacko, or starving," O'Brien said.

The cops laughed.

Steve grimaced. He never understood gallows humor. He knew the homicide officers used it to mask the uneasiness they felt for the horrors they had to confront, but he couldn't get past the fact that the beautiful young woman they were gathered around had been a living, breathing human a few hours earlier. She was someone's daughter, a family member who possessed a history and once had a future, but it had been snuffed out, just like that. No tomorrow, only an obituary.

O'Brien turned, and spotting Steve, changed his tack. "What do you think, Steve?"

"Looks like a bite, probably human. I'll take impressions and let you know as soon as I can."

"If it is, we got ourselves the Dizzy Dean of weirdo killers. I'm out of here. I have to get the blood work and DNA samples started."

O'Brien packed his gear while Steve opened his case and snapped on a pair of latex gloves. The police photographer kneeled next to the bed and snapped his last shot.

"I got good close-up shots of the wound Doc, different angles, in black and white, color, and ultraviolet. I'll have the prints ready tomorrow," he said.

Steve preferred the contrasting illumination of ultraviolet light and the photographer knew it after they had worked on a tough bite-mark case the year before.

"Make sure you print the direct shots on a one-to-one ratio, or I'm dead meat in court," Steve reminded him.

"How come you always bust my balls over the ratio?" the photographer asked.

"Cause if we get lucky enough and catch this sicko, I have to convince the good people of New York, who have been plucked from the jury pool for a homicide case, that he's our man. I do, this by matching up the models of his teeth, with your prints of the wound. If it's not one-to-one, any defense attorney worth his salt would gobble me up and spit out my remains."

"I wouldn't let a lawyer jerk your chain, Doc. You might not use Novocain the next time I'm in your chair. Adios, amigo."

Once in charge of the body, Steve opened his bag and removed the supplies he had devised to fit the unique needs of his specialty. On a large pad he squeezed out a ten-inch roll of impression material and matched it with the same amount of accelerator. Next, he picked up a packet that resembled an oversized sausage, removed the wrapper and kneaded it until it looked like a large omelet. He placed it over the wound and the surrounding area to form a tray. With the excess, he fashioned a handle on the top. When the substance conformed to the contours of the abdomen, he switched on a portable ultraviolet light and directed it at the light-sensitive tray. It hardened in thirty seconds. He sprayed the inside with adhesive, and after it dried, mixed the lines of base and accelerator impression material, filled the tray, and placed it over the wound. After two minutes, he removed the set impression to reveal a perfect negative imprint of the site. The familiar routine calmed the fluttering in his stomach.

Steve packed his satchel while the coroner's men zipped the victim into a black nylon body bag, and loaded it onto a gurney. He accompanied them on the elevator ride to the lobby. No one spoke. Steve unlocked his car while the attendants slid the body into a waiting morgue ambulance. Too numb to move, he leaned against the Porsche, and watched the flashing lights disappear before he climbed into the driver's seat.

As he drove the wet streets to his Greenwich Village office, he reflected on how he'd come to perform root canals on tigers and take impressions of wounds on mutilated corpses. It was not what he had in mind as a student in dental school.

He felt a tinge of guilt that he had not told his retired parents in Florida, that private patients were no longer his main source of income.

He still maintained a small practice, but only on two weekdays and Saturdays. The rest of the week he examined bite marks, identified skeletons, and treated the residents of the Bronx Zoo.

As he eased around a fender-bender in front of the Chrysler Building, he began to dwell on the accidental turning point which motivated him to

7

become a dentist. He often thought about it, and could reconstruct the event almost moment-to-moment.

He was sixteen, waiting for his mother in the reception room of the family dentist, Dr. Jack Feinberg, a sweet, gentle man with an offbeat sense of humor.

The doctor opened the door and said, "My assistant's out with the flu today Steve. How about helping me do some dental work on your mother?"

"Cool!" He almost tripped over himself rushing through the waiting room.

Dr. Feinberg led him into his treatment room. His mother, already anesthetized, sat in the dental chair. "Your mom's missing these teeth," he pointed to her X-rays mounted on a viewfinder. "We're going to replace them by preparing the teeth on either side for crowns, and then make a bridge by connecting them to the false teeth."

Steve nodded enthusiastically. His mother smiled up at him through numb, lopsided lips.

"I'm so nervous," she said thickly.

Dr. Feinberg smiled. "Not to worry, Mrs. Landau, as long as I stay calm."

His mother shot Steve one of her looks. "You may be my only child, but if you hurt me, I'll sic your father on you."

Steve laughed. He knew the worst his father would do, was have an intense conversation with him about the Mets.

"And," his mother continued, "your allowance will go through a serious depression."

This time, Dr. Feinberg laughed, but Steve gritted his teeth.

The gentle, caring way in which Dr. Feinberg performed the exacting dental procedures made a lasting impression on Steve. He remembered how clear his future had become after he left the office with his mother grinning ear to ear with her new smile.

"Must be a night for nostalgia," he said softly to himself, as the slanting rain sparkled in the headlights, "murder scene must have jogged my memory." A Fifth Avenue bus splattered a wall of water over the windshield, which jump-started his reminiscing again. He pictured the torrential downpour that had greeted his arrival at Keesler Air Force Base in Biloxi, Mississippi, after he had been drafted following four grueling years of dental school.

A Gypsy cab cut him off, bringing him back to the present. He stopped at a red light at Sheridan Square, and looked in the rear-view mirror at his dark brown eyes, set a little too close to his patrician nose, before he concentrated on his straight black hair. "Almost long enough for a ponytail," he said to his image. "Sure beats the nerdy crew cuts I wore back in the Air Force. It was cool being an officer, but I sure as hell was no gentleman."

He broke into a broad grin when he recalled the besotted, raucous melee at the Keesler Officer's Club, when he and his fifteen fellow dentists were automatically promoted to captains.

The light changed, and a truck honked, breaking his reverie. His mood changed abruptly when he thought, *Shit! The promotion party was where I met Carol Ann.*

He clenched his jaws, rammed the gear shift into first, and rabbited the Porsche onto Bleecker Street.

2

Carol Ann

Steve had downed his fifth tequila shooter at the bar of the Keesler Officers Club with the other celebrants to start their promotion party. He was licking salt off the back of his hand, when two attractive, well built blondes in matching miniskirts and low-cut sweaters walked into the room. They smiled at him through ruby lips. He broke away from his buddies and concentrated on walking a straight line toward them.

He had been a little shy in High School due to self-conscious doubts about his nose, and that his ribs were so obvious in his basketball jersey. He couldn't do much about his beak-like snout, but at the coach's recommendation he started to lift weights. By the end of his senior year, the cheerleaders began to look at him in a different way. At Syracuse University his basketball prowess increased as did his social skills which led to two semiserious relationships, and later, another more serious one with a dental hygienist in Dental School. None of them lasted, but his confidence had ratcheted up, and he looked forward to new adventures in the service.

"Hey!" he had said through concrete lips. "You twins look terrific in those shorrt skirts. Wha's your names?"

"Carol Ann, but..."

"Whish one's Carol?"

"Captain, if ya'll would uncross your eyes, ya'll would see there's no one else here 'cept lil' ol' me."

When he finally was able to focus on her, he couldn't help but notice her major league cleavage, plus model's legs, that never seemed to end, and a face that reminded him of the old movie star Betty Grable.

He was hooked as much as any trout would be on a dancing jitterbug lure.

Their affair began as a stock pot of simmering spices, which quickly boiled over into a torrid Cajun feast.

Despite all their deeply ingrained differences they married six months later. Their wedding at the Officer's Club was the highlight of the Biloxi social season. Carol Ann's daddy, a shrimp boat captain, didn't appear too happy with his daughter's choice and acted like a jealous suitor. Steve overheard him complaining to his wife, "There's a shit load of eligible good ol' boys around here. Why in hell, did she have to hitch up with a goddamn Yankee Jew?"

Steve's parents took their first plane ride to attend, and when they were introduced to Carol Ann at the New Orleans airport, Steve's father Lou Landau took his son aside and whispered, "Nice going Champ, she's a hottie. Does she have any sisters?"

Steve punched Lou on the shoulder, but it soon became apparent his mother wasn't thrilled with his bride-to-be. The two women looked as if they were circling each other in anticipation of the big bout. Ann Landau kept shooting tiny, under the radar, but piercing barbs at every opportunity, while Carol Ann smiled graciously and used all her Southern charm to deflect them.

He remembered Carol Ann's laugh had been like wind chimes. Now, if something tickled her, his ex-wife sounded like a wounded screech owl.

The previous women in his life had all been released from the same mold. Tall, lithe, not too much chest, short dark hair, Semitic backgrounds, and noses. Who'd have thought, this luscious Southern Baptist blonde bombshell in her red hot-pants would turn out to be the Queen of Ice, and turn off any thought of sex during their last year of marriage.

11

Jesus! My life has taken some weird turns, he thought as he pulled into the parking garage around the corner from his office. After the divorce, he had sold his practice and bought a brownstone on a tree-lined, West Greenwich Village street. He had set up an office and a small studio apartment on the first floor, and rented the upper stories to two artists. On nights like this, when he was too tired for the drive to his one indulgence, a forty-five foot sailboat docked at City Island, he slept in his studio.

He dragged up the steps of the brownstone, went directly to his laboratory, and stopped for a moment to survey his domain. He had designed his office, unlike most traditional dental offices to accommodate the needs of his unorthodox practice. The lab was three times the size of each treatment room.

He opened his case and removed the impression he had taken of the victim's abdomen. He rotated it in his hand and studied the green material, but was brought up short when he spotted splotches of dried blood on the edges. He slammed his hand on the lab bench as he thought of the mutilated image of the young blonde woman.

"If I have anything to do with capturing you, you sick mother fucker, I'll make sure you never get a chance to use your teeth again," he bellowed in to the empty lab.

His emotions cooled slowly as he mixed a batch of dental stone and vibrated it into the impression. While he waited for the model to set, he washed the strainer for his espresso machine, filled it with an ounce of finely ground espresso beans, poured water into the reservoir, and turned it on. He checked the stone models and estimated they still needed another twenty minutes for the final set. He removed the steaming cup from the espresso maker and called his marina neighbor.

"Hey, Agatha, I need a favor."

"Let me guess! You want me to take Captain Bill for the night."

"You must be a psychic."

"Bullshit! It's the only reason you ever call me."

"That's not true. I called you last week when I ran out of ice."

"You're all heart. I can't take your cat tonight."

"Hey, if it's the ice, I'll buy you a bag —"

"It's not the ice, you testosterone turkey. I have a guest tonight and she's allergic."

Steve snorted. "Tanya the veterinarian?"

"Don't ever mention her name again!" Agatha said stiffly. "My new friend is Jill, she's a computer analyst."

Steve almost choked on his espresso. "Jesus, Aggie, a suit! You hate suits."

"If you continue to call me that name, Landau, I'll petition the dock master to move your boat to another slip."

"Sorry Agatha. What about Captain Bill? Our Captain Bill?"

"I'll fill his dish, but he stays aboard Impressions tonight."

"You know how he gets when he's alone all night. Leave the forward hatch open and let him tomcat around. I think he has a new girlfriend."

"At least one member of your crew is scoring. You can take lessons from your feline buddy."

"Thanks for reminding me. Hey, does Tanya with the tight ass swing both ways? Maybe she can end my celibacy."

"Not likely. She left me for a dike cop —"

The crash of the phone hurt Steve's ear. He washed out his coffee cup, and checked the stone again. It was hard. He separated the model from the impression, and quickly vibrated a new batch of stone for a second model. He tidied up before collapsing on the bed in his tiny apartment and immediately fell asleep.

It didn't take long for him to settle into a REM state. He dreamt he was back in the Air Force, walking down the path to his off-base house in Biloxi. He entered the bedroom to find Carol Ann curled up, on their antique four-poster bed in her wedding dress. The windows were open and the curtains blew in a frenzied dance, but not enough to dissipate the familiar morgue-like scent of sweet decay. He turned Carol Ann over to find her throat slit. With each arterial beat, bright red blood pumped out, staining her white dress in grotesque shapes and intermingling with her blonde locks. He grabbed her around the neck and squeezed it tightly to stanch the flow, but blood kept spurting out between his fingers. Her eyes bulged in terror.

13

He bolted upright screaming, and drenched in sweat. The electric clock read one-fifteen. He sat stock still, waiting for his heart rate to return to normal, but a knock on the door set it racing again.

"Who is it?" he called, in a shaky voice.

"It's Bruce. Are you all right? We heard you scream."

Steve opened the door to find his tenants, Bruce and Philip nervously fingering their silk bathrobes.

"Bad dream," Steve said, "sorry I disturbed you."

"Try warm milk," Philip said. "It's a neat and natural tranquilizer."

"Neat," Steve repeated, "I'll give it a try. Thanks for your concern."

"Sleep tight and don't let the bedbugs bite," Bruce said from the staircase.

The warm milk failed miserably. The unsettling nightmare kept him wrapped in his sheets for the rest of the night.

The next morning Steve separated the second model from the impression. He labeled the two sets with the time, date, and location before he stored one in his case and wrapped the other for delivery to the evidence depository. Still unnerved by his restless night, he decided to go for a run along the Hudson River to Battery Park. The contrast of the route always put him in a better frame of mind. He started with a slow warm-up run through the cobble-stoned streets of the West Village, and then burst into the heavy foot and bike traffic on the path along the West Side Highway. Running was more of a psychological release for him then exercise. He worked out his most nagging problems during the five-mile loop. He usually ran three or four times a week, but during his last month with Carol Ann, he had run every day — more a catharsis than a compulsion.

After a few blocks he settled into his normal stride, and started to enjoy the scenery, but almost stumbled when the memory of the murdered woman returned to haunt him. The QE2, cruising slowly up the Hudson, distracted him briefly, but images of the victim's face and her bloody open wounds, quickly shifted the views of the majestic ship into the background.

14

The downtown skyline and the Statue of Liberty, his usual morale boosters, could not distract him from his obsession.

With a conscious effort, he redirected his thoughts to the strange path his professional life had taken. After eight years, he had become bored with private practice. Not much had changed in the profession and, except for minor refinements, he was still using the techniques he had learned in dental school. Restless by nature, he chafed at the claustrophobic environment he had settled into.

He had read in his alumni bulletin that one of his former instructors, Teddy Kasmir, planned to retire as the veterinary dentist at the Bronx Zoo. Steve had called him immediately.

"Steve, how are you? It's been a while," Dr. Kasmir said.

"Twelve years. I'm surprised you remember me."

"All my mavericks are indelibly etched upstairs. What can I do for you?"

"Train me to take over when you retire."

"I hoped someone like you would apply."

"Should I take that as a compliment?"

Kasmir laughed. "This is a strange specialty. I need an oddball like myself to train as a replacement."

"And?"

"If you haven't lost the edge you had as a student, you'll do fine. I'll teach you all I know here at the zoo, but you still have to take a three-month residency at the American Veterinary Medical Association in Schaumburg, Illinois."

When he told Carol Ann about his decision, she had thrown her wet teabag at him. "How will we pay our bills while you're away?"

"The Bronx Zoo pays a stipend, and we have more than enough in savings."

"What will I do while you're gone?"

"What you've done for the last year — ignore me."

"Go to hell, shithead."

15

"I'd rather go to Illinois."

He ended his run with a sprint across the highway. I better change my line of work if it keeps dredging up my sorry-ass history, he thought. He cooled down as he walked along Christopher Street to Bleecker, ate breakfast in a neighborhood coffee shop, and after a second cup of coffee, went home to shower. While he was dressing, his private phone rang.

"Steve, we have to talk about Samantha," Carol Ann demanded without preamble

"Problem?"

"Not yet. I want to head it off before there is one."

"Stop being so melodramatic. What is it?"

"I'm sure she has a boyfriend, and I think you should talk to her when you see her this afternoon."

"Birds and bees stuff?"

"You know how she looks up to you and this subject is much easier for you than for me."

"I know."

"Let's not get into that. Please?"

"Okay, I'll fill her in on female anatomy, safe sex, and so on."

"You can be so coarse, sometimes. There's something else we have to discuss."

"Not now, I'm late for an appointment. Can it wait?"

"Call me when you have time, it's important"

During the cab ride to Police Plaza, Steve reviewed the conversation with Carol Ann. She was such a damned drama queen, but her instincts about Samantha were usually on the money.

Lieutenant Hank Gagliardi, Chief of Detectives at the 19th Precinct had scheduled a conference in his Police Plaza office to discuss the previous night's homicide. He assigned Steve to work with First Class Homicide

16

Detective, Sergeant Lonnie Wright. Wright, a six-foot-six and almost half as wide, black giant, sported a closely shaved head that reminded Steve of the back of a bowling ball. After Wright shook his hand, Steve checked to see if his fingers might have fused. Perez and Stone—the two detectives who initially responded to the call were also present, as well as Pearson from the crime lab, and O'Brien from the M.E.'s office.

Lieutenant Gagliardi was a no-nonsense cop. "Okay, paisans, whadda we got?"

Perez opened his notebook. "White female, Doris Walker, age thirty-two. Moved here from Wisconsin four years ago, worked as a computer analyst for one of the large downtown brokerage houses. Neighbors said she kept to herself. Doorman says she was a looker, and he tried to put moves on her with no luck. When she did go out, it was usually to one of the local First Avenue singles bars. We'll check them out tonight. She came home with a white dude last night, but the doorman couldn't identify him, cause he was helping a tenant unload her car. He did scope him from behind and said his threads looked expensive and he had a head fulla hair."

Gagliardi ran a hand over his slate black stubble. "Color?"

"Dark and wavy," responded Stone, the other partner who caught the call. "None of the neighbors heard anything out of the ordinary."

"All right, check her place of business and any friends you can dig up. Someone might know if she got hooked up with a guy who'd be pissed off enough to do her."

Stone flipped his notebook shut. "We'll get on it first thing, Loo."

Gagliardi turned to the medical examiner. "O'Brien, whaddaya got on the post?"

"She wasn't drunk and had no drugs. She was violently raped. Baseball-sized hematomas on her thighs, upper arms, and labia. Time of death was between one and three a.m., cause of death was obvious. Son of a bitch cut both carotid arteries, opened her up from ear to ear. Doubt if she lived more than two minutes after that. Before she died he mutilated her abdomen in the area of her umbilicus."

"Christ!" Gagliardi banged his gnarled fist on his desk. She was still conscious?"

"Probably not, Loo, but she could have been."

17

"What'd the bastard use?"

"Dr. Landau better pinch-hit on that."

Steve stopped doodling a stick figure holding a knife. "He bit a nice chunk out of her abdomen. Indentations around the wound site are definitely from human teeth."

"How the hell could he do that?" Gagliardi asked.

"I've never seen it before in that area, but the potential's there."

Gagliardi swatted at a circling fly. "Spell it out, Doc. Nuts-and-bolts are what we need here."

Steve waited a beat. "Before our caveman ancestors had tools and fire, they ate their meat raw. Their fossilized teeth and ours are the same size, but the Flintstones had much larger, massive jaws. As we evolved we became more civilized, and cooked our food so that it became easier to chew, and over time, our jaws shrunk. That's why most of us have our wisdom teeth extracted; there isn't enough room. With that said, our evolutionary jaws are still strong enough to bite off a chunk of anatomy."

Gagliardi scratched his stubble. "Thanks for the history lesson, Doc."

"Sorry about the lecture."

"No sweat. I'll have something to teach the kids tonight. Pearson, I know it's early, but what's the crime lab got?"

Pearson straightened his bow tie and read from his notes. "All the blood came from the victim. No traces of tissue under her fingernails, but we have semen and saliva samples to DNA-type once we get a suspect. No prints, he must've worn gloves, there were traces of latex. We found a clear footprint in the blood and estimate the killer to be between five-ten and six feet, 185 to 195 pounds. We're checking metal fragments we found in her neck wound. We'll get you the results as soon as the tests are complete."

"Okay, gents, good work. Detective Wright'll be our control officer. Everything goes through him," Gagliardi bellowed. "The next twenty-four hours is our critical time. Let's get us a perp for Doc Landau to match bites and wrap this up."

As the squad was leaving, Lonnie Wright cornered Steve. "Buy you a cup of coffee?"

They crossed the Bowery and Lonnie led them to a Chinese pastry shop. The owner grinned with widely spaced teeth as soon as she saw Lonnie. He flashed her two fingers. The old lady served two custard pastries with two mugs of coffee as soon as they sat down, and giggled at Lonnie before hurrying away.

"You got something going with our — proprietor?" Steve asked.

Lonnie smiled. "I cleared her son in a Tong gang war homicide. She's been baking me these little beauties ever since. I warn you, they're addictive."

"Mm! You're right. A steady diet of this'll turn your teeth to mush. This is a hell of a thing for a dentist to eat in the middle of the day."

"Did you hear about the woman who called her gynecologist to ask him if she left her panties in his office? When he assured her she hadn't, she answered, 'Oh, then I must have left them at the dentist.'"

Steve had heard the joke many times, but when Lonnie's hundred-watt smile lit up his face, Steve laughed any way.

"I hope this won't screw up our working together," Lonnie said.

"Probably."

Lonnie bit off a chunk of pastry while Steve stared at him, "You look so damn familiar. Have we worked on anything before?" he asked.

"Not unless we banged football helmets."

"Jesus! You're that Lonnie Wright? The middle linebacker for the Giants?"

"Guilty as charged. The same big, black, and beautiful scourge of NFL quarterbacks."

"The first two are obvious. I'll have to think about the third."

Lonnie laughed. "I think we'll get along fine. You play ball? You look like you're in good condition."

"Basketball guard at Syracuse. Mostly remembered for holding Sy Hugo Green to a mere thirty-two points in the NIT quarter-finals."

"Hey, no wonder I didn't recognize you. You still play?"

19

"Just pick up on Sixth Avenue in the Village. A coupl'a guys from the oh-six and me challenge some of the local talent and regularly get our asses kicked."

"I know that game. It's not for the faint-hearted. Maybe I'll join you one day, and we can show the gang-bangers how the game's played."

"We need all the help we can get. You in shape?"

"I could still outrun any perp in a hundred-yard dash."

Lonnie delicately fingered the last of the Chinese pastry into his mouth. "So what do you think, Doc? Is this case an isolated incident of a guy going berserk, or do we have a crazy on our hands?"

Steve finished his coffee. "You're probably a better judge than me. The only experience I've had in that area is with my nutty ex and I wouldn't classify her as a maddened killer."

"From the way this mutt did the vic, I'd say we're going to see a lot more of the fucker." Lonnie tried to get the attention of the proprietor.

"Something's bugging the shit out of me, Doc. Mind if I ask you a question?"

"Is it what every John asks his hooker?"

Lonnie threw his head back and laughed. "Very perceptive Bro, but no kidding, how the hell did you get into forensics?"

"Not so perceptive," Steve said. "Sooner or later, everyone asks me the same question. I'll give you the short version."

"Sounds like we need more fortification," Lonnie signaled the old lady.

"I had volunteered to attend to the dental needs of the animals in the Bronx Zoo, and I had to train at the veterinary school in Schaumburg Illinois. My second week there, a passenger jet out of O'Hare had collided with a private plane and they both went down in the Poplar Creek Preserve."

The owner set out two more pastries. Steve chewed one thoughtfully.

"C'mon, Doc, don't leave me hanging. What did that have to do with you?"

"My instructor was the chief of forensic dentists in the Chicago area, and he had asked me to help."

"Survivors?" Lonnie asked.

"No one made it. There were a hundred and thirty passengers."

Lonnie was about to take a bite, but put the pastry down. "Jesus! Ghoul City. It sounds almost insurmountable."

"That's the mother of understatements. I didn't realize how grisly it would be."

"How'd you make out?"

Steve shook his head with the memory. "Like I was on a grotesque roller coaster. There was so much commingling of body parts it looked like an obscene Picasso painting. Most of the time my guts were tied in knots, but the challenge of identifying the victims demanded all my intuitive and intellectual skills."

"Sounds like you were hooked."

"Intrigued was more like it. My instructor thought I had a good feel for forensics."

"That was it?" Lonnie picked up his pastry again.

"Yep! The following year I received accreditation from the American Board of Forensic Odontology and the College of Veterinary Dentistry. I sold my practice and was served with divorce papers.

"Lotta people I know don't have that much action in a lifetime. Lonnie called for the check.

"I have to temper some of my more outlandish actions since I have a teenage daughter to worry about," Steve said, "that reminds me, I have a date with my kid. I hate to eat and run, but I have to pick her up, I'm late."

"Have fun, Doc." Lonnie waved off Steve's offer to pay. "Talk to you later."

3

Sam

Steve came to a screeching halt in his former driveway, bolted up the steps of his old Westchester house, and almost ran into his ex-wife, standing in the doorway.

"Steven, I've left messages at your office and the boat. We have to talk."

"I'm late for my date with Sam. Can it wait?"

"If you insist, but it's important. You must call me later."

"Right."

Samantha suddenly appeared, squeezed in between her parents, and ran down to the car.

"C'mon Dad, you're late! We'll miss the best part of the day."

Steve paused on the porch, studying his teenage daughter. Sam had her mother's high cheekbones and blonde hair, which she wore long. Thank God, she inherited my height and not my humongous nose, he thought as he followed her to the car.

He gave her a quick hug and a kiss on her cheek, to which she made the predictable comic grimace.

Steve backed out of the driveway. "What do you feel like today, the museum or the boat?"

"Dad!"

"Sorry, thought you might like a change."

"If it was December, you might have a point. But since I'm the grand-daughter of a shrimp-boat captain and the daughter of a sailing nut, I'm hooked. Why would I want to change?"

"Aye, Samantha, me proud beauty, I was hoping ye'd say that."

"Your pirate impression is as lousy as ever."

She's also inherited my crappy sense of humor.

While Steve drove Sam to City Island, a powerfully built bald man stared at his expressionless gray eyes in the bathroom mirror of his downtown apartment. He slowly ran a double-edged razor over his lathered face in preparation for his rendezvous later that evening. He became erect picturing what he would do to his blonde date, and nicked his upper lip. While he licked the blood away his thoughts drifted.

He watched his mother comb her long yellow hair and apply red lipstick in front of a partially shattered mirror. She pouted her mouth after she finished and looked down at him reproachfully. "Nicholas is coming today and is bringing a friend for you."

"I don't want to be with his friend. The last one hurt me."

"Hush, you stupid boy, times are extremely bad. We have to do what is necessary to get by."

There was a sharp rap on the door and two men in uniform came into their squalid, apartment. The taller one was Nicholas, he didn't bother to introduce his comrade, but grinned lasciviously as he brusquely shoved his mother into the bedroom. The other soldier, a coarse, squat man with a week's stubble, grunted as he roughly pulled the boy's pants down, bent him over, and took him right there on the living room floor. It hurt even more than the last one, and he cried out in pain.

23

Stanley Woods-Frankel

The bald man's eyes came back into focus as he returned to the present. Nicholas patted his face dry with a terry cloth towel and splashed on an expensive aftershave. Naked, he walked with the grace of a panther to the large window. He watched a bunch of pre-kindergarten kids play hide-and-seek in the pocket park on the opposite side of the street while their nannies gossiped on a nearby bench. He could hear the children giggle and he began to hum the song they each sang when it was their turn to be the seeker. He turned and walked through the bedroom of his loft apartment singing:

> *Come out come out,*
> *wherever you are.*
> *I'll find all you blondes,*
> *no matter how far.*
> *So lock all your doors.*
> *Don't keep them ajar.*
> *Remain home tonight.*
> *Stay out of the bar.*
> *Or one bite from Dracula,*
> *Will make you a star.*

The bald man giggled like the kids downstairs, but the mood took over and he started to laugh until tears ran down his face. When he finally stopped, he started to chant again, "Anyone around my base is it." This time, he laughed so hard he fell back on his waterbed, but stopped as abruptly as he had started. He rose soberly and still naked, walked to a closet with a mirrored door. He stood for a moment, admiring his muscular body before he went inside and removed a chocolate sport jacket and a pair of tan slacks. He opened a drawer, withdrew a gleaming sharp object, ran his finger over the cutting edge, and slipped it into the inside pocket of the jacket.

Once on the boat, Sam hugged a purring Captain Bill and cooed in his ear, "Did my handsome, little Prince Charming miss me?"

24

Captain Bill meowed his approval when Sam set down his plate full of cat food.

"I'll start lunch while you get us ready to sail, lassie," Steve said from the galley.

Sam removed the mainsail cover with the imprint Impressions sewn on either side and led the sheets from the large Genoa sail back to the cockpit. She placed the boat hook and all the winch handles in their pockets before pressing the ignition switch. Steve came up through the hatch when he heard the engine turn over. "Think you're ready to take her out?"

"Get serious!"

"You've practiced enough."

"Well, what're you waiting for? Cast off the lines, Matey!"

Steve disconnected the phone and electric cables, untied the dock lines, and brought them aboard.

"Okay, Sam, remember you're going to shift into reverse, turn the wheel to starboard, and slowly back out. Good, now shift into neutral, and let the boat's motion carry you to the end of Agatha's slip."

Sam exhaled loudly. "I know, I've seen you do it so many times—"

"Cool it, kid. We're moving around some pretty expensive real estate. You even think of scratching her hull, and Agatha'll have your father's head swinging from a halyard."

"Sorry Dad."

"No sweat. Turn the wheel sharply to port and shift into forward gear. That's right, now give her gas, and let's go."

"Like this?" Sam's excitement was palpable.

"Whoa—slow down, Captain. Four knots, until you reach the entrance buoy."

When they reached open water, Sam turned the boat into the wind, and Steve winched up the main sail. After he cleated the main sheet, he came back to the cockpit, unfurled the big Genoa, shut the engine, and they were off.

Sam had a beatific look on her face as she expertly trimmed the boat for close-haul sailing. Steve pretended nonchalance as he commented, "Nice going, Skipper."

The sails snapped to attention and Impressions heeled as the speed increased. Wind whistled through the rigging, and waves slapped against the broadsides, reverberating through the hull as the boat sliced through the modest chop. The lopsided smiles of the captain and first mate broadened even wider as they drank in the sights of Long Island Sound.

They sailed around the end of City Island into open water, dodging all the sailboat races, the crazy power boaters, and the occasional tugs towing barges. Steve kept stealing glances at the fourteen-year-old, girl-woman, who was of his flesh, carried one-half his genes, and instilled such meaning and joy into his life. It seemed like only yesterday, he had put drops in her eyes after her birth in the Keesler Air Force Base hospital. Now she constantly amazed him with her intelligence and wit. The fact that she loved the sea and sailing as much, if not more than he did, cemented the special bond they shared.

They anchored in their favorite cove, ate lunch, and went for a swim while Captain Bill anxiously paced along the deck and monitored them.

While drying off, Sam noticed Steve's pensive expression. "Dad, are you all right?"

"What? Sorry, kitten, tough day in the office."

"Which one?"

"Forensic."

"Cool! What's happening?"

"Nothing for you to worry your pretty little head about."

Sam's eyes flashed. "Will you stop talking to me like a child?"

"You're not old enough to hear about this."

"A murder, I bet."

Steve nodded.

"That is so cool. Come on, Dad, was the victim shot or stabbed? And, like, why were you called in on the case? And —"

"Enough Sam. You've been watching too much TV."

26

"I hate when you treat me like some teenage geek."

"Big flash, Sam. You are a teenager, and a pretty recent one too. You'll have plenty of time to find out what Looney-Tooners there are in this world. Now knock it off!"

Sam sulked long enough to make her point, before she beat Steve at backgammon. After the second game, Sam's brow wrinkled in concentration.

"What's up kitten? You look as if the weight of the world's on your shoulders."

"Have you talked to Mom yet?"

"Briefly."

"She's spacing, cause I started to go out with this really neat guy."

"She is? Well — so am I."

"You are?"

"Yes, I'm not ready for this."

"Like, you don't have to be. I am."

Steve knew that one day he would have to accept the fact that his daughter would be sought after by horny, teenage boys trying to get rid of their pimples. He didn't think it would happen so soon. He told Sam about his reservations.

"Don't worry Dad, you'll outgrow it."

"I hope so. Bear with me."

"I promise to help you through it."

They both laughed. As they pulled up the anchor, Steve said, "Just promise me you'll be careful."

"Dad!"

4

Amy

Steve's mood plunged to a melancholic low after Sam shut the car door and ran up to the house they had once shared as a family. Mercifully, Carol Ann was out. His depression deepened during the ride back to City Island. Even Captain Bill couldn't cheer him up. He checked his messages, and spent the next half hour vacuuming Impression's main salon. He poured a stiff bourbon over ice, then, at the extreme of boredom, opened his latest professional journal and sipped his drink. That did the trick. He fell asleep in his queen-size bunk, before he completed the first page.

The phone jarred him awake at three in the morning.

"What?"

"Doc, sorry to wake you, it's Lonnie."

"Lonnie, whassup?" He shook his head to ward off the cobwebs.

"It's time to go to work, my man. We got another one."

"Shit! Where?"

"Upper West Side, 81st Street, opposite the Planetarium."

"Damn! We do have a crazy on our hands."

"Tell me about it. Better boogie down. I'll be waiting."

"Right."

Steve jotted down the street and apartment numbers, dressed in a rush, and took the Harley, to make better time. He roared out of the marina parking lot and sped down the Bruckner expressway. Driving at high speeds down the empty highway with the wind screaming around his helmet would normally exhilarate him. The concentration he needed to operate the motorcycle usually cleared his mind, but lingering concerns about Sam exploring sex with some damn teen pecker-head, combined with what now, sounded like a sick-o serial killer preoccupied him. He risked a spinout when he braked hard and leaned into the turn for the F.D.R. Drive. He cut across the 79th Street Central Park transverse and pulled up to the address at 340.

The living room was decorated like a Laura Ashley advertisement. Lonnie was standing in the center giving instructions to a crime scene tech. He called Steve over once he spotted him. "A close duplicate of the first one, Doc. The vic was a young, attractive, blonde paralegal. Similar M.O. Throat slashed the same way. Bite marks are different, though."

"How's that?"

"He took chunks out of the inner part of both her thighs."

The bedroom was covered with bloody splotches and seemed like a madman's attempt to match the roses on the flowery wallpaper. Steve swallowed hard. The gory setting appeared too similar to the scene of the previous night with the exception of the victim's body which lay sprawled in an awkward position on the carpet. The wounds on both thighs stood out.

Steve went to work. By five thirty, he had completed his photos and impressions.

Lonnie kept stealing glances at him while he worked. After the morgue attendants removed the body, Lonnie asked, "How about breakfast? I know a decent greasy spoon on Amsterdam."

After they ordered, Lonnie shot Steve a sly grin. "Met a friend of mine six months after Dr. Jones made him a set of dentures in one hour for fifty bucks. I asked him how he was making out. He said he'd taken his son fishing that morning. The kid fell overboard and couldn't swim. My friend dived in, but caught his balls in the oarlock. He said it was the first time in six months he forgot about the dentures."

Steve almost choked on his pancakes. "I'll have to remember that one."

"Now that I have your attention, I'll bring you up to speed on the first homicide. We questioned the bartender at the joint where Doris Walker — that's the first victim — went the night she was murdered. He remembered she sat in a booth with some guy, but he couldn't add to the description the doorman gave us. She was well liked at her job, dated, but had no steady boyfriends, or enemies. Blood was all hers. Fiber samples of close-knit brown worsted like the kind used in trousers were found near the bed. The metal fragments from the wound were stainless steel. The murder weapon was not a knife — it tore, more than it sliced. We'll do DNA testing on this vic to confirm we're dealing with the same killer."

"If we get a match, he seems to prefer attractive blondes."

"So far… If you think of any other similarities, let me know."

"Will do," Steve stood. "Gotta run, I have a date with a female gorilla." He departed quickly leaving Lonnie with a questioning look.

Steve parked his motorcycle in the zoo employee parking lot and went with Dr. Emil Dolensek, the chief of veterinary medicine, to the Great Apes Exhibit. Dr. Dolensek's charge, Amy, was nearing the end of her final trimester.

Dolensek spoke with an East European accent. "Anytime we have a baby gorilla born in captivity, that's one we don't have to take from the wild. They're so difficult to breed we felt lucky when Amy finally became gravid."

Steve followed Dolensek's stare to the prospective mother sitting lackadaisically in a corner of the man-made jungle, nursing a swollen jaw.

"What do you think?" Dolensek asked, while Steve scrutinized the ape.

"Probably an abscessed tooth. I certainly don't want to anesthetize or X-ray her at this point in her pregnancy."

"You think antibiotics will do the job?"

"For the time being. Most dental abscesses are from gram-positive bacteria. Amoxycillin should take care of it without harming the fetus. Is she eating?"

"Not enough to take the medication orally."

"Okay, let's do it by injection. We can dart her."

"Sounds good."

"If it doesn't work, as a last resort we can put her out and I'll either lance the abscess or extract the tooth."

"I hope it doesn't come to that."

"Ditto."

"I have more. Dolensek led Steve to the African Plains compound. "See the Ibex in the corner?"

Steve nodded.

"He's getting a little obstreperous, biting the other antelopes."

Steve borrowed Dolensek's binoculars and focused in on the Ibex. "Set him up for next Wednesday. I'll contour his front teeth."

Before leaving, Steve visited his friend the Bengal tiger. He was chomping down on a large leg of lamb without apparent discomfort. One for our side, he thought.

Steve delivered the stone models and copies of his photographs of the latest victim to One Police Plaza the following day. He stopped at both Lonnie's and Gagliardi's office to see if any new developments had surfaced, but both were out on assignment. He quick-walked the short distance to the courthouse on Center Street, where he was scheduled to appear as an expert witness for Neil Jordan, a cop who had shot a prisoner he had been escorting to an upstate prison.

Steve climbed the steps and passed in between the two huge columns guarding the entrance to the Criminal Court Building. His heels clicked as he walked across the marble floors, inlaid with the New York State seal. Familiar with the routine, he waited patiently in line for his turn to go through the metal detector. He opened his case containing his slide projec-

31

tor and slides for a burly security guard to inspect, and once he got the go-ahead, caught an elevator to the seventh floor. Arnold Weiss, Jordan's lawyer was pacing the hallway outside the courtroom. "Am I glad to see you, Dr. Landau. I was beginning to think you forgot about us."

"Moi? No way counselor. Blame the metal detectors."

Weiss hurriedly rehearsed Steve with the type of questions he would ask. They were winding down, when a bailiff stuck his head out the courtroom door and motioned them inside.

The courtroom was one of the smaller ones in service with half the spectators blocked from a full view of the proceedings by support columns. Steve was the first witness after the judge called the court to order. Weiss recited Steve's credentials, and the prosecuting attorney accepted him as an expert witness.

Weiss began his direct examination: "Dr. Landau can you tell us why you, a forensic dentist, worked on this case?"

"I was asked to check the bite marks on Detective John Cahill's arm, and see if they matched the prisoner Mark Davis's teeth. Davis was being transported to jail in the back seat of a police car with Detective Cahill. Detective Neil Jordan, Cahill's partner was the driver. The cops had humanely handcuffed Davis's hands in front, and he started a fight.

"It is alleged, that Davis had bit Detective Cahill's arm hard enough to force him to drop his gun. During the ensuing battle, Davis grabbed Cahill's gun, and pointed it at him. That was when Neil Jordan shot him."

"Objection!" The prosecutor said. "Hearsay."

"Overruled. These facts have already been established with the jury," the judge stated, "you may continue, Mr. Weiss."

"What were your findings?"

Steve set up his slide projector while the bailiff unfolded a screen in front of the jury. Steve asked for the lights to be turned down. He clicked on the first slide. A lacerated arm filled the screen, and he aimed a laser pointer at the center. "These bite wounds were deep enough to require ten sutures and two weeks of antibiotics —"

Weiss interrupted, "And traumatic enough to force Cahill to drop his loaded pistol?"

Steve thought for a moment, "I would say so."

"How did you prove that the teeth marks on the detective's arm belonged to Davis?"

"I was getting to that, counselor." Steve advanced the slide projector. "This slide is a photograph I had taken with a forensic ruler in the foreground to illustrate it is on a one-to-one basis. The next slide shows the acetate square I had placed over the photo. The blue markings are where I traced the edges of the anterior or front teeth. I took impressions of the dead prisoner's mouth, and as you can see on the final slide, the models I made from those impressions match perfectly with the blue indentations on the acetate."

"Your witness," Weiss sat down.

The prosecutor rose to begin his cross-examination. "Just a few brief questions, Dr. Landau. Isn't there a possibility that someone else's models could fit your marks?"

"Slim, extremely so, in this case." Steve directed his laser pointer to the slide. "As you can see, Davis was missing a lateral incisor, and the other lateral was not fully formed. We call those peg-shaped laterals. The chances of someone else having that configuration and fitting the marks are extremely rare."

"Rare, but not impossible."

"Everything's possible, counselor, but in this case, I don't think so."

Weiss called Steve a few days later to thank him for his testimony and told him that after a short deliberation, the jury had exonerated Jordan.

The following week, Steve was in his office cementing a crown on one of his private patients. Nancy called him over the intercom. "Señor Doctor, un hombre named Lonnie's on the teléfono. Says it's muy importante."

"She's been driving me crazy since she started taking Spanish lessons," he told the patient. "Stay closed, I'll be right back."

Steve shucked his gloves and picked up the phone in his private office.

"At least I didn't have to wake you again," Lonnie said. "We got another one, Doc. This one's a little closer to you, in Chelsea."

Steve's heart sank. After a few beats he spoke in a subdued voice, "Same M.O.?"

"No doubt about it. See you in the lobby of the Alhambra Building, next to the 23rd Street Y."

"Give me twenty minutes." Steve hung up, his good mood gone. He told Nancy to reschedule his last two patients.

Lonnie met Steve in a lobby filled with overstuffed relics of the pre-war era. "Better wear your mask; this one's a little ripe." He handed Steve a jar of Vicks.

"Time of death?"

"Thursday night, with another new twist. This fucker's writing a new chapter on grisly"

The Homicide Investigative Unit marched out en masse, creating a major bottleneck at the apartment entrance. Steve had to wait to ask about the new development.

"O'Brien's come and gone," Lonnie told Steve in the confusion. "The scene's been dusted, vacuumed, photographed, and investigated. Body's in the bedroom again," Lonnie led the way, between spare modern living room furniture, surrounded by chrome and glass end tables. Steve noted antique posters of Paris lining the walls as they passed through.

Steve smeared a blob of Vicks under his nose before he slapped on his mask. The stench, even in the living room, made his eyes water. He paused in the doorway to take in the scene. The room seemed even more chaotic, and the wounds more vicious. At closer range, the odor emanating from the body, even through the mask, was almost unbearable. Steve slipped on his gloves, too upset to speak, and shook his head. Another beautiful blonde lay sprawled on a bed, completely covered with dried blood. Tiny creatures Steve did not want to identify crawled around and out of her gaping mouth. Her throat was even more savagely ripped open than the previous victims. Both her nipples had been bitten off.

5

Nita

Lieutenant Gagliardi called another meeting the following morning. Steve raised an eyebrow, as he and Lonnie entered the crowded anteroom. "We're a task force now," Gagliardi said.

Steve nodded to Perez, Stone, O'Brien and Pearson. The four detectives who caught the rotation on the last two murders were added to the team. Police commissioner Warren Stenvall marched into the room followed by his adjutant, and the chief of detectives. The cops had been standing around in small groups studying the photos of the latest homicide, but immediately stopped their banter to make way for the group. Stenvall and his entourage joined Gagliardi on the podium, while the task force seated themselves on municipal issued metal chairs. No one spoke after the clatter died down. The click of the door closing in the rear broke the silence. A statuesque blonde with shoulder length, curly hair, entered the room. She wore a black business suit, pink blouse, and Nike running shoes. She bore a confident look as she paused to look for a seat.

"Sorry I'm late, gentlemen; there was a fire in the subway." She sat down, removed her running shoes, and slipped on a pair of black pumps that she withdrew from a capacious leather bag. All male eyes in the room followed her every move. Her well-shaped runner's calves got Steve's undivided attention.

The police commissioner, impeccably attired, including a ready-for-TV powder blue shirt, announced, "Gentlemen, I would like to introduce Dr. Nita Lazar, consulting forensic psychologist for the N.Y.P.D. It appears we have a serial killer on our hands, and we'll need her expertise to put together a profile. You all know my adjutant, Pete Christopher, and are familiar with each other. There's no need to remind you that whatever takes place in this room is absolutely confidential. The press would have a field day." Stenvall's icy glare pressed his point. "Lieutenant Gagliardi will preside over this meeting." He turned to Gagliardi, "Lieutenant, whatever manpower and resources you need, they're yours."

Gagliardi tucked a rumpled tie into a five-year-old sport jacket that he could no longer button over his expanding torso, before he exchanged places with the commissioner.

"Okay, paisans." He pointed to the wall behind him. "We'll keep an outline of evidence on this blackboard. Feel free to add to it as needed. It's gonna be in my office for task force eyes only. As you can see, the first homicide's already posted. Wright, whadda we got on the others?"

Lonnie referred to his notebook as he spoke. "First, there were a number of obvious similarities. All the vics were attractive young professionals in their mid-twenties to early thirties, lived alone and most importantly, blondes."

Nita Lazar tore her eyes away from studying the blackboard to shift slightly in her seat, and unconsciously finger her golden curls.

Gagliardi, in his best parochial-school printing, chalked the facts on the blackboard.

"Each had been in a singles bar the night she was murdered. All either had consensual sex or were raped by the killer. Semen, saliva, and pubic hair DNA tests confirm we're dealing with the same mutt. He killed all the vics the same way; slashed their throats. The sick bastard also bit off various parts of their anatomy. Two of the women were ravaged ante mortem.

"The murder weapon has not been identified, or recovered, and is probably still in possession of the perp. We know it is stainless steel, but not a knife, because the jagged ends of the wounds suggest a ripping or tearing action."

Lonnie turned a page, inked in a correction, and continued. "The killer's pattern so far, is restricted to Manhattan, with no specific time schedule. Probably depends on how lucky he is in the bars."

Gagliardi chalked in Lonnie's reading of the suspect's description.

(1) *White.*

(2) *Five-ten to Six feet.*

(3) *185 to 200 lbs.*

(4) *Long, dark, wavy hair.*

(5) *Favors brown clothes.*

"None of the witnesses could make a positive ID." Lonnie pointed to Steve, "Doc Landau informs me…"

All eyes turned to Steve. As Nita Lazar's cobalt blues locked on to his, he felt a flush of heat.

"Perp has a moderate overbite, and his right cuspid, or eye tooth, is longer than normal and overlaps his right lateral incisor." Lonnie tapped his own teeth to illustrate. "We still haven't found usable prints. Each homicide shows basically the same M.O., but they're becoming more brutal."

A few members of the team concentrated on absorbing the information. Others scribbled in their notebooks. The only sound in the room after Lonnie completed his summary was the screech of chalk on the blackboard as Gagliardi meticulously completed his printing.

"That's all we got, so far, gents." Gagliardi laid down the chalk. "Nice goin', Detective Wright. Anyone got anything to add? You wanna comment at this time, Dr. Lazar?"

"It's too premature for me to give you a meaningful evaluation. I need more time to study the police reports. Have you sent your findings to the FBI. Science Unit in Quantico?" Her voice had a husky quality.

"Yeah, all of it," Gagliardi said.

"Good," said Nita. "The BSU has some of the sharpest criminal specialists in the field. They should come up with an initial profile."

"Any hunches?" Gagliardi tried.

Nita narrowed her eyes in concentration. "My initial reaction is we're dealing with a psychopath, rather than a psychotic."

Stenvall scowled. "What do you base your opinion on, Dr. Lazar?"

"The killer apparently has an extremely calculating and devious criminal mind. He must be charming, if he seduced three sophisticated women. Obviously, he's able to mask his true anti-social behavior."

"Please continue, Doctor," Stenvall insisted.

Nita crossed her legs. Steve's eyes widened. "I don't have a lot more to add," she said, "other than my research of prior patterns. After committing two or three murders in a short time, most serial killers feel their blood lust satiated and take a rest."

"For how long?"

"That depends. Each one's different. The only thing I can say with any certainty is that when they resume the murders, they're even more vicious."

"A theory then, Dr. Lazar?"

She compressed her lips but shook her head. "I'm sorry, Commissioner, I really need more time to be accurate. I would hate to give you the wrong opinion based on sketchy facts."

"Fair enough," Stenvall nodded.

Gagliardi spoke up. "Okay, Wright, will coordinate our plan of action. First, check the habits and hobbies of all the vics and the places they frequented and shopped. Maybe there's a connection where the killer made his mark. Get a composite of whadever description we got to the bartenders in all the singles hangouts, from 110th Street down to the Battery. They see anyone who fits the description putting the make on attractive young blondes, they call us on our special number."

Gagliardi scratched at his stubble. "Get a make on his threads. Check which designers or manufacturers use the materials we found, and find out which retail stores sell them. Use the uniforms, if you have to, but follow up all leads. Ask the FBI if any similar killings occurred in any other city and stopped when ours began."

Gagliardi looked around the room, "Suggestions?"

"You might want to check with city and neighboring mental hospitals and find out if anyone with a violent history was discharged before the killings started." Nita volunteered.

"Good idea," Gagliardi said.

Brilliant, Steve mentally corrected him.

"Anyone else? You want to add anything Commissioner?"

"You seem to have everything under control, Lieutenant. There's no need to remind all of you that every day this madman is on the loose, another young woman's life is at stake. Get him, and get him fast."

Steve lingered in the conference room, waiting for Nita to gather her notes. When she rose to leave, he made his move, "You said you came by subway. Can I give you a lift?"

"Only if you're going to the Upper East Side." She gave him an encouraging smile.

"Just the way I'm going," he said with a straight face.

He did fine opening the car door for her, but she caught him staring at her hiked skirt as she slid into the passenger seat. He covered with a nervous snort. She laughed, and looked as if she was born to ride in a Porsche. He stalled twice getting out of the Police Plaza garage, and tried to recover with his killer grin. He knew it didn't work, from the look she gave him. He eased onto the entrance ramp of the F.D.R. drive and drove directly into a traffic jam, a situation that usually drove him crazy, but he relaxed. It extended his time with Nita. Then, he stalled again.

She raised her eyebrows. "Is this a new car?"

"No, I've had it a few years. Why?"

"Oh, I was just wondering," her startling cobalt eyes zeroed in on his. A warm and almost forgotten feeling, spread through his groin.

"Do I make you nervous?"

"What do you mean?" he said too quickly.

"That I'm a therapist, who treats a lot of heavy-duty deviates." She raised an eyebrow.

He cleared his throat. "That's part of it, but hey, you should see some of the animals I treat." The traffic inched forward. Steve shifted into first gear

39

and concentrated on letting the clutch out slowly. "Aren't you worried one of your bozos might try to act out one of his sick fantasies?"

"I'm a black belt," she said.

He gave her an appraising look.

"Maybe you think I don't look like a shrink?"

"That's part of it, too. Are you always so direct?"

"Only when I meet someone interesting."

"Jesus! All I've done is blabber incoherently and stall the car a lot."

She put her hand on his arm. "I think there's more to you than that. Tell me about yourself."

He laughed nervously. "I don't know where to begin."

"Start with your parents."

"Sounds like a therapy session."

She flashed him a radiant smile full of white, even teeth. His temperature went up a few degrees.

"Being a shrink has its drawbacks, but I find it's a good way to get to know someone."

"My parents were immigrants and — "

"So were mine," Nita said.

"That's neat!" *Shit! I'm starting to sound like Bruce, he thought. I hope she doesn't think I'm gay.* "They worked their tails off trying to make ends meet. I was an only child."

"Me too. Oh good, we're starting to move. I have an appointment in half an hour with a very nervous patient."

"Not to worry; I'll get you there in plenty of time. But back to my Rich-and-Famous life story. My father had a heart attack when I was in my second year of dental school. He survived, but couldn't work so I had to drive a cab to pay my tuition."

"Must have been tough."

Steve shrugged. He gave Nita as brief a synopsis as he could of his education, before he said, "Your turn."

40

"My parents had to escape from France during World War II, because Papa's great grandfather was Jewish. My Papa and I are non-practicing religionists, and practicing seculars, but Mama occasionally attends mass. They're both university professors."

"I bet they sacrificed as much as mine to give you your education."

Nita nodded. Steve relaxed.

"I got my B.A. from N.Y.U., my master's and Ph.D. from Columbia," she continued.

"My thesis in abnormal psychology concentrated on psychopathic and psychotic behavior. I interviewed a dozen serial killers, including Ted Bundy and David Berkowitz."

Steve started to ask why, but realized how nerdy that would sound and nodded wisely instead.

Nita's look hardened. "They were sick, and horribly deranged murderess, the psychopath we're looking for now appears to be auditioning for their club."

"You didn't have a chance to see the crime scene pictures. This son of a bitch would make Attila the Hun look tame."

Nita nodded. "I've been a consultant for the NYPD for over four years," she continued, "and I was involved in the investigation and apprehension of two serial killers. I have their tapes, and those of the Bundy interviews. Maybe I should bring them in for the task force to see what they're up against."

"I, for one, would really be interested in seeing them," Steve said a bit too eager.

She adjusted her position in the cramped bucket seat and crossed her long legs.

Steve altered his position to hide his growing discomfort. He downshifted to exit at 68th Street, and cleared his throat. "Is there anyone special in your life?"

"Here's my block. Second awning on the right's my building." She turned back to him. "I had a relationship with one of my former professors, but I'm currently unattached." Her teeth sparkled in another smile as she reached for the door handle.

Steve jumped out of the car, and hustled around to her side in a Groucho Marx crouch, only to find the doorman holding the door for her.

"Thanks for the lift. Take care of yourself," she winked, and walked briskly to her building.

What the hell did she mean? He thought forlornly. He leaned against the car and watched the rewarding rear view of her retreating figure disappear through the lobby door.

He smacked his forehead with the heel of his hand. *Shit! I really blew that. She must think I'm some kind of a wussy, thumb-sucking, beetle-brained asshole. I didn't even get her number.* The doorman stared at him with an amused look. Steve beat a hasty retreat to the driver's side and burned rubber pulling away from the curb. *No sweat; I can get it from Gagliardi, and we'll see a lot of each other during the investigation.*

Steve headed up to City Island and his floating forty-five-foot apartment. He had chosen the island as the place to berth his boat, because it resembled a New England fishing village, and was only thirty minutes from downtown Manhattan.

As he walked down the dock to Impressions, he took out a bosun's whistle and blew three shrill notes. A furry white head popped up from behind Agatha's footlocker and Captain Bill dashed out. "C'mon, buddy. I know what a pain in the ass you can be when you're hungry." Steve picked up his cat and scratched his favorite spot under the jaw.

Captain Bill rubbed vigorously against Steve's leg while he opened a can of gourmet cat food. Afterward, Steve polished the bright work on deck, while a contented Captain Bill curled up atop the folded mainsail and monitored his master's progress.

The next morning, several angry seagulls, fighting over the remains of a filleted bluefish, woke Steve at five. He spent a few restless minutes fighting with his sheets before he decided to go for an early run. He trotted slowly through the tree-lined island streets bordered by imposing Victorian houses. By the time he reached the wooded areas of Pelham Bay Park, he hit his stride and continued out to the packed sands of Orchard Beach. The sun rose over Long Island Sound as Steve headed back to the boat. He realized he had spent the entire run thinking about Nita Lazar.

He showered, dressed, and filled Captain Bill's bowl. Chores done, he went to the City Island Diner for breakfast. After a second cup of coffee, he drove to his office.

His first patient of the day, Michael Herman, a Broadway producer, rinsed his mouth after Steve had completed a filling. "Dr. Landau, I'm in a bind, and I was hoping you could help me."

"I'll be glad to, if I can. What's the problem?"

Herman wiped his glasses. "I'm starting rehearsals for the musical *Dracula!* We lucked out and got Art Powers, the movie star, to play the lead. He has to sing two crucial songs while wearing vampire fangs. Do you think you can make him a set of teeth that looks good but will allow the audience to hear and understand him?"

"I've heard some wild questions before, but at least I have a working knowledge of this kind of dental problem."

"Wonderful! You've worked on theater productions before?" Herman asked, excitement in his voice.

"Not exactly. But I've done dental work on vampire bats."

The smile froze on Herman's face.

"I'll check with my laboratory and let you know." Steve didn't crack a smile until the director left.

Steve called Gagliardi from his private office and his adjutant told him he was out in the field.

"I have to consult with the psychologist on the case we're working. Can you help me?"

"You mean Dr. Lazar?"

Steve tried to keep his voice level. "Yes, that's the one."

"I don't know Doc, the Loo doesn't usually give out that information."

"For crying out loud, we're all on the same team."

"I know, but—"

"I'll tell you what. How about you give me Doctor what's her name's number, and I'll give you a free cleaning."

43

"Since you put it that way," he recited both her home, and cell phone number. "Don't forget my cleaning now."

"Call my nurse for an appointment."

"What's your number?"

"Ask Gagliardi," Steve hung up, and immediately dialed the home number he was given. While waiting for Nita to pick up, his pulse ratcheted up to race speed, and he became more fidgety than he had been before the final game for the NIT championship.

"Hello." Nita's throaty voice came through the ear piece. Steve took a deep breath and tried to keep his voice level.

"Hey Nita, how's it going?"

"Great. Who is this?

"Uh, Steve, Steve Landau. I gave you a lift…" Nita laughed. It sounded like wind chimes to Steve.

"I know who you are, I recognized your voice. What took you so long to call?"

"I had to get up the nerve."

"You don't have to do that with me Steve. I told you, I think you're interesting, and I don't pay idle compliments."

Steve gave himself a thumbs up. "If that's the case, and you're free this afternoon, I thought you might want to go for a sail."

"Sounds wonderful, but I'll have to take a rain check. I was planning to edit the tape of my interview with Ted Bundy for the task force.

"Do you want some feedback?"

"Sure, I can always use that."

"I'll bring lunch. What time?"

"Now is good. You know the building, Apartment 5A. I'll tell the doorman"

"Not exactly a cool way to start a friendship," he quipped, "see you in a little while."

Steve set down the large bag loaded with avocados, stuffed with shrimp salad from Citarella's gourmet counter, and a bottle of Chablis, and rang the bell for 5A. When Nita opened the door, dressed in jeans and a white blouse that showed a lot of midriff, Steve could feel his heart hammer away like a starving woodpecker. When she took the lunch bag and kissed his cheek, he had to concentrate on staying upright.

"I thought we could eat while I edit," she said and placed the lunch on a table already set with plates and cutlery before a thirty-six inch TV. "I've deleted all the extraneous introductory stuff, except for this section." Nita slipped a DVD into the player, while Steve laid out the food.

The screen filled with the title *Interview with Ted Bundy on Death Row, January 14th, 1989, conducted by psychologist Nita Lazar.* A scene of a room painted in gunmetal gray came on with a dining room sized metal table fastened to the floor, and two folding chairs on either side. One side had a large steel ring bolted to the table, and on the other side sat a younger looking Nita Lazar, with her long, blonde hair tied in a pony tail, and professional looking white lab coat. Steve spooned a healthy portion of shrimp salad and avocado into his mouth, and moved closer to the screen.

"You look good in a pony tail."

"Thank you, kind sir," Nita's voice on the screen diverted their attention back to the TV.

"This will be the final interview of Theodore Bundy, who had spent the last ten years on Death Row, but is now slated to be executed by electric chair here at Florida State Penitentiary in nine days.

Nita filled their wine glasses, nibbled on her avocado, and took a sip.

"For most of his time on death row, he claimed to be innocent of the charges, but recently, he recanted and confessed to the murder of thirty young women, the authorities believe it may have been closer to fifty. This interview, is to examine what possible motive Ted Bundy might have had to commit these violent crimes."

The door in the back of the room opened and a tall, nice-looking man in an orange jumpsuit shuffled into the room in leg irons and handcuffs with two guards supporting him on either side, one guard stood back, while the other locked his handcuffs to the table ring. When the other guard bent to do the same with the leg irons, Nita waved him off. "Mr. Bundy and I will be fine. If you will just hang around outside the door, I'll call you if I need

45

you." Both guards looked at her as if she claimed to fly, and backed out. Steve put his wine glass down, and stared at the real Nita sitting next to him in the same way the guards had done.

"Jesus Nita. You just said this crazy weirdo had admitted to setting records in the murder league, why on earth did you do that?" Nita clicked the pause button on her remote.

"I thought he would be more open, and I would get a better interview if I allowed him a little freedom, and —"

"And?"

"I was young, impetuous, and stupid."

Steve was about to say something, but changed his mind at the last second. He had never come across anyone as honest as Nita. "You must have been a great girl scout."

Nita laughed. "I did, after all get a terrific interview, as you will see." She clicked on the play button, and took another delicate spoonful of the shrimp salad.

"Why did you insist you were innocent of all the charges against you, early in your incarceration, and then recently recant?" the screen Nita asked.

"I had my reasons," Bundy replied.

"Do you care to elaborate?"

Bundy donned his famously winning smile. "You're the shrink, you tell me."

"Not until you give me something to work with."

Bundy shrugged, answering in an almost bored tone. "Normal childhood, simple loving parents, good student, graduated college, majored in political science, got a job in D.C. and also worked on a committee to elect the Governor of Vermont. Pretty girlfriend, considered marriage…"

Steve studied Bundy. "He's so normal looking, he could have been a boy scout."

"He had been," Nita said, "just wait for the rest of the interview. Watch his eyes."

"Mr. Bundy, I have all that background information in your file. How about fast-forwarding through the bullshit and cutting to the chase."

"Whoa, a tiger in a lab coat," Bundy said, "tell you what, sweet lips, call me Ted, and I'll give you everything you want."

Nita's facial expression remained neutral. "Your girlfriends name was Stephanie. How come you didn't get married?"

"The bitch broke up with me."

"You sound angry now. How pissed were you then?" Nita asked.

Bundy worked his jaw muscles. "I was enraged enough to kill, and I did."

"You raped and strangled your first victim. She was tall, had long straight hair, and bore a resemblance to Stephanie. Was that a coincidence.?"

"What do you think, shrink?"

"I'll take that as a no. Since most of your victims had similar characteristics, was sex your primary motive with all the women?"

Bundy's coal black eyes bore into Nita's "Fucking was definitely a factor, but I was more interested in controlling the bitches. I wasn't about to let another broad cancel my subscription."

Nita made a notation in her notebook, and looked up. "How were you able to gain so much power over so many women?"

Bundy's smile reminded Steve of a fox ready to break into the hen house. "I played a different role with each one," he said. "I had asked a college co-ed to help me get my books in my car, and then bopped her over her head with a tire iron. I had a fake police badge and handcuffs, and made false arrests."

Nita nodded. "I remember reading about a woman you stopped, in her car, and when you tried to handcuff her, she ran out onto the highway, flagged a passing motorist and got away."

"Her claim to fame," he snickered, "The only one who got away from the infamous Ted Bundy."

"Why didn't you kill Stephanie, the source of all your angst?"

"I did better than that with her. We eventually got back together again. She was more serious about it this time, and I just walked out on her without a word."

"Is that when you murdered the twelve year old girl?" Bundy's eyes grew even darker.

"I'd rather not talk about it. You know sweet lips, all this yakking about my past conquests has given me a humongous boner. He shot out his handcuffed hand as far as it would go, and grabbed Nita's wrist. "How's about rubbing it, so Teddy boy can sit on the thousand watt chair with a smiling face?"

Nita sat absolutely still for a few seconds, staring back into those cold eyes, and then without warning stood up, shouted out a karate *kiai*, and brought her free hand down in a blurred bone rattling chop on Bundy's forearm.

He instantly let her go, and screamed out "The bitch broke my arm!" The two prison guards rushed into the room and the screen went blank.

"Holy crap, Nita!" Steve exclaimed. "You are my super heroine. You have bigger *cojones* than ten of my biggest jock friends. You didn't bat an eyelash when that crazy bastard grabbed your wrist" He got up and hugged her after she ejected the disc, and when she lifted her head, he kissed her lightly at first, and then, with more passion. When the tip of her tongue brushed his own, the current jolted him to his core. He hugged her even tighter, and hoped she couldn't feel his mach speed heart beat. Nita was definitely aware of his hardness, and she gently stroked his cheek, and backed away. "Sorry big guy, this is as far as we can go," she whispered into his ear. "I have a patient coming in half an hour."

Steve had to refrain from telling her that in his present condition, he only needed half of those precious minutes.

6

Scotty

Steve met Nancy in the lobby of the Medical Examiner's Office a few days after Gagliardi's conference.

"Any idea what this is about?" he asked.

"Dr. O'Brien called after you left yesterday. He has two unidentifiables for you. Don't you get a warm, fuzzy feeling to know how much you're wanted?"

"You brought my forensic kit?"

"Does a pigeon leave bird doo on your car?"

"What happened to that sweet, innocent, choir girl I hired ten years ago?" Steve asked as the M.E. motioned them into his office. The walls were lined with team pictures of the three New York teams that had won World Series pennants with a place of honor for one photo of Mickey Mantle, Duke Snider, and Willie Mays with their arms around each other. In the corner, a mounted skeleton had a cigar in its mouth and a New York Yankees cap rakishly perched on its head.

"How come every time I see you two, my teeth hurt?" O'Brien asked.

"How come every time I see you, I end up growing icicles off my rear end in that ice box downstairs?" Nancy snapped back.

"Now, now, children," Steve said, "are you going to tell me why we're here, O'Brien?"

"We fished two out of a sunken car up around your ballpark."

"Not enough left for fingerprints?"

"You need skin for prints. The crabs and other aquatic beasties must have thought it was Thanksgiving. We have two Gray's Anatomy skeletons for you to play with down in the bullpen. One male and one of the opposite sex."

"How can you tell, if you just have the skeletons?" Nancy asked.

"Our forensic anthropologist examined their pelvic configurations. You and your sisters need more space to have babies."

"The things we do for you men. What'd you mean by Dr. Landau's ballpark?"

"A boat with a shallow enough draft to pass easily under the Hutchinson River Drawbridge by City Island banged into an underwater obstruction. Turned out to be a new Lincoln that had been reported stolen two months ago by its owner, a Scarsdale chiropractor. Our bag of bones was inside."

"How the hell did it end up under the bridge?" Steve asked.

"Cops in a blue-and-white had spotted it on the road and gave chase. They thought the thieves got lucky and made it across the bridge before it was raised. Now we know the perps were called out by the big ump in the sky."

"O'Brien, can you finish one sentence without using a baseball metaphor?" Steve asked.

O'Brien shrugged and led them down to the autopsy room. Nancy breathed a sigh of relief, when she saw that the two skulls placed jaw-to-jaw on one of the stainless steel autopsy tables were the only occupants.

"Our anthropologist said they were caucasian, between twenty and thirty. This one's the male." O'Brien tapped it with a gloved finger.

"Set up the portable X-ray, Nancy. We'll shoot a few films." Steve took O'Brien aside, "anything new on our serial killer?"

"We found tissue fragments under the nails of the latest victim," O'Brien said.

"How much?"

"Enough to blood type the killer: O negative."

Steve flashed a thumbs-up. "We can probably add scratches to his description."

"I hope she put a few dents in the bastard's face."

"Anything else?" Steve asked.

"A couple of loose hairs on the body, near the bite marks. Forensic comparison makes them Asian origin. Killer could be Oriental or wearing a wig."

"Which means?"

"It's a shutout, till we find a bald Asian to match our findings."

Steve shook his head, "You are weird, O'Brien. You're doing it again."

"Señor Doctor," Nancy called out, "El machino's ready I just need usted to set up the Yoricks."

Steve rolled his eyes

"I'm sure you two want to be alone," O'Brien said at the door.

Steve positioned each skull and stabilized them with a bar of soap. Nancy angled the X-ray cone to shoot a full mouth series of both jaws. While Nancy developed the films in the morgue darkroom, Steve snapped a half-dozen photos of each skull, charted both mouths and listed the missing teeth, the fillings, and crowns. After Nancy brought him the developed X-rays, he drew in the shape of the root canals.

"Fax the chart to the National Crime Information Center. Maybe we'll get lucky," Steve said, "I'll be in O'Brien's office."

Steve settled on the M.E.'s leather couch. "What do you know about Nita Lazar?"

"You have that lean and hungry look. Is there more than a professional interest here?"

51

"You know me. I go bonkers over foxy blondes with great legs."

"Her brains equal her looks. You might be a little outmatched, Steve my boy."

"Thanks for your vote of confidence."

"Just calling a strike a strike. Are John and Jane Doe going to end up in Potter's field?" O'Brien asked.

"Depends on what we get back from the NCIC."

"How's the new computer imaging process working out?"

"After sweating blood to get it on line, I've only used it a couple of times. Two were remarkably accurate. One wasn't even close."

"I haven't been briefed yet. How does it work?"

"I enter measurements for more than one hundred points on the skull. The software program chooses among thousands of facial characteristics and prints a mockup of a victim's face. Then the fun begins."

"What do you mean?"

"I have more arguments with my colleagues over the computer images than any other procedure."

"Now, I know why forensic comes from the Latin translation for debate."

The door flew open and Nancy burst in. "Boss it's unbelievable. The NCIC has already faxed back three possibles."

Steve and Nancy rushed back to the morgue, where Steve matched his chart against the NCIC record. He discarded two, and then brandished the third. "This one's real close," he grinned.

Nancy read the report aloud, "Nineteen-year-old girl reported missing by her mother three weeks ago. We have a phone number for her dentist, Dr. Paul Roberts."

"Can you get him for me?"

"He's on hold. Line two."

"I should've known." Steve picked up the phone, "Dr. Roberts, I'm Dr. Steve Landau, forensic dentist for the NYPD. Do you have a patient named Janet Ryan?"

"Yes, she lives across the street from my office on Douglaston Parkway. Is she all right?"

"I won't know until I get a match. Can you fax me a copy of her records and last X-rays?"

"You'll have them in ten minutes."

Dr. Roberts's time estimate was on the money. Steve fastened his X-rays next to the faxed ones on a view box. "Bingo!" he exclaimed.

He called Detective Gallagher, who took the original missing person report and notified him of the positive ID, and then called Dr. Roberts with the bad news.

The following day, Gallagher called Steve. "Nice work Doc. The mother told us that against her wishes, her daughter was dating a mutt with a marathon rap sheet, name is Ron Carilli. If you woulda bet a grand larceny car theft—you'da won! Asshole wasn't very good at it, either. Bagged four times, copped a plea, did a short stretch at Cocksaxie. We're sending you his dental records for confirmation."

That evening, Steve drove Sam to Yankee Stadium to see her heartthrob Andy Petit pitch against the Red Sox. "What's up kitten? You look as if we've already lost the game," Steve said.

Sam stared at the bleak Bronx landscape for a long time as they sped down the Major Deegan Highway. "When you and Mom broke up, I always felt there was a chance you would get back together. I don't think you realized how upset I was. Every night I dreamt you were still living at home."

"What happened to change your feelings?"

"Mom told me she's planning to marry Nick."

Steve's foot goosed the accelerator. "I didn't know they were that serious."

"Mom told me she tried to tell you, but you never had the time to talk to her."

"I try to keep contact with your mother to a minimum."

Sam turned to Steve with a disdained look. "Dad, you have to discuss this with her. I don't want to live with Nickie. He's a real jerk."

Steve zipped around a station wagon. "He's a pretty decent guy, and I'm not going anywhere. We'll spend more time together. You can always sleep on the boat, if things get too rough."

"Are you serious? That would be super."

"Sure, you can start this weekend."

"Oh, Dad, I'm really sorry, I'm going with Dale and her family to their lake house."

During the game, Sam's mood reverted back to her animated disposition, and she cheered wildly every time Petit struck out a batter.

Steve couldn't stay focused on the game. Dark thoughts of another man living in his house, making love to Carol Ann in their old bed, blurred the action on the field. Visions of Sam belonging to a new family grouping escalated his jealousy. He would become the outsider. He couldn't share Sam's joy when the Yankees won and her heartthrob was credited with the win even though Mario Riviera pitched the last two innings. He grew more morose as he drove Sam home, while she chattered on about Petit. He hugged her tightly before dropping her off, then headed back to Impressions. He had a few stiff bourbons and spent a restless night sorting demons.

Carol Ann's impending marriage was a relentless intruder during Steve's morning run, but by the time he'd completed his five-mile loop, endorphins pumping through his body, he was able to move the thought to the backburner of his mind.

After he returned to Impressions he realized he had the whole day to himself. Even Captain Bill had deserted ship to cat around on the docks. Good time to install the new wind indicator and work on the engine, he thought. He spotted the squat figure of his neighbor, Agatha, in her customary cut-off jeans and T-shirt, emerging from her cabin, coffee cup in hand.

"Hey, if it isn't my best and most beautiful neighbor?"

"Stow it, Landau. What do you want?"

"I need a lift."

"My car's in the shop."

Steve shook his head. "A ride up my pole's what I mean."

"Watch your language, Buster."

"Jesus, Agatha!" Steve pointed to the bosun's chair hanging on the main halyard.

"Why didn't you just say you wanted me to winch you up?"

After Steve arranged his tools and the wind indicator in the instrument pockets of the bosun's chair, Agatha handed him an air horn. "Call me when you're ready to come down. My palms get too sweaty if I watch you swinging around the top of your mast."

Agatha turned the winch handle, and as Steve slowly rose up past the spreaders, his attention was diverted to a bikini-clad blonde coming out of Agatha's cabin. He cupped his hands over his breasts and motioned an okay sign to Agatha. His head snapped back as Agatha muscled him up so rapidly he thought he might fly past the masthead.

He replaced the faulty indicator then paused to enjoy the view of the harbor. When he had enough of the cooling breeze, he sounded a blast on the horn. As Agatha eased him down, he waved to her blonde friend and shouted, "Enjoying the sun, Jill?"

Agatha stopped in mid-turn. Steve bounced ten feet above the deck. "Her name is Lydia," she said through clenched jaws.

"What happened to Jill?"

"She was a one-timer."

"Didn't I tell you to stay away from suits?"

"Shove it, Landau," Agatha hissed, and lowered him to the deck in an almost free-fall drop. "It's been nice and quiet these last few weeks. Can't you stay away more often?"

"Then you wouldn't have me to kick around anymore." Steve rubbed his rear end. "I've been working on a case."

Agatha's eyebrows shot up. "It's about time. I want to hear all the gory details."

"Not yet. I can tell you to keep your blonde friend out of singles joints, but of course that would be the last place she'd go, if she's with you."

"I wouldn't count on it," Agatha said wistfully. "I'm sort of an experiment."

"No shit! How's it working out?"

"She'll make up her mind after our next date."

"Jesus! If I had that type of pressure, I'd probably stay at half mast."

"It's been so long, you probably forgot where to put it."

"Thanks, Agatha. If I had more neighbors like you, I wouldn't ever have sex. If it doesn't pan out, you'll give her my number?"

"Fuck off, Landau," she furrowed her brow. "Are you serious about the singles bars?"

Steve nodded. "We have a sicko who preys on blondes he meets in pick up joints."

"I'll pass it along."

After Agatha returned to her guest, Steve took his toolbox below. Working in the confines of the engine room was a numbing experience after working outside. In a few minutes, sweat was running down his face, stinging his eyes and dripping onto the propeller shaft while he repaired an exhaust valve.

He went topsides and started the engine to see if he'd made any progress.

"Shit!" he exclaimed, after reading the temperature gauge.

"Problem?" the sharp-eared Agatha called over.

"The intake valve must be clogged. I'll have to dive to clean it out.

"You go underwater with all the electric lines around here, you'll be one fried sailor," Lydia volunteered.

"You sure?" Steve asked.

"Trust me, I'm in the fire department."

"How about you girls joining me for a sail?"

Agatha's eyes rolled skyward. "Sorry turkey. We women already have plans. We're anchoring off Huckleberry Island for the afternoon."

"Looks like a job for me and the captain." He blew three quick notes on his whistle, and in a flash, Captain Bill jumped on board. Steve backed Impressions out of her berth, and after he motored past the harbor buoy, turned on the autopilot, raised the sails, and cut the engine.

The wind was blowing fifteen knots from the southwest, just right for an open-reach sail to Roslyn Harbor on the Long Island side. Steve decided to sail for a while before he did his dive.

Impressions sliced through the choppy waves at seven knots, port gunnel spilling water as Steve stroked a purring Captain Bill in his lap. Details of the murders flashed through his mind to intrude on the sunny day. Even with all the new evidence, the team was no closer to apprehending the murderer then when they started. The killer always seemed to be one step ahead of them. He'd have to make a dumb mistake or get caught in the act, but neither held much promise. From the team's problems, Steve's thoughts turned to erotic daydreams about Nita Lazar, when he caught sight of his friend Scotty McPherson's ketch, Athena, on a direct heading towards Impressions. Scotty, Steve's closest confidante, owned the most popular restaurant on City Island. Steve eased off the wind, and the two boats sailed alongside each other.

Scotty called over on his bullhorn, "Hi, ho, Steverino, what're you doing out on the briny all by your lonesome?"

Steve switched on his bullhorn. "Got some repair work to do — thought I'd enjoy a sail, first."

"Where you heading?"

"Roslyn Harbor."

"Race?"

Steve squinted at the bikini-clad crew scurrying about Scotty's deck, he winked at his own crewmate — Captain Bill, and answered on his hailer, "You're on. I'll wait for you at our usual spot."

Scotty gave him the finger, let out his mizzen and mainsail, and the race was on.

Steve had rigged Impressions for living aboard, rather than sailing efficiently, and consistently lost upwind races to Athena. Roslyn was downwind, though, and the two boats were evenly matched. They were bow-and-bowsprit approaching the harbor entrance when Steve eased off, came up behind Scotty, and stole the wind destined for Athena's sails to slow her down. Impressions burst ahead, beating Scotty by two boat lengths. By tradition, Scottie anchored first and Steve claimed his spoils by rafting to Scottie's boat.

Gentle ribbing and cries of "foul" and "cheater" reached Steve as he cleated the final spring line. He was about to cross over to Athena, but nearly fell overboard when he saw Nita Lazar emerge from Scotty's hatchway.

"Holy sh— what on earth are you doing on this pirate's boat?" Steve blurted.

"We had an engagement party for one of my staff at Scotty's restaurant last night, and he invited the entire party out today," Nita's smile was even more dazzling out on the water.

"What an extraordinary coincidence. I was just thinking about you, when I spotted his boat."

"How nice for both of us."

Steve felt awkward and knew Scotty would call him on it later. Scotty popped the cork from a bottle of chilled French wine filled glasses and raised his own. "May all my old friends remain old friends and all my new friends soon become old friends."

Steve's *Here, here!* was a few decibels louder than those of the other guests.

"How about a toast from the victor of the race?" Scotty asked.

Steve tore his eyes away from Nita's long shapely legs, and lifted his glass, "To our gracious host and fierce competitor. Good thighs — uh good times."

The women in Nita's party giggled, and Steve could feel his face grow hot. "Excuse me, people, I have to get back and repair my boat." He beat a hasty retreat to Impressions while the rest of the party went swimming.

While squirming into his scuba gear, Steve questioned Captain Bill, "What the hell's the matter with me? She must think I'm Shmuck of the Year."

The Captain tilted his head with a questioning look.

"You're a great help," Steve spit into his mask, held it tightly against his face, and jumped over the side. He removed the last of the eelgrass caught in the intake valve and turned to see Nita swimming underwater toward him. He waited until she motioned him up. When she broke the surface, Steve said, "Nice of you to visit."

"Actually I wanted to tell you we heard the marine operator calling you on Scotty's radio."

"Thanks. Come on aboard, I'll get it on my VHF."

They climbed down into his main cabin and heard, "Marine operator on channel sixteen, calling the yacht Impressions. Answer and call on channel twenty-six."

Steve set down his tanks and punched in channel twenty-six. "This is the yacht Impressions, Whiskey-Radar-Yankee-2-6-5, calling the marine operator."

"Impressions, stand by." Twenty seconds of silence passed, broken by occasional static.

"Steve, I mean, Impressions, do you read me?"

Steve and Nita recognized Lonnie's deep bass voice. "Lonnie, this is Steve. How the hell did you find me? Over."

"Hey, they don't call me a detective for nothing. I got in touch with your daughter, Sam, and she told me how to reach you. I'm patched into headquarters and calling from a patrol car. Over."

"Before you tell me why you had to track me down, remember Marine VHF's an open channel. Anyone can monitor our conversation. Over."

"Roger, Doc. I read you loud and clear. I called to tell you we need your services again. Over."

"Another incident? Over."

"Seems to be, even though there are discrepancies. Over."

"Where are you? Over."

59

"Pelham Bay Park. Fifty yards before the firing range on a path off the road leading to City Island. Over."

"Must be my day for coincidences. I just went running past that area this morning. Nita Lazar's on board. You want me to bring her? Over."

"Nita? Fast work, Doc." Steve could hear Lonnie chuckle. "I thought you had the hots for her. Sure, if she wants to come, it's okay. Over."

"May I remind you this is an open channel, and Nita is standing right next to my red-faced self."

"Oops, sorry, and you forgot to say 'over.' Over."

"Will you zip it up? We're leaving now. See you in an hour. Over and out."

Nita crossed back to Scotty's boat to change. Steve slipped out of his wet suit and dressed in jeans and a polo shirt. Nita returned quickly wearing shorts and a halter-top.

"Not exactly the right statement for a murder investigation," she said.

Steve made time by motor sailing back to City Island. They discussed the case during the tense sail back. Steve was concerned about Nita witnessing a homicide scene investigation.

"How many fresh murder scenes have you attended?" he asked.

"Including this one?"

Steve nodded.

"One."

"You don't have to go. Lonnie couldn't talk about it on the radio, but it'll probably be more grisly than the earlier ones, and the others were gruesome."

Nita swallowed hard. "I know, but if I can see the actual results of his sick mind, instead of photographs, I can get a better handle on what motivates our man."

"I remember how I felt the first time I saw one. If you start to feel queasy, don't be a heroine. Leave immediately, sit down somewhere, put your head between your legs, and take a few, deep breaths through your nose."

"I promise."

"Good, I don't want to see Scotty's good food going to waste."

"Okay, let's change the subject. Scotty mentioned you were divorced. You want to talk about it?"

"Scotty's the number one Island yenta," Steve lamented, he wasn't exactly thrilled about discussing his former wife. "There's not much to tell. I met my ex, Carol Ann, in Mississippi when I was stationed there in the Air Force. Before my discharge we got married, even though, we were as different as any two people could be."

"In what way?"

Steve needed time to think and adjusted the jib sheet. "Initially, her looks and Southern manners knocked me for a loop. She dressed each day like she was going to a party, while I have been accused of being sartorially challenged. I know it doesn't seem like much, but she doesn't have a single athletic bone in her body, while I'm a crazy jock, and with her at five-one, we were like the Mutt and Jeff of Biloxi."

Nita laughed, "Surely not reasons for splitting."

Steve looked at her sheepishly. "Well, there was this religion and sex thing, but you and I just met, and I'm not sure I feel comfortable talking about it."

"I understand." Captain Bill jumped on Nita's lap and she rubbed his back. "I just want you to know I think you're an exciting renaissance man and don't forget I'm a therapist who has heard things that would probably make Hugh Hefner blush."

Steve took a beer from the cockpit cooler, and held one up for Nita, but she declined. He stared at her for a moment and exchanged it for a club soda. "Everything was fine in the sack while we were down South, but once we got back to New York, she started to find excuses for not making love, until it reached a point where she completely rejected any type of intimate contact."

"Did you know why?"

Steve took a long pull on his soda. "Not at first. It came out in dribs and drabs. Turns out her father, a rough and tough shrimp boat captain, had been sexually molesting her for years."

Nita nodded slowly. "Did she get help?"

61

"I begged her, but she was adamant. She didn't want to be branded as crazy."

"But..."

Steve waved his hand. "I know, I know. I pleaded with her till I was hoarse. It got to the point where we had absolutely no physical contact. She wouldn't even hold my hand. Then, she started to go to church every day and spout scripture at me, ad nauseam. I decided I didn't want to live my life like that anymore."

"How did you feel after the breakup?"

"Gut wrenching guilty and totally torn up about the effect it had on my daughter."

Nita put her hand on his. "For what it's worth, you can't be responsible for another person's decisions. Your ex-wife could have seen someone and worked out her problems. You did all you could. Just make sure you stay close with your daughter."

Steve finished his soda and crumpled the can. "You must be a hell of a shrink."

"Thank you, kind sir. I feel bad for Carol Ann, she blew a choice opportunity."

"My feelings exactly. We better take down the sails, City Island is dead ahead."

Steve gunned Impressions into her berth, hitting reverse just in time to stop her dead in the slip. He jumped onto the pier, took the dock lines from Nita, secured Impressions and connected the electric and phone lines.

Leaving the boat to Captain Bill, Steve grabbed his forensic kit and camera with one hand and Nita's hand with the other, and led them on a foot race up the pier to the parking lot. He jumped on the Harley and started the engine with a roar.

Nita stared wide-eyed. "You're kidding?"

"No, hop on, we'll make better time."

"You own this monster?" She took a hesitant step.

"Me and the bank." He handed her Sam's helmet.

"What the hell," she strapped it on. "I always wanted to ride with a forensic Hell's Angel." She lifted the visor and fixed Steve with an ice blue look, "I hope you handle this one better than your car."

Nita threw her leg over the passenger seat, grabbed Steve around his mid-section, and they roared off. "I'm going to have to hold on real tight," she shouted over the engine and rush of air.

"I was counting on that."

Steve felt intoxicated by the closeness of Nita's body pressing tightly against his back. He inhaled her perfume at every red light. Her breath on his neck made him tingle all over and he had to use every ounce of self-control to concentrate on staying upright.

She gasped when Steve had to cut through the heavy traffic over the City Island bridge. The ride was all too brief as far as Steve was concerned, and dejectedly, he kicked down the rest stand to allow Nita to disembark.

Eight police cruisers and an ambulance with flashing lights confirmed they had reached the crime scene. Unmarked police cars sat askew on either side of a path that ran through Pelham Bay Park. The area directly in front of the path was clear and cordoned off with yellow crime scene tape. A specialist lifted a plaster cast of two tire prints from the soft earth adjoining the trail. Other technicians were methodically combing the area, plucking barely visible slivers off the surrounding bushes. Morbid onlookers parked in the remaining spots on the opposite shoulder. A uniformed cop tried to speed up the procession of cars full of curiosity seekers who, no doubt, would theorize about the scene while eating their island seafood dinners. A full contingent of TV vans, newspaper crime reporters, and photographers added to the congestion.

The homicide investigators emerged from the woods with grim expressions on their faces. No gallows humor on this one. Lonnie and O'Brien came around a bend, so engrossed in their discussion they almost missed Steve and Nita.

Lonnie called Steve aside. "This is the nastiest one yet, Doc. I thought I'd seen everything, but this one's a real shit kicker. The scene's the freshest so far, and we're still checking it out. We've got two clear footprints, so stick to the marked path. We don't want to fuck up the casts. The body is just around the bend. Perp probably pulled over late last night, waited till there was no traffic, then carried her up the path and dumped her. Two kids found her late this morning. Perez is questioning them over there." He pointed to the small group inside the tapes. "Two precinct cops checked out the squeal, didn't touch anything, and called us. She looks...well, you'll see. Has Nita done homicide scenes? It's a fucking mess."

Steve shook his head. "This bastard makes a point of that, doesn't he? I spoke to her. She thinks viewing the scene will help her develop a more accurate profile. She's a big girl, and if she thinks she can handle it, she can."

"Whatever. Walk directly behind me; we don't want to track up the path. O'Brien and the photographer are finished."

Steve motioned Nita to follow. As they rounded the bend, Steve saw the naked body, limbs spread at odd angles, sprawled on top of two crushed azalea bushes. From his perspective, he could not see beyond her breasts to her neck and head. The body was a much deeper shade of blue than the other victims, as if all her blood had been drained. Up close, he saw her long, blonde hair spread over the leaves of the bushes. He was within a few feet of her when he stopped short, and involuntarily held up his hand to stop Nita, but she was already alongside him.

She gasped and recoiled. The victim's throat had been ripped out from the bottom of her lower jaw to her shoulder blade. Steve thought of a zebra he'd once seen, right after a lioness had completed her kill.

Nita stayed back, sucking in large gulps of air, while Lonnie and Steve conferred.

Steve clenched his jaws. "If this is the same perp, the crazy bastard used his own teeth to murder her."

"O'Brien thought so, too. Can you get a good impression?"

"It'll be rough, it's a big area. I'll do a direct acetate imprint as a back-up."

Steve screwed the close up lens on his Nikon and bent down for a closer look. "One thing's for sure—these bite marks are not the same as on the other victims."

"How can you tell?"

Steve slipped on a pair of gloves and used his finger as a pointer. "The teeth marks are larger, and the bite is wider. Also, from the shape of the wound, I would say the teeth were sharper."

Nita lifted her head to listen, but avoided looking at the corpse while Steve pointed out the differences to Lonnie.

"Help me turn her on her side," Steve said. "It'll be easier to get better impressions, and a clearer acetate imprint."

Steve and Lonnie slowly turned the stiffened body over.

"Hold it!" Steve shouted. He bent down and pointed to a long, shiny object at the base of the azalea bush. Lonnie picked it up with a pair of tweezers. Steve's eyes widened to half dollars when he stared at the ten-inch stainless steel instrument. "It's a laboratory Vee Hee carver."

"Come again, Doc?" Lonnie placed it in an evidence bag.

"An instrument dentists and lab technicians use to mold wax on an unfinished denture."

"It's cutting through the bag. Are they always this sharp?"

"No. They're usually dull. This one's been honed."

"Nice going, Doc. This could be the murder weapon we've been looking for."

Steve shot a roll of film, then opened his case to take out the materials he needed for an impression and an acetate imprint.

7

The Deadly Tourist

Nita quietly backed away, then fled down the path to the shoulder. As Steve had advised, she sat on a rock, placed her head between her legs, and drew deep draughts of fresh air to control the intense gagging feeling in the back of her palate.

Across the road, an aged blue Ford was parked on the shoulder. The driver, a powerfully built, balding man in his early forties snapped to attention. He zeroed in on Nita with cold raptor eyes that were hidden behind mirrored sunglasses. His muscular forearms flexed as he gripped the steering wheel and relaxed in rhythm with her labored breathing. An electrified sensation coursed through his body when he saw how his handiwork affected her.

He knew he shouldn't be seen in the vicinity of the crime scene, but he couldn't resist the temptation. The thrill of being nearly face-to-face with his adversaries gave him an omnipotent feeling that he found hard to suppress. He had deduced early on that the massive black detective was in charge of the investigation. He also observed the deference given to the couple who had driven up on the motorcycle.

Why's the blonde bitch involved, if she's so fucking squeamish? he thought. *She does have a long, sexy neck, just like a swan.* He stared at it with hawk-like intensity, and constantly wet his lips. *I better get the hell out of here, before I call attention to myself.*

He started to turn the key in the ignition, but stopped when he spied the motorcycle driver emerge from the path carrying a leather case and a camera slung over his shoulder. The man stopped to talk to the blonde. The black man joined the couple, and they had a five-minute conversation. The motorcycle man and the blonde mounted the bike and headed back toward City Island. The black detective followed shortly in a green Chevrolet Caprice.

The observer started his car, waited for an SUV to pass, and keeping the larger vehicle between them, tailed behind at a discreet distance. He drove past, when the black man pulled into the parking lot of a rundown bar. *Anchors Aweigh* blinked erratically on a smoke-encrusted neon sign. He parked a few blocks away and walked back to the bar. He knew he was taking a big risk, but the excitement aroused him.

Inside the dark bar, Steve and Nita sat in a booth in the back of the room. Four men with a local boatyard emblazoned on their work shirts, shot pool while their coworkers sat at the cigarette-scarred bar watching the final inning of a Mets game. Lonnie paused at the entrance until his eyes become accustomed to the gloom before he spotted them. He ordered a beer and walked to their table.

"Sorry, Doc, I'm too depressed to tell you a joke. That was a tough sucker."

Steve waved him off. "No sweat. We're not in the mood to hear any."

"Feeling better, Nita?"

"I'm coping. This should help." She lifted a double Scotch and took a sip.

"You guys think this sicko's our man? I can't recall a homicide where the victim was so drained of blood," Lonnie said.

Nita paled at the memory.

"Sorry, Nita, we can do this later," Lonnie said.

"No, it's important we review the facts while they're still fresh in our minds."

"How about finding her outdoors and not in a Manhattan apartment?" Steve offered.

"She was killed elsewhere and dumped there," Lonnie took a long swallow from his Michelob, "That was O'Brien's theory."

"Maybe she lived with her parents or roommates," Nita said.

"So far, the only clues linking her to our mutt are: she was blonde, she was raped, and she was bitten," Lonnie said.

"Only this time, the bite itself was the cause of death," Steve added.

Nita downed a heavy belt of her Scotch.

The muscular man with mirrored sunglasses, now wearing a baseball cap to cover his smoothly shaved head, entered the bar, ordered a gin martini from the bartender, and carried it to a small table near the entrance, facing the threesome. The stranger looked over the top of his glasses and fixated on Nita's neck while sipping his drink. He paid particular attention, and his breath quickened, when he watched the way her swan like neck rose when her drink slowly passed down her throat.

She's a lush, he thought, *just like the other whores. But swan necks are no match for a hawk's bill.* He pulled his hat down, lifted the dark glasses back onto his nose and covered his mouth with his hand, before the trio passed his table on their way out. The black detective looked even bigger, close up.

"Steve, Nita, I'll see you at the conference Wednesday morning," the black man said as they stopped at the door.

"Right, Lonnie," the motorcycle man said.

The killer repeated their names silently, while he threw some bills on the table, and then left the bar as the man called Steve roared by on the motorcycle with the woman named Nita hugging his back. He watched them stop a few blocks down, next to where he had parked his car. Quickly, he walked the few blocks, arriving just as a parking attendant delivered a white Acura to the entrance of Scotty's restaurant. The bald man unlocked his blue Ford as Nita and a group of women emerged from the restaurant and got into the car. He watched her wave to the man called Steve and drove off.

Steve started the Harley, rode another four blocks, and made a right turn into the City Island Marina. The man in the blue car followed close behind. He pulled alongside the curb next to the marina entrance. The image of Steve parking the Harley in the parking lot reflected in the stranger's mirrored glasses. His peregrine eyes followed Steve as he walked down the gangplank to a sailboat with the name Impressions on the stern. A white cat was pacing the deck.

The man asked a passing launch boy, "Can you tell me who owns that sailboat?" He gestured in Steve's direction. "I thought I recognized him as an old army buddy named Steve."

"Got that right, Cap. Dr. Steven Landau."

"Doctor?"

"Yeah, he's a dentist."

As he walked back to his car he thought, *a dentist, of course, no wonder he's so important. They can't make a case against me without him. Better still, he's involved with the blonde tramp. Maybe I can get two birds with one stone.*

8

Dr. H. Hugh Nagle

The next day, Steve called Frank Tintrup, the owner of his dental laboratory to ask about the Broadway director's request for a set of Dracula teeth.

"Shouldn't be a problem," Tintrup assured him.

"I'm not comfortable that the actor has to sing, while wearing them."

"Call Dr. H. Hugh Nagle. He's a theatrical makeup dentist and I've been told he's *numero uno* in that limited field. He's probably your best bet."

Steve looked Nagle up in the New York State directory and recognized his address as a prestigious professional building on West 57th Street. He called the listed number, and an officious female voice answered after the first ring.

"Good morning. This is the office of Dr. H. Hugh Nagle."

High class, presumptuous, expensive, Steve doodled on his pad. "Good morning, I'm Dr. Steven Landau. I'd like to speak to Dr. Nagle."

"What is this in reference to?"

"One of my patients has a dental problem involving a theatrical performance. I want to consult with Dr. Nagle about a solution."

"I can give you an appointment in three weeks."

"I thought lunch would be more appropriate. Of course, as a professional courtesy, it would be my treat."

"Dr H. Hugh Nagle is a very busy man. He usually has his lunch delivered to the office."

"My plate is pretty full, too. Could you please check with the Doctor?" Steve kept his tone as pleasant as possible.

"If you insist," she put Steve on hold. He thought he would gag as he listened to a recorded message relating all the fabulous services offered by Dr. H. Hugh Nagle over the background of a Liberace concerto.

He scrunched up his nose and wrote, monumental royal pain in the butt, on his pad, and circled it a few times before he heard, "Dr. H. Hugh Nagle speaking."

"Dr. Nagle, my name's Steve Landau, and I'm a fellow dentist. My lab had recommended you. I'm making a set of Dracula teeth for an actor in a Broadway play, and I can use some advice. I'd be pleased to take you to lunch for a conference."

"Nice try Doctor, but I consider my work a personal specialty. If you don't have any experience in this field, you can introduce me to the director and I'll pay you a finder's fee."

"Nice try yourself Doctor, but, I'm sure I can work it out on my own. Thanks, for your time."

"Thursday would be good for me. One o'clock at Lutece."

"You're on." *What a pissy, pompous ass,* Steve thought as he hung up. He hoped he wasn't making a mistake that would rear up and kick him in the butt.

Lieutenant Gagliardi slammed his big paw on the desk in the conference room and admonished the team. "Goddammit paisans! Someone ran off at the mouth and now the newspaper and TV geeks are calling our skell,

71

the `Dracula Killer.' We're gonna need all the breaks we can get, cause the vultures are goin' to ratchet up the heat. Lonnie, whadda we got?"

"Our perp's raised the ante. Doc Landau figures this time he used a different set of teeth over his own as the murder weapon. Blood tests confirm he murdered Thelma Lewis, the victim in Pelham Bay Park. Ms. Lewis lives — make that lived — with her parents in a duplex apartment in Gramercy Park. She told her parents she had a date with a man she had met the night before at a singles bar.

"Stomach contents showed a full meal about two hours before she was offed. Time of death was between twelve and one a.m. Our perp's now wining, dining, and drugging his blondes before killing them. Enough chloral hydrate was found in her system to knock her out. The M.E.'s not sure how it was done, but over three quarters of her blood was gone. That's a helluva lot more than she would've lost before her heart quit."

Lonnie waited until latecomer Perez found a seat, and was rewarded with one of Gagliardi's withering looks.

"We found traces of stainless steel in the wound again," Lonnie went on. "The instrument Doc Landau found under the body is a dental tool called a Vee Hee carver. The blade had been sharpened and could have been the murder weapon in the previous homicides. We lifted a partial thumb print off one end. Len, in fingerprints, says he can make only three and a half points. Not enough for court, but it can help us with an ID."

Lonnie paused, waited until Gagliardi caught up scratching his notes on the blackboard, and continued. "The footprint matches the one we found in the blood of the first vic's apartment. Tire treads were from two moderately worn Goodyear radials. Lucky break! A fireman coming home to City Island, after a late tour, remembers seeing an old blue car parked in the area around four a.m. Unfortunately, he didn't get a make or model but he thought it was a fifties or sixties vintage. Threads on the bushes at the location are the same brown material we found at the other sites. Blood sample: Type O negative, are also the same as the earlier findings. Finally, there were traces of gypsum or plaster of Paris on her backside and upper torso."

Gagliardi put down the chalk with a flourish and turned to face the team. "I got six more detectives assigned to us. I'm gonna have them check the car angle. I know it's a long shot, but I want a team on all the Goodyear dealers in Manhattan. Tell them to computer-check for an old blue car or call us if one comes in for replacement tires. Canvass all the parking garages in Manhattan, and notify the uniforms on patrol to check the streets. Maybe, we can catch a break.

"Perez and Stone, run down the singles bars and restaurants in the Gramercy Park area with pictures of the victims and whatever descriptions we have of the perp. Lonnie, assign a team to question her friends. Maybe, they were with her when she met him, or, she coulda described her date for 'em. Recheck the retail men's stores, for customers who prefer brown suits and sports jackets. Let's work on the fireman. Maybe hypnosis will help him remember more about the car.

"Listen up, everyone. Because of the dental tool we found, we could be dealing with a dentist. Lonnie, call the New York Dental Society and the American Dental Association to see if they have information about dentists who've done time or lost their licenses due to sexual misconduct. Doc Landau, you can help, also. Contact the dental supply companies and find out who sells that brand of Vee Hee instrument."

Gagliardi paused to let Lonnie finish taking notes. He turned to Nita, "Dr. Lazar, you got anything we can use?"

"Yes, Lieutenant, I think I have a handle on him, now," Nita stood and moved to the front of the room. "There's no need to tell you we're dealing with a very disturbed, but intelligent, and seductive individual. Unfortunately, none of us will be able to pick up on his illness since he looks and acts normal, and was suave enough to seduce a lot of attractive, professional type women. Don't be fooled. He's an extremely troubled person who was probably sexually abused as a child. I'm certain his mother or a woman close to him was an attractive blonde and actively involved in the abuse.

"Serial killers have a need for power. They want to dominate their victims, be a godlike figure, who controls their lives. He thinks, he's a supreme being who can't be caught, so, he's getting careless. That slip can be a major factor in capturing him."

Nita stopped and took a sip of water. "Sociopaths have pathologic character disorders, that allow them to kill and inflict the most brutal and unspeakable acts of violence with impunity. They have absolutely no regret, conscience, or guilt about what they do, but kill for the thrill of what they know, are perverted acts. A few even believe their acts are justified."

A murmur rose among the team as a few members nodded to each other. Nita waited until the whispering died down. "As our man's murders increase, he needs more gratification, more arousal. He has, as Detective Wright said, raised the ante by changing his M.O., but he's revealing more of himself as he takes more chances. His actions are becoming more bizarre and gruesome. He's challenging us, trying to outwit us, and maybe, in an oblique way, confronting us."

Nita paused for a moment, held up a bound notebook, and continued, "Data from the FBI's B.S.U. unit, as well as my own observations, confirm that serial killers are mostly white males between twenty-five and forty with a lower-class upbringing. They vent their aggressions in an effort to gain entrance to the higher levels of society. In reality, they're psychologically emasculated sociopaths, frustrated by their cultural obstacles. They target upper-middle class females, to rape, murder, or mutilate to achieve celebrity.

"Serial murderers are captured because they get sloppy and make mistakes. As you all know, David Berkowitz was caught by accident, when he illegally parked in front of a fire hydrant the night of one of his murders. Joel Rifkin was pulled over because of a broken taillight. Our killer can be more closely associated with Ted Bundy, since he uses his teeth on his victims."

Nita stopped, but no one spoke. All eyes were riveted on her. As long-time homicide detectives, they had developed an indifference to murder. But the brutality of this killer seemed the ultimate nightmare. One of the newer members of the team, a female detective from central homicide, could only shake her head.

Finally, Lonnie asked. "Can you add anything to what we know about his physical appearance, Dr. Lazar?"

Nita pursed her lips. "He's probably attractive and very concerned about how he looks. I'd guess—and it's only speculation—that he works out and might have a weightlifter's physique. Also, he has powerful jaws, so he probably has a square face. So, ladies and gentlemen, all we have to do is add this information to our earlier evidence, find a perp that fits our profile, and snap a pair of cuffs on him, before the Fibbies get in our way."

A lot of amen's eased the tension. Gagliardi rose to wrap up the meeting. "Thanks, Dr. Lazar," he said, "your input's gotta help. Okay, ladies and gents, lets hit the streets."

Steve folded his notes. "Your talk got everyone's attention," he told her at the door.

"Thanks, I gave it a lot of thought."

They left the conference room together. "Can I interest you in a more leisurely sail this Sunday?" Steve asked.

"I'd love to," Nita answered, "But, I promised my parents I'd go there for a late lunch. You're welcome to join me."

Steve could have done a cartwheel. "That'd be terrific. Where do they live?"

"Riverside Drive and 81st Street."

"I have a great idea. Why don't I pick you up at the East 23rd Street Boat Basin, and sail around Manhattan to the West 79th Street Marina? We could walk to your parents from there."

"You're right, that is a great idea. Meet you Sunday at 23rd Street at noon."

"I'll be there." Steve's step was considerably lighter as he left One Police Plaza.

The next day, Steve remade his rarely used tie three times before he slipped on his best sports coat. "I must be crazy, letting that jerk Nagle pick the most expensive restaurant in the city," he told his image in the mirror. "I'll just have to charge it to the show." He winked to himself before turning out the light.

Steve arrived early by his customary ten minutes and was shown to Nagle's table. At exactly one o'clock, Nagle arrived with great flourish, followed by the fawning Maître d'. He sported a deep tan and a look of aristocratic nonchalance. *Probably cultivated* **both** *in the Hamptons*, Steve thought. Nagle's jaw was strong and his hair fashionably long, with every dark wavy strand in place. His slate-gray eyes took Steve in without expression. He was impeccably dressed in tan slacks, an expensive sports coat, and a silk chestnut shirt opened to reveal a yellow ascot.

Christ, an ascot. Do you believe this guy? Steve thought

Nagle's dazzling smile was accentuated by some of the whitest porcelain caps Steve had ever seen.

"Dr. Landau, I presume?"

"Dr. Nagle, good to meet you." The two men shook hands. Steve thought, *Nagle must work out to have that firm a handshake.*

"How do you get away with not wearing a tie at Lutece?"

"Rank does have its privileges."

Steve kept his look impassive. "Why don't we order first? Then we can talk."

Nagle ordered, in French, the most costly items on the menu, as well as a vintage bottle of wine. Nagle looked vaguely familiar, but Steve couldn't put his finger on where he might have met him. A few queries failed to jog his memory. Nagle dominated the conversation with tales of his many successes and his prowess in treating a long list of celebrities.

Steve stifled a yawn and looked at his watch. "If it's alright with you, I'd like to discuss the type of teeth I could make for a singing Dracula."

A look of annoyance flickered for an instant over Nagle's tan face. "Yes, of course, that is the reason for our lunch."

Steve flinched and plunged ahead. "I'm undecided about using porcelain or acrylic. Which material would you suggest?"

"For motion pictures, I've used porcelain, but for the theater, and repeated use, acrylic works best." Nagle pronounced theater like an English drama critic.

"Then, I'd have to make a few sets, since the acrylic will either wear or stain."

"Precisely, and of course use the lightest shade. But I'm sure you must know that."

"Of course." *This egotistical schmuck is a lot worse than I anticipated,* thought Steve. "How will I get around the phonics? Remember, he has to sing with these teeth."

"That does present a problem. Let's see. Suppose you make them only as an anterior laminate with no material on the inside of the front teeth."

"Then, I won't be able to get any retention. What if, I rolled the incisal edge of the acrylic around the tips of the anterior teeth? The actor would have security during his high notes, with no interference to his diction."

"Excellent, Doctor — you might turn into a theatrical dentist after all."

Steve had to restrain himself.

"Are you a G.P. or do you specialize?" Nagle continued.

"Specialist, Doctor. But like you, in a very limited field, or should I say fields?"

Nagle furrowed his tan brow. "Fields?"

"Yes, I specialize in veterinary dentistry, and most of my patients are residents of the Bronx Zoo. I also have a part-time general practice in the West Village. In addition, I'm certified by the Forensic Board of Odontology and work as a consultant for the NYPD."

Nagle's eyes opened wide. "Are you working on the cases that are presently terrorizing our fair city?"

"As a matter of fact, I am."

"How interesting. Please, tell me about them," Nagle's voice took on a conspiratorial tone

"Sorry, Doctor, I'm not at liberty to discuss them." Steve snapped his fingers. "Wait a second! Maybe you can help. Didn't you make a set of metal teeth for the villain in one of those action adventure movies?"

"You must be referring to *Iron Jaw*. Yes, of course I did." Nagle waved it off with an impatient gesture.

"Could they be cast in stainless steel with extremely sharp edges and a special mechanism to add strength to the bite?"

Nagle grabbed the napkin off his lap, folded it, snapped it on the table, and shoved his chair back as he stood. "Yes, they can. I'm sorry, but I have to get back to the office. My next patient is a Prima Donna, and is extremely rude when I'm late. I'm sure you have your share of them."

"Yeah sure. I have a tiger named Tony who roars before all his appointments."

Nagle looked down at Steve for a moment. "Nice chatting with you. Ciao."

Stanley Woods-Frankel

What a piece of work! Steve reflected as he signed his credit card for an outrageously expensive bill.

9

Old Friends

The next day, Steve went to jail. He met Assistant D.A., Oscar Fuentes, on the steps of the 26th Precinct. "Thanks for coming on such short notice, Doc." Fuentes held the door to the station house for Steve.

"No sweat. What's the story?"

"The suspect, Simon DeLeon, was arrested last night by two uniforms two blocks from a Korean market holdup. He was carrying an unloaded pistol, a pocket full of bills, and he had chocolate on his fingers," Fuentes said.

"Chocolate?" Steve asked.

"That's right. The proprietor was pistol whipped, but before he passed out, he pointed to a candy bar the perp had bitten into."

"I hope New York's finest didn't knock any of his teeth out."

"Nah, it was a good bust. Asshole still hollered police brutality. Maybe you can rip out a few of his molars when you do your thing."

"That stuff went out with the Inquisition. And, by-the-way, that is what your ancestors did to mine back in medieval Spain."

"I apologize for them. How about just chipping a front tooth?"

The desk sergeant called Steve aside. "He's not thrilled about having impressions taken of his teeth."

Steve shrugged. "So, what else is new?"

"Watch yourself, Doc. The mutt's not what I'd call cooperative."

Two cops accompanied Steve and Fuentes to the holding tank and held DeLeon while Steve checked his mouth. The prisoner tried to bite Steve's finger.

Steve put down the impression tray, crossed his arms and stared hard at the prisoner. "We can do this in one of two ways. Cooperate and let me do my job, or I get a court order to put you in la-la land. Either way toad, I'm taking your impressions. Be cool, and the judge might go easier on you. If not, forget copping a plea. The prosecutor will gladly barbecue your sorry ass into well-done strips. Your choice amigo."

The man glared at the guards on either side of him. "Go ahead," he snarled. "Jus remember Dentist, you hurt me, I gotta long memory."

"Hey man, this is not the time to make my hands shake. Open wide." Steve performed the procedures and poured up the models in the visitor's bathroom. Later, the set stone model and teeth marks in the chocolate bar matched perfectly. Steve unpacked his Nikon and snapped a few shots of the labeled chocolate bar next to a forensic ruler and DeLeon's models. He changed to a close-up lens and finished the roll, shooting from different angles to illustrate their alignment in court.

With no emergencies the following day, Steve was free to join his associates at an all-day seminar on implants at the First District Dental Society. During the lunch break he and two of his classmates, Norm Wagshul and Herm Bressack, went to a nearby kosher deli. They retold their favorite dental school stories over hot pastrami and cream sodas.

Herm said, "All I can remember, is those beautiful aspiring actresses and models who came to the clinic to get their teeth capped, because the price was right."

"Is that why you were always walking around with a hard-on?" Norm asked.

"Watch it old son. Remember I married one of 'em," Herm bit into a sour pickle. "That reminds me, Steve. My wife wants to know what exciting things have been happening in your lonely bachelor existence."

Steve's lips parted in a sly smile. "Same old, same old, except there's someone new in my life."

"That's all you're going to tell us?" Norm chided. "Come on, Stevie baby! What's she look like? Is she a flake like you? What does she do? How is she in the sack?"

Steve laughed. "She's smart, beautiful, athletic, has a black belt, and is a forensic psychologist. The rest is none of your business."

"You guys working together on that case in the papers?" Herm asked.

"That's how we met."

"Who would have thought, you'd become a forensic expert?" Norm quipped.

Steve smiled. "Who would have thought, you'd become an oral surgeon, after me and Herm had to carry you out of the surgery clinic every day of our rotation?"

"Ouch, old buddy!"

During the apple strudel and tea, Steve described what a debacle his session with Nagle had been. "Lunch with that egomaniac is on my short list of unpleasant experiences."

Norm nodded. "My current office manager used to work for the snake. She told me, in confidence, of course — that Nagle's a horny bastard who tried to make her, and every blonde actress who walked through the door."

"I attended a cosmetic dentistry lecture he gave last year and heard rumors he had to buy his way out of a raid on a S and M club in Chelsea," Herm added, "Leather whips, chains, the whole bit."

Steve had trouble focusing on the implant course after the lunch break.

10

The Date

Steve took extra care shaving, splashed on his killer lotion and left a half hour early for his date with Nita. He cursed the current running against him as he motored down the East River, and arrived ten minutes late at the 23rd Street boat basin. When he caught sight of Nita waving to him from the pier, he became acutely aware that his heart rate had ratcheted up to match the beat of the engine pistons.

"Haven't felt like this since I was a teenager," Steve said under his quickening breath as he turned Impressions into the wind and nosed slowly up to the dock. Nita, wearing hip-hugging capri pants and a cotton shirt tied off at her midriff, gracefully jumped on board. Steve gunned the engine, pulled away from the dock, and fought the current to head down-stream. He started to apologize for arriving late, but Nita shut him up with an unexpected brush of her lips.

"Keep that up, and I'll be late for all our dates," he said.

"I'm just really glad to see you."

"Double that for me," he said, trying not to stare at her bare midsection.

"Nita picked up Captain Bill and laid him in her lap. "Hey handsome, are you going to be our chaperone for the day?"

They motored down the East River around the tip of Manhattan before Nita helped Steve set the sails for the trip up the Hudson to the 79th Street Marina.

"Are you all right?" Nita asked.

"Sure. Why, do I look different?" Steve asked, certain his thumping heart was visible through his polo shirt.

Nita appraised Steve. "I don't know, you seem kind of nervous. Have you sailed up the Hudson before?"

"I could probably do it with my eyes closed," he assured her.

"You can't fool a shrink. Something's bothering you. Why don't you lie down on the boat cushion and tell ol' Doc Lazar about it."

Nita's reassuring smile loosened Steve up. After a nervous laugh he confessed, "The last time I met a girl's parents, I was with the woman who would later become my ex-wife, and that was months after I met her."

"Are you afraid I have designs on you?"

He laughed nervously again. "That would make my day. I'm apprehensive about meeting them. I just hope they like me. Silly, huh?"

"Not to worry dear Steve. If you appeal to my discriminating taste, they'll adore you."

"And do I?"

"With flying colors. Don't worry about mom and dad. They have a lotta, lotta smarts, and will have your agile mind spinning."

"They must have, if you're their daughter."

Nita squeezed his hand. They were quiet for a while, enjoying the beam reach sail past the Chelsea Piers.

"Have you come up with any new theories about the Dracula Killer?" Steve asked.

"The BSU faxed us their findings. Our profiles are fairly close."

"That must be a boost to your confidence."

"Not really. We're far apart on the causative factor in the killer's life. I strongly believe it was his mother."

"And the mucky mucks at Quantico?"

"They think it could have been any female, blonde authoritative figure who damaged him in his formative years."

"Hold on." Steve let the Genoa sail out to catch more wind. "So where do you go from here?"

"We duke it out, and eventually throw a compromised profile into the computer and come up with the usual suspects, or not. The FBI agrees with you that the killer may have a dental background. We're adding that to the mix."

"Makes a lot of sense. Most of the dentists I know are borderline certifiable."

"I hope you're one of the exceptions."

Captain Bill jumped off Nita's lap and started to patrol the deck.

"I'm the maverick of my profession, if everyone's sane, I'm Loony Toons, and vice-versa."

Nita smiled. "That's part of your appeal."

"I hate to change the subject, but how much can we expect from a profile. Have they really helped capture the bad guys?"

Nita pursed her lips. "At the very least, a profile narrows the field to a workable number of suspects. On a few occasions, it pinpointed the killer exactly. Other times, it kept the investigation moving in the right direction, until some unforeseen incident finally broke the case."

They were quiet again as Impressions glided past the Intrepid Aircraft Carrier museum permanently docked at 44th Street.

"Enough shop talk," Steve said, "I feel like you know all about me, and I haven't a clue what makes you tick."

"You've uncovered one of my shrink tricks. Where do I begin?"

"I've spilled my guts about my failed marriage, how about telling me what happened with your relationship with the college professor?"

"Actually the two of you have a lot of similar traits, but are totally opposite in other ways, and vive la difference." Nita's pronunciation bore a French nasality.

Steve turned the wheel and started to unwind the sheet from the winch. "Can't wait to hear about it, but the wind shifted and we have to tack."

After Impressions picked up speed on the new course, he turned to Nita. "The good news first."

Nita laughed. "So far in our very brief relationship, there is no bad news. But here goes, you're both tall, good-looking, although, I think you have him beat there, and very intelligent. You are more proactive and analytical while Charles is more of a detached academic. "

"That's it?"

Nita turned serious. "Be patient, I know you think since I'm a therapist, I'm a very open person, but in reality I'm extremely private and get stage fright when I have to talk about myself."

Steve winched the sheet another revolution. "I promise to behave myself. How dissimilar am I from this Charles character?"

"In many ways, the two of you are poles apart. In the first place he's a lot older, and he was still married when we started."

Steve looked at Nita over his sunglasses. "How'd you handle that little dilemma?"

"Not well. I almost fell apart when he left her and wanted to move in with me."

"Did he?"

Nita nodded. "For about two weeks but neither of us could handle the guilt. During that brief little interlude, I found out he expected me to be his little housekeeper, and contributed zero to the daily chores. That was the first step in a long breakup."

"Any other differences?"

Nita watched the joggers along the Riverside Park path for a while. "Charles is totally un-athletic, terribly out of shape, and looks it, unlike the buff sea captain who is now transporting me to my parents. He couldn't handle my competitiveness and didn't have a clue why I had taken up Karate. He didn't came to my black-belt ceremony when he knew how important it was to me."

"Sounds like he felt you weren't connected."

85

Nita stared at Steve. "Hmm, perceptive and compassionate. You'd make a good shrink."

Steve laughed. "No thanks. My dance card is full enough for now. There's the 79th Street marina. If you take the wheel, I'll go below and radio them," Steve said.

He returned after a few minutes, "They assigned us to an upriver mooring."

Nita eased up to the pennant, and Steve pulled the line aboard with a boat hook. They worked the tricky maneuver effortlessly, as if they had been doing it for years. Once the boat was secured, they lowered the inflatable Zodiac and, leaving Captain Bill in charge, motored to the dinghy dock. They walked up the ramp, through the security gate, and climbed the steps to Riverside Drive. Steve's anxiety eased when Nita took his hand during the short walk to her parents building.

Nita stopped before they got to the entrance. "I should warn you, my father hated Charles after his first visit, and Charles never came back. My mother wasn't exactly overjoyed with the way he treated me either. Since I'm an only child, they dote on me, so you better be on your best behavior."

Steve saluted her. "Yes Ma'am. Just give me a signal when it's time to kiss your feet. Us, only kids have to stick together."

"*Bonjour, mon amour*," said Nita's mother as she kissed her daughter lightly on both cheeks, European style. Nita's father gave her a bear hug and smiled at Steve. Nita took Steve's hand. "Mama et Papa, I would like you to meet *mon très cher ami*, Dr. Steven Landau."

Nita's mother, Micheline, kissed him on both cheeks. "*Enchanté*, Steven," she said warmly. "We are so glad to meet you. Nita has told us all about you."

Steve almost blushed. "I'm afraid, there's not much to tell."

Micheline smiled seductively and waved her finger at him. "You would be surprised."

Before Steve could catch Nita's eye, her father, Dr. Claude Lazar, a ruggedly handsome man with a trimmed goatee and athletic build, firmly shook Steve's hand, then clapped him on the back "What can I get you to drink?" his smile was generous.

86

Steve visualized Madame Lazar as a knockout in her younger years. She wore her auburn hair, flecked with gray, in a chignon held in place with a flamboyant antique comb. Her features were sharper than Nita's, but the two women shared the same captivating, cobalt eyes. She still had a trim figure and could easily have passed as Nita's older sister. Like Nita, she had beautiful skin and wore little make-up. She also had the same knack as her husband for putting Steve at ease.

Madame Lazar, a creative chef, specialized in Parisian cuisine. For appetizers she offered *"Pâté de foies de Volailles et terrine de poisson."*

Nita translated for Steve by whispering in his ear, "Chicken liver pate and chilled fish terrine."

Steve looked apprehensively at the Lazars to see if they noticed the goose pimples break out on his arms.

A frigid, dry Sauvignon Blanc accompanied the colorful arrangement. Steve smacked his lips after tasting the soup, a chilled vichyssoise. He thought nothing could possibly be any better, until Micheline Lazar served the main course, announcing, *"Canard au poivre vert."* Nita again whispered in Steve's ear, "Roast duckling with green peppercorn sauce." Steve didn't know which he liked better, the crisp, piquant duckling or Nita's breath on his ear. Steve thought he could not eat another bite, when Nita sent a shiver down his spine, titillating his ear one more time. "Chestnut mousse." She helped her mother serve *Mousse aux marrons*, for dessert.

Epicurean heaven, Steve thought.

During an after-dinner brandy, Steve and Claude held a spirited debate about the upcoming mayoral election and the death penalty until Nita nudged Steve. "If you want to catch the current, we should leave now."

"Can't it wait?" Claude lamented. "We didn't get a chance to talk about the Yankee's chances for winning the pennant."

Nita laughed. "If I left it up to you, Papa, we'd be here all night. I promise to bring Steve back."

Bearing a kitty bag full of leftovers, Nita and Steve returned to an eager Captain Bill and got underway a half-hour before sunset. They skimmed lazily down the Hudson, watching the red sun sink behind the Statue of Liberty and the Jersey skyline beyond. As they rounded the Battery, the lights of downtown Manhattan commenced their nightly glitter. Nita sighed moments later, when the sparkling diamond arch over the Brooklyn Bridge blinked on, complemented by the illumination from the South Street Seaport. The wind, uncharacteristically right for raising the multi-colored balloon-like spinnaker, along with the current going to flood, gave them a boost upriver. Nita snuggled in Steve's arms as they glided past the United Nations with the summer-tinted lights of the Empire State building in the background. After a rocky passage through the whirlpools of Hell's Gate, they sailed under the Throggs Neck Bridge and into the expanse of Long Island Sound. Steve bypassed the busy anchorage of City Island and headed east toward the quieter Little Neck Bay.

He dropped the sails as they drifted into a small cove and set the anchor. After securing Impressions, Steve joined Nita in the cockpit with a split of champagne.

"Your relationship with your parents is very special, and I think they're great," he said, "I'd like to propose a toast to them for giving me you."

"Thank you, kind sir, and I'll drink to Mr. and Mrs. Landau for giving me you."

They tapped glasses and drained the champagne. Steve threw his glass into the dark water, and Nita's followed. He took her in his arms and their lips met eagerly in a tongue-searching kiss.

Lips still connected, their fingers flew, as they removed each other's clothes. Naked, Steve hoisted the laughing Nita over his shoulder and carried her, fireman style, down the gangway steps. He laid her gently on his raised bed in the aft cabin. He stood at the foot of the bed for a moment, hostage to her beauty. He kneeled and slowly kissed her toes, one-by-one. Nita moaned with joy as he tenderly worked his way up to her knees. He lifted her thighs over his shoulders and kissed her into a state of rapture. When he could hold off no longer, he slid into her. She exhaled a powerful mysterious sound, a combination of scream and song. Moments later Steve sang out his own chorus. Exhausted, they fell asleep in each other's arms to the gentle, rhythmic rocking of the boat.

Steve sleepily reached for Nita at sunrise, but felt the bed beside him empty. He rose with a start. Movement from the clear hatch-cover overhead drew his attention. He blinked twice to make sure the vision he saw was real. Nita, clad only in his tee shirt and her bikini panties, was performing a sunrise yoga exercise. He thoroughly enjoyed the view, and saw no reason to disturb her. He stretched and lay back until she was finished. When she stepped off the cover, he lifted the hatch and said, "Good morning. If you would like to see a perfect example of homo erectus, the captain suggests you come below."

He barely got out of the way as she dove through the hatch onto the bed.

11

Dracula

Monday morning, Steve and Nita clung to each other, in front of her building, unwilling to let go, until they agreed to go sailing again the following weekend. Steve drove south on F.D.R. Drive to his office in Greenwich Village. His first patient was Art Powers, the actor playing Dracula on Broadway.

Powers had been a matinee idol in the eighties. Steve, a movie buff had seen him star in his most memorable films, including his last two disastrous flops. Nancy was one of his biggest fans and was passionate about her loyalty. She had read a gossip column to Steve after she had inked Powers' name in the appointment book the week before. "It says the only reason Art Powers took the role of Dracula was to save his career." She slammed the paper down. "Jealous bitch! She wouldn't know talent if it bit her on the ass."

Steve had tried to calm her down, but she continued to rant that her hero had been wrongly maligned.

After Steve walked into the office, Nancy stopped primping. "Your producer friend wants you to call him before my heartthrob comes in for his appointment," she said.

Steve assumed a severe expression. "I expect you to act professionally when Art Powers is here."

"Don't worry, boss. I'll be *Miss Dignified* until I jump on his bones." She picked up the ringing phone and looked up at Steve. "Lonnie Wright?"

Steve went back to his private office and picked up the receiver.

"Hey Steve. What's the difference between a dentist and a lawyer?" Lonnie's voice boomed through the receiver, loud enough for Steve to hold it away from his ear.

"I give up."

"Shit, I thought you could help me. I'm having lunch with a few ADA's today, and I need lawyer jokes."

"You're on your own." Steve shifted the phone to his other ear. "Whassup?"

"We got a few live ones out of the computer after cross checking Nita's and the BSU files."

"She told me the report came in."

"She did? You two getting it on?"

Steve thought for a second. "You could say that, but you better not."

"I'm cool, man. Anyway you want to sit in on some of the interrogations? We could use your input."

"No can do. My appointment book over-floweth. Call me here if you get snagged on a dental question."

"Appreciate the offer. Don't drill into too many nerves today. You know what I'm sayin."

"You're confusing me with Lawrence Olivier. Just make sure you never become a patient. Keep me posted."

Steve hung up, and seconds later Nancy announced over the intercom, "Mike Herrman, line two."

"Mike, what can I do for you today?"

"Promise me you'll stay calm for your session with Art Powers."

"Problem?"

"That's putting it mildly. My star, soon to become your patient, is close to a nervous breakdown. He expected this play to boost him back on top, but he became apoplectic when he found out he had to sing two crucial songs on stage wearing a set of false fangs."

"I thought he had a good voice."

"He does, but he hasn't sung in public for years—and rehearsals are not going well. We had to do mucho stroking, just to get him to meet you."

"How'd you do that?" Steve doodled a figure with fangs and a pitch-fork.

"We told him how much free publicity we're getting with this Dracula Killer in the news every day. You've heard about that, haven't you?"

"Who hasn't?" Steve's voice had a sardonic edge.

"Why do you say it like that?"

"I'm working on the case."

"Don't breathe a word to Powers. He'll go apeshit."

Steve drew horns on his figure. "Nice to know I'll be working with an eager and agreeable actor."

"No such animal exists. Lots of luck, Dr. Landau."

Powers, fifteen minutes late, fulfilled Herrman's prophesy.

"I am not an actor; I am a movie star," he said, immediately setting things straight. "Therefore Doctor, don't screw up, or you'll never practice in this town again."

Jesus! He uses dialogue from his movies, Steve thought. *Can I pull this off and satisfy this raving egomaniac, or should I just refer him to that jerk Nagle and save myself a lot of aggravation?* "Mr. Powers, I understand your reluctance, but you'll have to trust me. You have to wear artificial fangs, if you're going to play Dracula."

"I don't trust dentists."

"Bad experience as a child?"

Powers raised his eyebrows, "Yes, how did you know? I've been phobic ever since."

"Your secret's safe with me. I'm not going to minimize your fear, but what we have to do today is easy. I don't even have to use the drill."

Powers relaxed. "No needle?"

"Right. It's that simple. I'll fill this tray with a doughy material and gently place it over your teeth."

"How long will it stay in my mouth?"

"Forty-five to sixty seconds."

Promise."

"Cross my heart."

Steve fitted a tray for Art's mouth. *Arghh!* Powers was a gagger. Steve quickly removed the tray from Art's mouth. *Never a dull day in the wonderful world of dentistry,* Steve thought. "Stay cool, Art. I'll spray the back of your throat with a topical anesthetic. That'll take care of the gagging."

Powers sputtered, "You're sure it'll work?"

"Trust me!" Steve said with a confidence he didn't feel, but Powers came through. While waiting for the alginate to set, Steve, in an effort to take Powers' mind off the procedure, said, "It's appropriate that you need a dentist like me to have a successful show. Bela Lugosi, the original Dracula, became terminally ill while filming his last movie. He insisted that his dentist stand in for him to complete the film."

Powers' eyes remained wide until Steve removed the impression from his mouth. "You're not planning on a career change?" he sputtered.

Steve laughed. "Nope, I'm up to my ears with my practice. Rinse out."

The next procedure, measuring his freeway space — the amount of space between his teeth when his jaws were completely at rest was much easier and proceeded without protest. Powers became so relaxed that he even cracked a few off-color jokes when his mouth was free.

By the time Powers left the office, he and Steve were on a first-name basis. A nonchalant, comeback-confident matinee idol made his appointment to fit the fangs with tongue-tied Nancy.

"Nancy?" Steve stared into her eyes, but her faraway gaze showed no comprehension. *"Como está, Señorita?"*

She still didn't respond. He waved his hand in front of her face. "Hello? Is anyone home?

"Oh boss, isn't he wonderful?"

"He's not exactly my type. Is Mrs. Austron here?"

"She just came in." Nancy sighed.

"When you're through dreaming about your hero, say three hail Mary's and seat her. My session with Mr. Wonderful was intense. I need a break."

He poured a cup of coffee and sank into the leather chair in his private office. He took a sip, dialed the dental lab, and asked for his favorite technician, Frank.

"Frank's mother is seriously ill. He won't be in for two weeks," the lab receptionist informed him.

Steve hung up, knowing he had a problem. The work was too delicate to trust with any other lab tech.

He knew the best solution was to use Nagle's lab. He gritted his teeth and dialed his office.

The teutonic receptionist answered. "This is the office of Dr. H. Hugh Nagle."

"Hi, this is Dr. Landau, I need a few seconds of Dr. Nagle's time."

"You mean now?"

"That would be nice. If not, he can call me back at his convenience. I'll be in all day."

"I'll see what I can do," she said in a clipped tone.

I'm not going to let this bitch get to me. "Thank you, I would appreciate it. I just realized I don't know your name."

"The patients in Dr. Nagle's practice call me Nurse. My name is Etta Rausher."

"Ok, Etta. I won't have any trouble remembering, since I have an Aunt Etta. I appreciate your cooperation."

"I would prefer if you called me Miss Rausher or Nurse. Please hold."

"Ja wohl, Frau Rausher," Steve said in his best Colonel Klink accent to the dead line.

Nagle came on the line.

"Well, the Gestapo put me through," Steve said.

"I beg your pardon?"

"Your nurse, Miss Rausher, is a real charmer."

"She's just following orders."

"Of course." *Standard Nazi excuse.* "I won't take up any of your valuable time, Doctor — I need the name of the lab person you use for your specialty work."

"Don't you have a laboratory?"

"My lab tech's away, and I'd rather use someone with experience in this field."

"My man's name is Hans Dieter. He used to work for me, until he opened his own lab. I tried a few others, but they couldn't hold a candle to Dieter's artistry. He works out of his loft in Soho. He's a bit of a strange duck, but a perfectionist." Nagle reeled off the phone number.

"Thanks for your time, Doctor."

"Think nothing of it. By the way, do you play tennis?" he asked unexpectedly.

"Yes," Steve tried not to sound surprised.

"Are you any good?"

"I've won my share of matches, but I'm a little rusty. Why?"

"I'd like to invite you to my club. We can bang the ball around and play a few sets. I promise to go easy on you."

Steve grimaced. "That won't be necessary. What club?"

"Premium Point Beach and Tennis, a little north of your neck of the woods, on Orienta Point, in Rye."

Predictable, Steve thought. One of the most exclusive and pretentious clubs in the New York area.

"I know it, but I'm going to be tied up next week. Suppose I give you a call when I know I'll be free."

"Are you still working on the case of those murdered blondes?"

"Yes, plus a few others."

"How's the investigation going?"

"It's like playing tennis with a ping pong racket."

"You mean you don't want to talk about it."

"I mean, I can't."

"Not even a tidbit to titillate my clientele?"

"Not even a morsel."

"Yes, of course. Well old chap, call me when you have time. Ciao."

What the hell was that all about? Steve wondered. All of a sudden he wants to be my buddy. Steve smiled to himself. *It would be nice to cream his egotistical ass on the tennis court.*

As he was pondering the phone call, Nancy poked her head into his office. "Mrs. Austron's going to have kittens, if you don't get your tush into the treatment room and insert her new dentures."

Nancy's efficient scheduling kept Steve busy until lunch. Finally, he got the chance to call Hans Dieter. "Mr. Dieter, my name's Dr. Steven Landau. Dr. Nagle recommended you highly."

"I should hope so, I've been doing his lab work for years."

Steve detected a slight German accent, a personal prejudice he found difficult to overcome, but Dieter's pleasant voice softened the edge.

"Landau?" Dieter said. "Is that a German name?"

"My father was born in Austria. He emigrated from Vienna, before the Nazi takeover."

"I see. How lucky for you. The Viennese are an ill-mannered bunch."

"And lucky for you too or I wouldn't be talking to you now."

"Ha, ha! You have a good sense of humor, Dr. Landau."

And you don't, Herr Dieter. "I just took impressions of an actor. I need an acrylic set of Dracula fangs with overly long canines."

"No problem, Dr. Landau, I'll be able to send you the exact teeth you need in less than a week. I hope you are not as big a pain in the rear end as the *great* Dr. H. Hugh Nagle. I've had to bail him out of a lot of tight spots."

Steve doodled an angry peacock. "He speaks highly of you, too. I'll be easy to get along with, as long as you follow my prescription and your work is as good as you and Dr. Nagle say it is."

"Believe me, Doctor, you will be very pleased with the results."

Another teutonic prima donna, thought Steve. *With as big an ego as Nagle's, they must have interesting discussions.* He gave Dieter his address for the delivery service.

Dieter and his arrogant sarcasm rankled Steve throughout the afternoon. Finally, at six-thirty, Nancy told him Mr. Casconi had been his last patient for the day.

"Way to go! I couldn't look at one more mouth," Steve said. "I can't wait to call my two best girls."

"Two?" Nancy asked with a quizzical look. "Last I heard, you only had Samantha. You slip one in on me?"

"Looks like it, Nance. I might have a new girlfriend."

"Congratulations! I hope she knows about your crazy schedule."

"She does, and it's okay. Her dance cards are even more chaotic."

Nancy put her hands on her hips. "And when were you planning to let your poor suffering nurse in on your secret paramour?"

"As soon as I caught my breath after meeting the hectic schedule my poor nurse set up for me."

"Hah! Well congratulations, the two of you should make an interesting couple as you charge off into the sunset."

97

12

Scotty's Restaurant

Steve returned to Impressions, fed Captain Bill, and called Sam. "Hi, kitten, I miss you. How're you doing?"

"Dad this is so cool! I was just going to phone you. School has an early enrollment program, and I have to meet with my counselor Wednesday morning to work out my college prep courses. Mom can't make it. Think you can?"

"College prep? That can't be possible! You were just in elementary school."

"Daaad!"

"You can count on me, Pumpkin."

"Are we sailing Sunday?"

"But of course, my little chickadee. I'm bringing someone I want you to meet."

Sam waited a beat before replying. "Dad, I'm not a little kid anymore. Can you eighty-six the vegetable and little animal names?"

Steve clucked his tongue. "No flora or fauna monikers shall pass through my lips again."

Sam exhaled an exasperated sigh. "Your guest male or female?"

"Definitely female. Her name's Nita."

"Then you won't mind if I bring a friend?"

Steve tried to keep the caution out of his voice. "Male or female?"

"His name's Cleveland."

"That's a city. What kind of name is that?"

"You can be so tacky sometimes. Everyone calls him Cleve, and please don't intimidate him."

"I promise. Pick you up Wednesday morning at ten."

"Love you, bye."

Before he could deal with the ramifications of meeting his daughter's first beau, he dialed Nita's number. "I've been thinking about you all day," he said, without preamble.

"I'm still high from yesterday."

"Me, too. Last night was very special. How lucky can a guy get? I just got off the phone with another beautiful woman."

"Oh! And who was that?"

"My daughter, Sam. You're going to meet her Sunday."

"If she's anything like you, I'll adore her."

"Let me tell you about Sam." They talked into the early hours of the morning.

The next morning Steve was in the morgue examining a three-month-old infant with a crushed skull. O'Brien and Olga Moore, a detective from the 23rd Precinct, stood beside him. "Her parents found her on the floor next to her crib after her christening party," Moore said.

"Check out these bruises on the triceps area," O'Brien said. He lifted the baby's limp, lifeless arm.

"Bite marks, for sure." Steve said

"Christ! Who the hell would do that to such a tiny baby?" Moore was pounding her fist into her other hand.

"Wasn't an adult," Steve said, he was looking through the close up lens on his Nikon. He snapped a half roll of film from different angles with a millimeter gauge from his forensic kit next to the two purple bruises on the fleshy part of the arm. "These marks are from anterior deciduous teeth."

"Don't kids lose their front baby teeth by the age of six?" O'Brien asked.

"Most do, but some late teethers can retain them until eight or nine."

"I'm outta here," Moore said, buttoning her jacket, "the party guest list beckons."

"Me, too," Steve said, "I'm testifying in a malpractice case."

Two hours later, a bailiff passed a note to Steve as he left the witness stand. "Call O'Brien."

Steve speed dialed his cellular phone as soon as he got out of the court-room. "Moore just called," O'Brien told him. "The only kid at the christen-ing was the baby's seven-year-old brother. She got a confession."

"From a seven-year-old?"

"She probably beat him with a rubber hose."

"O'Brien, you are by far the weirdest person I know. What'd the kid say?"

"He admitted he was jealous and bit his baby sister. When she started to cry, he got scared and pitched her out of the cradle. Kid's uncle, a transit cop, witnessed the confession."

"I'm glad I wasn't in Moore's shoes when she told the parents,"

"Yeah, you'd look funny in heels."

"Goddamn it, O'Brien! Give it a rest. This is a tragedy. I really hate it when you treat cases involving little kids so lightly."

"Lighten up, Steve. You can't let this stuff get to you."

Steve took a deep breath and let it out slowly. "It'd be great if we could solve the Dracula case as easily."

Steve could hear O'Brien slap his head over the static on his cell phone. "I don't know where my mind is lately. I keep having these Florida moments. I forgot to tell you about the big break we got. The culture of the last victim's vaginal swab developed into a parade of base stealing, gonorrheal diplococci."

"Our perp's walking around with a case of the clap?"

"Probably isn't even aware of it, yet. When a white, smelly secretion starts to drip from his pecker, he will be."

"Couldn't have happened to a nicer guy. How're you going to handle it?"

"My secretary's typing a general notice to distribute to all the metropolitan clinics, hospitals, and labs as we speak. We could get lucky if the killer seeks medical treatment."

"Keep me posted. Gotta go. My cell battery's low." Steve walked back to One Police Plaza, signed in, went through security, and took the elevator to the fifteenth floor. He eased into the tiny cubicle assigned to him. The prisoner's holding cells at the courthouse were more spacious. Whenever he rose from his metal chair he did it slowly, afraid he would dislodge an overhead tile. The area appeared even smaller, when Lonnie strolled in and sat down heavily in the chair facing Steve. Steve pushed aside his paperwork.

"Hey, Doc! Hear about the woman who told her dentist no matter what tooth she touched, it hurt?"

"Nooo," Steve groaned.

"Her dentist said, 'Every tooth?' She said, 'yes,' and touched each tooth in her mouth and cried out in pain. 'Do you know what the problem is?' she asked. 'Without a doubt,' he replied, 'Madam, you have a broken finger.'"

Steve chuckled, "Between you and O'Brien, who needs Comedy Central? I had a good laugh when he told me our perp has the clap. Any other progress on the case?"

"We narrowed down the men's stores that sell the tan sports coat that matches the fibers the techs found. Gagliardi's finished the list of convicted

101

dentists, and we've started to computer cross-check them with motor vehicles to see if any of them owns an early model blue car. By the way, the perp's left-handed."

"How'd you figure that out?"

"The angle of the cuts and the way he had to hold the victim's neck to bite her."

"Interesting. So now we're looking for a dark, wavy haired, left-handed clothes horse with the clap, a predilection for blondes, and a knowledge of dentistry."

"Sounds about right. And like Nita said, all we have to do is find a perp that fits that description."

"I wish it was that easy."

"Hey, Doc, I need advice. My wife had to go to North Carolina on business, and I promised my daughter I'd take her for a lobster dinner tomorrow night. You know any nice joints on City Island?"

"I not only can recommend a place, I'll meet you there with my daughter. It's Scotty's, half way down City Island Avenue, on the right."

"I like it, Doc. Seven-thirty okay?"

"You're on. How about, since we'll be socializing, you drop the Doc and make it Steve?"

"You got it—Steve."

The next morning Steve picked up Sam and they drove to New Rochelle High School. The last time he had driven her to school was for her fifth-grade play. It depressed Steve to realize how much of Sam's life he had missed and how fast time was flying. *Two more years, and she'll be in college. Where the hell did it go?*

Sam was her talkative, buoyant self as they walked down the empty corridors to the counselor's office.

Miss Bailey, a shapely redhead, ushered them into her office. After they were seated she said, "Samantha, as you know, you have to take the required courses to get into college. If you know what field you'd like to enter, there are a number of electives you can take that would help you get into the college of your choice."

"Well, I'm thinking of becoming a veterinarian."

Steve sat up in his chair. "You are? Since when?"

"I'm sorry, I didn't discuss it with you, Dad, because I wasn't sure. But you know how I love animals."

"Kitten, I don't disapprove. I think it's great, but I was hoping we could've talked about it. Does your mother know?"

"Nope. Just you and Miss Bailey."

"Hmm," Miss Bailey said. "I enjoy sharing your secret, Samantha, but I think it would be wise to let your mother in on it."

They spent the rest of the appointment outlining the courses Sam would take over the next two years.

Miss Bailey turned her hazel eyes to Steve. "I think it's terrific how interested you are in Samantha's future. If you have any questions, I mean any at all, please feel free to call me." She handed Steve her card, accompanied by a significant glance.

As they were getting into the car Sam said, "Dad, are you all right?"

"Yes, of course. Why do you ask?"

"That was a pretty good-looking lady coming on to you, like, with no holds barred, and you didn't pant once. I mean you gave her absolutely no encouragement. That is definitely not your shtick."

"Maybe she's not my type."

"Baloney. You have no type. What's up, Doc?"

"Well, I've just started to see someone, and I don't have eyes for anyone else right now."

"Hey, that's great. When do I meet the mystery lady?"

"Sunday, she's the friend I'm bringing sailing."

"That is so cool. She can meet me and Cleve at the same time."

Steve winced, hoping Sam and Cleveland didn't have the same relationship he had with Nita. He was too young for ulcers.

That evening, Scotty's was as busy as ever. A line of people stood outside waiting to get in. As soon as Scotty spotted Steve and Sam, he roared, "Dr. Landau, your table is ready."

"I thought you didn't take reservations," Sam said as they maneuvered through the crowded restaurant.

"I don't. I just couldn't bear to offend the beautiful date of the illustrious Dr. Landau."

"You must've won awards with the amount of bull you shovel, Scotty." Sam laughed.

"A friend and his daughter will be joining us." Steve said, after Scotty seated them in a small private room.

"How'll I know him?"

"He looks like Darth Vader and will tear the place apart, if he's not served right away."

"*Hoot, mon,* my kind of customer. They'll be shown to your table as soon as they arrive."

Five minutes later, Scotty delivered on his promise. Lonnie's daughter, Candy, had the color and sheen of milk chocolate and the high cheekbones of a fashion model. Her smile needed work. Steve guessed it was due to adolescent shyness. Sam had gone through the phase three years before.

"Who's your favorite singer?" Sam asked, shortly after Candy got comfortable. By the time the appetizers arrived, they were whispering secrets behind their fathers' backs.

Steve avoided swapping shoptalk with Lonnie by talking about the root canal he had performed on the Bengal tiger at the zoo. The girls were mesmerized.

"Can we spend a day with you at the zoo?" Sam asked.

Lonnie looked at Steve, and both fathers nodded.

"Yes!" The girls high-fived over the table. Lonnie told his captive audience a few antiseptic dental jokes. Steve was charitable and laughed along with the girls. Finally the girls excused themselves and giggled off to the ladies room.

Steve looked expectantly at Lonnie. "Well?" he asked.

"Lotsa action, but still no cigar," Lonnie said. "Clap squad's getting a workout. Jesus! In this day and age, you'd think more bozos would use rubbers."

"What do you mean?"

"Squad's getting thirty to thirty-five calls a day from doctors around the city.

Steve shook his head. "Guys better cross their fingers that dripping peckers are their only problem. Any of them come close to our killer's description?"

"Got a few good leads. Perez and Stone are checking them out tomorrow."

"That's encouraging."

Lonnie looked around to make sure the girls were not on their way back. "Got something even better. Remember the fireman who saw the old car by the crime scene?"

"Sure. Gagliardi wanted to hypnotize him."

"We used one of the department shrinks. He got the fireman to recall there was the letter Y and the number 6 on the plate."

"Cool! I never had that kind of success with hypnosis."

"You? I thought the subjects you saw were already stiff."

"Don't be such a wise guy. I took a course in hypnosis to use with extremely apprehensive patients."

"Did it work?"

"On a few subjects. With the others I felt like a schmuck in a white jacket. Steve shook his head with the memory. "What's this about the license plate?"

"Having two of the digits narrows the computer search. We're running it through the MVB."

Steve drained the last of his beer. "Where the hell are our daughters?"

"You know what happens when teenage girls get together," Lonnie said, "I'm more antsy wondering when our killer's going to strike again."

"Remember what Nita said."

"What did Nita say?" Sam asked as the girls swooped back to the table.

"Nothing that concerns you, Snoopy," Steve said.

"You guys working on a case?" Sam asked.

"My father never talks about that stuff at home," Candy said.

"Nor will he now," Lonnie said.

The discussion ended when Scotty joined them, and the party revved up. Finally, when they couldn't eat or laugh anymore, Steve called for the check.

On the way out, Steve's beeper went off. He excused himself to check the call and came back a few minutes later.

"Anything I should know about?" Lonnie asked.

Steve shook his head. "That was the zoo. Atlas the elephant has an abscess under his tusk. I have to operate first thing in the morning."

While waiting for their cars, Steve asked Lonnie to join the group sailing on Sunday.

13

Atlas

Nick, the head attendant, and his two assistants were waiting for Steve and Nancy when they arrived at the zoo the next morning. "Doc Dolensek had another emergency," Nick said. "He told me to tell ya, he gave Atlas 'nough Ketone to keep the big guy in dreamland for a coupla hours."

Atlas was lying on his side in his cage when Steve and his entourage entered the elephant compound. Steve walked around the animal's massive head, followed by Nancy. Steve pointed to the red area that extended from the base of Atlas's tusk, halfway up to his eye. "That's one mean-looking mother of an abscess. Nick, you and your assistants can help Nancy scrub down the area while I set up the equipment."

Steve fit a sterile five-gallon glass container into the reservoir and an evacuation tube with the diameter of a vacuum hose to the zoo's suction machine. After he had worked on the rhinoceros the year before he had designed a new cutting device. He had tooled and screwed a three-foot long handle onto a Central American machete. He wiped down the razor-sharp blade with alcohol.

"Pink Floyd should go well with this procedure." Steve said to Nancy as they donned their surgical gowns.

"Good choice." Nancy inserted *Dark Side of the Moon* into the CD player before she slipped on her gloves and mask.

Steve snapped on his gloves, adjusted his mask and, putting all his weight on the end of the scalpel handle, cut into the thick hide in front of the tusk. "Damn, this is like trying to cut through chain mail," he grunted. Once through, he extended the incision up to the apex of the abscess, a distance of about two feet. A foul greenish pus gushed out and filled the vacuum hose.

Nancy gasped. "Yuck, smells like the road kill of a dozen skunks."

Nick, fighting with the reservoir of the suction machine, shrugged apologetically as his two assistants, hands over their mouths, hustled out of the cage. It looked like the reservoir would overflow, but Nick had a reserve tank ready.

"Let's get a drain into the incision," Steve said after the green exudate stopped flowing.

Nancy and Nick retracted each flap of Atlas's hide while Steve inserted a three-by-one-foot strip of Iodoform gauze into the incised opening.

"It's time for the mother of all syringes of Tetracyclene." Nancy handed it to Steve.

He injected the contents into the elephant's rump. "We'll take a swab to culture, in case we need a more specific antibiotic."

The pale and apologetic assistants returned to help Nick place boards around the cage, isolating Atlas from the public.

"Nick, stay with him until he recovers from the anesthesia," Steve said. "I'm off to make rounds." He and Nancy left to check the rest of their zoo charges.

They met Dolensek at the Great Apes compound. The veterinarian pointed to Amy.

"She just started labor. We should have a new addition to our family in a couple of hours."

After Atlas regained consciousness and Steve was sure the elephant was out of danger, he returned to Impressions. Captain Bill detected the elephant's scent and scooted away until he got hungry and started his leg-rubbing act.

The next morning, the preliminary set of Dracula teeth arrived at Steve's office, the workmanship was exceptional. Dieter had done everything Steve had asked, plus he had added grooves into the long canine fangs to increase the dramatic effect.

Nancy vowed to herself that she would not exhibit her usual exuberant idolatry, when Art Powers came in, but still lost her power of speech as soon as he entered the reception room. She couldn't find the words to chide him for being fifteen minutes late. Art was unusually subdued, and even more anxious than he had been on his first visit. Steve needed ten minutes to calm his hyperventilating patient. When Steve thought Powers was relaxed enough, he withdrew the Dracula teeth from the lab bag. Powers stared at them wordlessly, but followed them with his eyes until they crossed as Steve brought them up to his mouth. Tentatively, Steve placed the false teeth over Art's natural ones and heard a satisfactory snap as they settled in.

"That'th it?" Art Powers asked.

Steve smiled. "You want more?"

"No, that'th all right. Why am I lithping tho much?"

"You'll get over that. You just have to learn the new placement for your tongue when making the 'th' and 's' sounds."

"How can I do dat?"

"After they're completed, wear them day and night for the next two weeks."

"You mean in my houth and during rehearthals?"

Steve nodded."Especially then. The more you wear them, the faster you'll overcome the lisp. Also, you'll be forming a lot of saliva. That's your body's reaction to something new in your mouth. That, too, will pass in a few days."

"Thteve, you're a geniuth."

Steve laughed and removed the teeth from Art's mouth.

"They'll be finished and ready to be put to work next week," Steve said, while he made a few minor adjustments.

109

Nancy's flush returned when Art came out to her area. Her voice raised an octave when she asked, "Next Thursday at ten, okay?"

Flashing his famous smile, Art replied, "That's fine, Nancy, and thanks, I couldn't have done this without you."

Steve found Nancy lying prostrate over the appointment book.

14

The Cruise

Although Steve's schedule was full, the week dragged by in slow motion. Perpetually on edge, he constantly examined the appointment book, impatient for Saturday afternoon. His heart sank Saturday morning when he looked out the porthole of Impressions to see overcast skies and a steady drizzle. The weather forecast was not promising. His dejection increased as he drove downtown to see the morning roster of patients.

Nancy threatened to throw the phone book at him, when he checked his watch every five minutes. "Hey, Boss, that's not going to make the time go any faster, and the patients are starting to notice. Trust me she'll still be waiting for you."

"Thanks, Nance. I didn't realize it was so obvious." He checked his watch again.

Steve bolted out of the office as soon as he completed the filling on his last patient, and sprinted to the garage. After a fast trip uptown, he braked to a halt in front of Nita's apartment building. Nita, who had been pacing the sidewalk, jumped into the car, and they sped away.

She let out a sigh of relief, "I thought this week would never end."

"Ditto for me; seemed like fourteen days. Just have to make a quick stop at the zoo to check on one of my emergency patients."

"Great! I get a chance to see you at work."

Nick and Atlas's keeper opened the door to the elephant area and escorted Steve and Nita into the compound. Nita took two giant steps back, when she saw the size of the gigantic bull with a drain hanging out above his tusk. She stood behind Steve while he read the culture results.

"Why is he looking at me like that?" she asked.

"You're a new presence in his cage."

"What if he doesn't like me?"

"Atlas? He's a pussycat. Besides he'll love you because you're with me."

"Suppose he's psychotic and gets jealous?"

"Don't worry — we'll have plenty of notice."

"How?"

"He always lowers his head before he charges."

Nita punched Steve in the arm. "I wasn't aware you had a sadistic streak."

Steve rubbed his arm and turned to Nick. "We'll change the antibiotic to Streptomycin."

"You got it, Doc."

"How'd he do last night?"

"The old boy was restless, but he seemed comfortable."

Steve studied the incision. "The area above the tusk still looks swollen. We'll leave the drain in for another few days."

"Whadever."

After they left the elephant area, Steve took Nita to the Great Apes compound to see how Amy was getting along.

"Oh, Steve," Nita squeezed his arm. "Look how the baby gorilla clings to her mother."

"Unfortunately we have to separate them for a little while, next week. Mama has to have an abscessed tooth extracted."

"Isn't there another way to do it?"

"It'll only be for a little while, and we want to do it before the baby ingests too much of Mama's antibiotics." Steve nudged Nita away from Amy, who was tenderly nursing her tiny newborn.

When Steve and Nita left the zoo for the boat, the weather, although still overcast, was improving. They cast off at two-thirty and set sail for Eaton's Neck, Steve's favorite anchorage on the Long Island side of the Sound. The wind freshened from the northwest, and they had to tack up the sound. After the seventh tack, Steve said, "At this rate, we'll never get there. I'll furl the jib, and we'll motor the rest of the way."

"Good," Nita said, "I have to talk to you, but we've been too busy."

"Fire away, Goddess of the Seas."

Nita smiled but no mirth was in her eyes.

"Uh, oh, this looks serious. You going to tell me you're going back to your old boyfriend?"

"What I'm about to tell you is strictly between you and me. I can't even tell you the whole story, or I'll betray a patient's confidence."

Steve had never seen Nita's eyes burn with such intensity. "Hold on!" He switched on the auto-pilot. "You have my undivided attention."

"My final patient last night told me he knows who the Dracula Killer is."

Steve's jaw dropped. "Jesus, Nita! Why did you wait until we got out here to tell me? I'll call Lonnie and he can cuff the bastard. Who the hell is he?"

Nita shook her head. "I thought you'd react like that. I didn't sleep a wink last night, thinking about it. You'll have to hear me out before I make a decision."

"But—"

Nita put her finger over Steve's lips. "You'll need some background first. My patient was convicted as a sex offender, but was paroled four years ago after serving eight years of a twelve-year sentence. He had enrolled in a rehabilitation program while at an upstate prison and has been undergoing intensive psychotherapy with me since his release."

"What was the charge?"

"He kidnapped his former girlfriend after she broke up with him, dragged her to an abandoned warehouse and raped her."

"Man, oh, man! You sure have some doozies for patients. Give me Atlas any day."

Nita fixed Steve with a disdainful look. "Don't tell me you're one of those NYPD closet conservatives."

"Moi? No way"

"That's a relief. Anyway, my patient's been one of my success stories and is in the final stages of treatment. I was planning to discharge him in the fall."

"Your patient lucked out with you as his therapist. How does he know who the Dracula Killer is?"

"While in the joint, my client had a few run-ins with a con in his cell block. A former pro wrestler doing eight-to-ten for beating his wife. She almost died and still has massive headaches."

"For crying out loud, Nita. There must be dozens of guys in the slammer for the same offense."

"True—but how many of them bit off chunks of their victim's anatomy?"

"Ah, so, Number One Shrink. Continue."

"This wrestler intimidated fresh young inmates to become his playmates and when he tired of them, he beat them up, biting them in the process. My patient said you could pick his former lovers out of the general prison population by the scars on their bodies."

"A real sweetheart. Is he still doing time?"

"He was due to be released a month before Doris Walker was killed."

Steve looked at Nita over his sunglasses "Did your patient tell you the guy's name?"

"No. He said he was always referred to by his alias, his professional name."

"Which is?"

"I can't tell you."

"How about your patient's name?"

Nita nervously hand brushed her hair back into a ponytail with a look of uncertainty on her face. "Now you can understand my dilemma," she said. "I'm bound by my professional code of ethics not to divulge any information obtained during a therapy session."

"Jesus, Nita. We have a Hannibal the Cannibal running amuck in the Apple. Can't you make an exception?"

"No—and neither can priests or lawyers. I'd be breaking the law, if I did. The only exception I can make is discussing it with a control analyst"

"Do you have one?"

"Not anymore," Nita lowered her eyes, "not since we broke up."

Steve nodded. "He was the professor you had the affair with?"

"Yes," she said in a low voice. She took a deep breath. "I'm on thin ice just by telling you as much as I have. I can't tell you my patient's name or even the name of the prison."

"Can I at least tell Lonnie some of what you've told me?"

Nita's cobalt eyes flashed in anger. "You do, and our budding relationship will come to a crashing halt."

"You're that serious about it?"

"You bet. A relationship is based on trust. If you go behind my back on this, I could never be comfortable with you."

"Message received loud and clear. This will be our little secret."

"I just wanted you to know there is someone out there who fits the profile."

115

"What about the dental theory? Wait. Don't tell me. He worked in the prison's clinic."

Nita nodded.

"What happens when the Dracula Killer gets hungry again?"

"I'll cross that bridge when I have to."

They motored the next few minutes in silence, deep in their own thoughts. As they approached the Long Island shoreline, Nita exclaimed, "Steve, aren't we sailing into the beach?"

Steve shook his head. "Not to worry, matey. The entrance to Eaton's Neck is camouflaged by the breakwater and stand of trees behind it. That's why we're going here — not many sailors know it exists."

He slowly steered Impressions through the tortuous channel into a small inlet surrounded by a long winding beach and a green wall of dense pine woods. "It's so pristine and quiet here," Nita whispered.

A cabin cruiser at the far end of the cove was the only sign of civilization. They set the big Danforth anchor just as the other boat was leaving. The receding throaty sound of the yacht's engine accentuated the solitude of the anchorage. Only an occasional call of a sea bird disrupted the peace of the refuge emphasizing the illusion they were far from the New York metropolitan area.

Nita settled into Steve's arms as the sun broke out from under the cover of low hanging clouds to erupt into a fiery sunset. Wordlessly, they watched the evening sky shift from crimson to ultramarine, leaving a pink afterglow on the underside of the remaining clouds. Nita pointed downward, and they murmured appreciatively as the quiet water of the cove mirrored the range of colors, before it turned to charcoal. Steve lit a kerosene lamp, hung it from the underside of the boom, and fired up the grill on the aft pulpit. "Swordfish steaks okay?"

"You sure know how to seduce a girl."

"This should help." Steve flourished a bottle of Dom Pérignon.

The champagne worked and Nita's earlier misgivings softened. Relaxed, she lay down on an air mattress that Steve had placed on the aft deck after their dinner. Nita was finally able to block out her ethical dilemma. Their lovemaking was less frantic and more sensual than the first time.

Later, as they lay on their backs watching the August display of shooting stars, Nita said, "I'll ask my patient if he wants to volunteer his information."

Steve rolled over and brushed her lips with his. "It's your call, sweetheart. I'll go along with whatever you decide." They fell asleep in each other's arms to a rising new moon.

Nita was awakened by a group of gyrating gulls dropping mussels on a nearby rock outcropping, and then fighting over the remains. The smell of coffee and pancakes, blended with Steve's off key singing, restored her to consciousness. She and Steve watched the stately procession of Botero-sculpted clouds drift across the azure sky while they ate breakfast. A light breeze barely rippled the blue-green water in the protected cove as Steve pulled up the anchor.

The breeze freshened when they entered the Sound, and they set sail in a ten-knot following wind for the New Rochelle Marina. An hour later, Lonnie, Candy, Sam, and her friend Cleveland climbed aboard and Steve conducted the introductions. The light gusts died, and Steve had to motor back out. Nita, Candy, and Sam, who carried Captain Bill, went forward to settle on the port side with their legs dangling over the gunwales.

"Your father told me you're planning to become a veterinarian," Nita said to Sam.

"Exactly. I enjoy assisting Dad when he works on the zoo animals, and I thought it'd be so cool if I could work with him." Sam chucked Captain Bill under his jowls.

"If you need any help with your science courses, I have a lot of books you can use."

"That'd be super, Nita."

Back in the cockpit, Lonnie asked Cleveland, "Did you hear about the man who, after receiving his bill, asked his orthopedic surgeon to give him a break? The surgeon said, 'Sure, do you want an arm or a leg?'"

"No." Cleve's face stayed blank.

Lonnie tried a few more jokes on Sam's preppy friend, but got the same response. He looked at Steve and dropped his arms with his palms extended. "Tzu gornischt!"

117

Steve cracked up. "Where the hell did you learn Yiddish?"

"I play second clarinet in a Klezmer band."

"You must be a big hit at Hasidic weddings," Steve said.

"My favorite gig. Ya know what I'm sayin?"

Steve shook his head. "How about steering, Cleve?"

"I don't know how."

"It's easy, while we're under power. Just turn the wheel in the direction you want to go. You'll do fine."

After a few bumpy turns, a smile finally spread across Cleve's freckled face. Later, Steve anchored off the Larchmont breakwater and everyone went swimming. Afterwards they returned to the boat ate a picnic lunch, and lounged on deck. Finally, Steve said, "Time for the younger contingent to go to the beach. Cleve, help Sam lower the dinghy."

As Steve, Nita and Lonnie watched the younger people motor away, Steve, wasted no time. "Here's a list of the dental supply companies that sell the Vee Hee carvers." Steve handed Lonnie the copy.

Lonnie put the list in his pocket. "I'll get a man on it as soon as I get back. Gagliardi finished compiling the file of convicted dentists and wants you to go over it on Monday. We cross-checked their prints with the partials on the carver you found, then again to see if any of them owned an older blue car with license plates that had the two letters the fireman remembered. We've narrowed it down to three suspects. Two of them bought the larger type carver at least two years before losing their licenses."

Steve nodded. "I'll be there bright and early. It's been kind of quiet. Think it'll last?"

Nita shook her head. "Let's not become complacent just because there's been a lull for the past few weeks. The next time he strikes," she warned, "it'll be with a vengeance."

"Did the clap squad turn up anything?" Steve asked.

"Nope. All the leads fizzled. There's always the possibility he's taking care of it himself. Hey, you lose one and then you win one. We got a good hit with the motor vehicle computers. A blue 46 Plymouth's registered to a recently freed, heavy-duty sex offender. He had worked as a dental assistant in the Elmira prison clinic. He skipped from his last known address shortly before Doris Walker was murdered. Gag got a few guys working on that."

"What kind of sex offense?" Steve asked.

"He kidnapped and brutally raped a college co-ed," Lonnie said

Steve shot Nita a questioning look.

Nita turned abruptly from Steve. "Any luck with the APBs?"

"A few false alarms, men who fit the composite descriptions trying to pick up attractive blondes in singles bars. I've been married so long, I forgot it's a sanctioned sport for horny guys." Lonnie chuckled. "One incident involved an assistant D.A. and got a little nasty, until Gagliardi threatened to tell the guy's wife. Otherwise nothing else is shaking loose."

"With each murder, the killer is getting bolder. He's bound to make bigger mistakes," Nita reminded them.

The sound of the dinghy outboard alerted them to the return of the kids. "To be continued," Steve said. "How come you're back so fast?" he asked Sam and company as they climbed aboard and winched the dinghy up to the davits.

"A guy in uniform kicked us off," Sam said. "He claims the beach is now private."

Steve shrugged. "The good news is the wind picked up—we can sail back to New Rochelle. Sam, you handle the helm, while Lonnie and I pull up the anchor. Cleve, help Nita raise the main sail."

Steve let Sam remain at the wheel. She used the opportunity to give Candy and Cleveland lessons on how to steer the boat.

After Steve motored up to the gas dock at the New Rochelle Marina, Lonnie said, "Thanks for a great day, Steve. I'll take Sam home. When're we going to kick some butt on the basketball court?"

"I'll be tied up in court for a few days. I'll call you as soon as I'm free."

"Lucky you. I always get flustered on the stand."

"You?" Steve laughed. "Just tell them a few of your lousy lawyer jokes, and they'll get you out of there as soon as possible."

"That reminds me. Did you hear the one about—"

"Bye Lonnie," Steve and Nita said in unison as Steve wheeled Impressions around to head back to City Island.

As they passed the entrance buoy, Steve said, "The guy never knows when to quit."

"I wonder how many people would laugh at his stories if he was just a short, skinny accountant?"

"He probably would have given up long ago."

"I want to get serious for a moment."

"You have an uncanny knack of reading my mind," Steve said.

"You have to give me time to try to work this out with my patient."

"What if he refuses to cooperate?"

"I'll work something out with Lonnie, but it has to be on my terms. Let's forget that for a moment. It was torture waiting for the weekend to see you. I want to be with you during the week too."

"Yes!" Steve raised a thumb. "Does that mean we're an item?"

"Yes, you crazy nut, we're an item." Nita kissed him so passionately he put Impressions into irons. The flapping sails sent Captain Bill scurrying below decks.

After docking at City Island, Steve drove Nita home and stayed the night.

15

Number One Suspect

Steve attended a cut-and-dry coroner's inquest in downtown Manhattan Monday morning. The proceedings were over in half an hour. After a short walk from the courthouse, he walked into Gagliardi's office.

"Yo, Doc," Gagliardi greeted him. "I got an interesting list for you to peruse — some of your brethren who've gone astray. Why doncha see if you know any of 'em and lay a few pearls of wisdom on me."

Steve took the printed sheet, scanned it, and whistled. "Twenty-three? I didn't realize there were so many fucked up associates."

"These are only the hard-core cases. They've already done their time. Woulda been longer," Gagliardi assured him, "'cept a few are still in the joint, and the others are either too old or sick to commit this type of homicide."

Steve pointed to the second name on the list. "This man practiced in my former hometown. He got a lot of heat in the local press after he was convicted of fondling female patients while they were intravenously sedated. I had to listen to a lot of crappy innuendos from my patients, until that one blew over."

"Is he a contender?" Gagliardi asked.

"You can cross him off, Loo. The publicity sent him off the deep end and he had to undergo intensive psychiatric therapy in the joint. He's been keeping it up since his release."

Steve continued scrutinizing the names. "I testified as an expert witness at this man's trial. He was convicted of child molesting, so I don't think he's our man, either. The only other one I know is number nineteen. Is he out on the street already?"

Gagliardi flipped through a few pages. "Medical pardon three months ago."

"Must be something serious. He's a wimp who actually tried to rape one of his patients while she was under analgesia. She came out of it and beat the shit out of him, so I think you can cross him off, too. I don't recognize anyone else."

"Lonnie tell you we picked up some likely candidates on the computer cross-check?"

Steve nodded.

"One was your number nineteen." Gagliardi used a marking pencil to slash a red line through the name. That leaves numbers eleven, sixteen, and twenty-three."

"Eleven and sixteen did time for forcible rape. At least we have two live ones."

While Gagliardi and Steve studied the list, Lonnie came into the room. "Hey, Steve, hear about the woman who was about to have a tooth extracted and told the dentist, 'I don't know what's worse, having my tooth extracted or having a baby.' The dentist replied, 'Madam, please let me know what you prefer, so I'll know how to adjust the chair.'"

"I heard that in my freshman year at dental school. That's just what the lieutenant and I were talking about."

"You tell the Loo about your high class, perverted dentist friend?"

"You holdin out on me, Doc?" Gagliardi said.

Steve snorted. "His name's H. Hugh Nagle, and he tops my list for weirdo of the year."

"How so?"

"His ego's bigger than the Donald's, and he has a real crappy attitude toward women. One of my colleagues informed me he's a charter member of an S and M club."

"Which end of the equation is he?"

"Definitely not the masochistic type. But he does have a morbid interest in the case."

"What kinda dresser is he?" Gagliardi pressed.

"I only met him once. You could call him stylish, if you like yellow ascots."

Gagliardi's eyes narrowed. "Yellow ascot, huh? What color suit?"

"He wasn't wearing a suit. He wore a brown sport jacket with leather patches and tan slacks."

Gaglardi perked up. "Height and weight?"

"A couple of inches shorter than me, about five-eleven; one-ninety, one-ninety-five."

"Flabby or solid?"

"He's definitely in good shape. My fingers were a little worse for wear after I shook hands with him."

"Ladies man?"

"Not my type. I guess women who are attracted to conceited bullshit artists might think so."

"Car?"

"I don't know. I'd guess he has expensive wheels, a Mercedes or Jaguar. I don't think he would be caught in anything less."

"Hair?"

"Dark and anchorman-styled."

"Well, Doc, until someone else comes along, I like your dandy as a genuine, grade-A, super-duper, ace, number-one suspect. Any way we can check this what's-his-name without arousing any suspicion?

"Too bad we can't tap his phone." Lonnie said.

"Ya got that right," Gagliardi countered, "too early for a court order."

"Why don't you let me see what I can find out?" Steve interjected. "He invited me to his club to play tennis. I think it's just a ploy to find out what progress we're making, but what the hell, like the Trojans said, 'Why look at the mouth of a gift horse?'"

"Musta been a genius to stick that name on a contraceptive," Gagliardi went to the blackboard and chalked in Nagle's name.

Steve rolled his eyes at Lonnie who only shrugged. Gagliardi rubbed the chalk off his hand. "Okay Doc, you got a deal. Be cool, act natural, and try to find out what he drives and where he shops. If you can, get us a left thumb print and a shoe size,"

"Whoa! I get a gold shield for all this snooping?"

"Sure, and I'm gonna start doin root canals," Gagliardi said. "By the way, try to beat the shit out of him on the tennis court and see how he reacts."

"That could be a problem. I haven't played in a while."

"C'mon, Doc, you can do it. We're counting on you."

"At least one of us is confident. I'll call him after my court case."

"Anything we should know about?"

"Insurance case, possibly a homicide. You might want to check it out. Case depends on the identity of a burn victim."

"Keep me posted," Gagliardi said, and went back to the blackboard.

16

The Trial

"Shit!" Steve muttered under his breath as he tripped over a television cable in the Center Street courtroom. "Court TV — I should've worn a tie." He slipped into a seat in the rear while Larry Piergrossi, an insurance company lawyer, questioned Ken Chasin, a fire department investigator Steve had worked with in the past.

The case involved a young widow who was suing an insurance company for payment on her husband's policy. The insurance company had claimed his death was suspicious and therefore not covered.

"Could you tell the jury what you found in the charred remains of the Zorn mansion, inspector?" Piergrossi asked.

"The partial remains of a skeleton. The top half of the skull was missing. There were also a few scorched Indian jewelry pieces."

"Did you identify the jewelry?"

"Yes, there was a ring, a bracelet, and a belt buckle which, according to records, was bought three years ago by Joseph Zorn during a trip to Taos, New Mexico."

"Did you find evidence of arson?"

"We found traces of flammable liquids."

"Your witness," Piergrossi turned and sat down amid a battery of litigation lawyers who were all dressed in designer suits, wingtips and gold Rolex watches. *Got to be mucho bucks involved for that much artillery,* Steve concluded.

"One question Inspector." The plaintiff's lawyer approached Chasin. "Were arson charges brought against anyone after your investigation?"

"No, the D.A. felt there wasn't enough physical evidence."

The insurance company investigator was the next defense witness sworn in.

Piergrossi remained seated. "Mr. Chicko, how much was the Zorn mansion insured for?"

"Ten million dollars."

"Who is the beneficiary?"

"Joseph Zorn's wife—Sheila Zorn. She also stands to collect an additional ten million in life insurance."

Steve's attention shifted to a heavily made up, thirty-something redhead, dressed in a severely cut conservative suit. She re-crossed her legs, but her gaze remained glued on the witness.

Piergrossi pressed on, "What had been the state of Mr. Zorn's finances before the fire?"

"To be charitable, he had been dangerously close to bankruptcy. Creditors were virtually at his doorstep, and the bank was about to foreclose on the mansion. Three months prior to the fire, Mr. Zorn had cashed in all his CDs and sold his yacht and Rolls Royce."

"What happened to the proceeds?"

"To date we have not been able to trace their disbursement."

Mrs. Zorn's attorney only asked one question on cross-examination, "Did the sale of Mr. Zorn's assets constitute any crime?"

Chicko shook his head. "Only if it wasn't declared on his tax return."

The lawyers spent the rest of the morning questioning Zorn's associates, and business partners. A picture of a major league wheeler-dealer formed in Steve's mind.

Following the lunch break, Dr. Richard Corbin, Joseph Zorn's dentist, was called to the witness stand. Piergrossi went to the evidence table and brandished a manila envelope. "Dr. Corbin, we have a copy of your dental records for Joseph Zorn. Instead of going over them line by line, would you give us a brief summary?"

"Objection!" interjected Mrs. Zorn's attorney.

The judge looked over her glasses. "Noted," she said. I'll reserve judgment until I hear more. Proceed, Doctor."

Dr. Corbin, whose owlish appearance was reinforced by his thick glasses, squinted into the television lights. "I treated Joseph Zorn's periodontal condition for almost twenty years."

Piergrossi cut in. "Translate periodontal condition."

"Gum disease. But it was hopeless. Eventually he lost all his upper teeth as well as all the lower molars and the two second bicuspids."

"Did you replace the missing teeth?"

"Yes. Three years ago, I made him a set of full upper and partial lower dentures with clasps on the remaining lower first bicuspids."

"How old was Mr. Zorn?"

"Sixty-four."

"Thirty years older than his wife?"

Mrs. Zorn's lawyer popped up, like a piece of toast. "Objection!"

"Overruled. The witness will answer the question." The judge nodded at Dr. Corbin.

"I wouldn't know. She was not a patient," Corbin answered.

"Did you see him professionally after that?"

"Contrary to my advice, he didn't come in for regular check-ups. I didn't hear from him until five months ago."

"And what was that for?"

127

Corbin referred to the chart through his thick glasses. "An emergency visit. His lower left first bicuspid fractured, and I restored the tooth with a gold inlay."

"Do you have the X-rays?"

Corbin cleared his throat. "No, Mr. Zorn refused to have X-rays taken, because he said he just had a great many taken for a GI series. When the X-rays were requisitioned for the trial, I could send only the old films."

The plaintiff's attorney made the point on cross-examination that none of the films showed the gold inlay.

Steve was the next witness. He was sworn in, questioned about his credentials, and certified as an expert witness. Piergrossi led him through the methods he used to identify bodies burned beyond recognition in fires. Then he asked, "So after you made an incision in the victim's cheek to expose the teeth, what did you do?"

"Identification was complicated since the victim had only eight lower natural teeth. His full upper and partial lower dentures were presumably consumed in the fire."

"Then how were you able to establish the identity of the body found in the ashes of this fire, Dr. Landau?"

"I couldn't."

Piergrossi locked into the eyes of each front-row juror. "Are you saying you could not with certainty say that the body found was that of Joseph Zorn?"

"I don't know whose body was found. I do know it was not Joseph Zorn."

All twelve jurors snapped to attention.

"On what do you base your conclusion?"

"I removed the mandible, the lower jaw from the skull found in the wreckage of the fire and cleaned it. It's on the exhibit table marked *Exhibit H*, if I may?"

The judge nodded.

Steve went to the table, retrieved the mandible, and returned to the stand. The jury and the spectators in the courtroom craned to get a closer look. Steve continued, "This lower jaw has the same number of teeth as Joseph Zorn had, and the right alignment: two centrals, two laterals, two cuspids, and two bicuspids."

"Then what is different?" Piergrossi inquired.

"Both bicuspids are in perfect condition. There are no fillings of any kind in either tooth. There are definitely no gold inlays."

The judge had to bang her gavel three times, to restore order.

"Your witness," Piergrossi smugly said to the opposing lawyer.

The attorneys for Mrs. Zorn requested a brief recess, then spent the rest of the afternoon going over Steve's testimony word by word, in an attempt to discredit the damage it had done to their client. Reluctantly, they had to let him leave the witness stand with his statements intact.

Steve rubbed his numb rear-end in the booth outside the courtroom, waiting for Nita to pick up the phone. "I hope you weren't planning anything for tonight—I'm drained."

"Poor baby. What happened?"

"I just spent the afternoon fighting off a school of ferocious, man-eating sharks."

"Who won?"

"It was a draw. I lost my stamina, and they lost their case."

"My hero! Come home—I'll order in Chinese and show you the lascivious tricks I can do with chopsticks."

"You've whetted my appetite."

"And you've wet mine. Hurry, lover."

They ate dim sum on a glass cocktail table in Nita's living room watching the Court TV replay of the trial and cheered when Steve appeared. Finally Nita turned off the TV and said, "It's time for the chopsticks show."

When Steve regained his breath an hour later, he said, "We'll be a big hit if we try that at Hung Fat's joint."

The next morning, during a run they were taking through Central Park, Steve said, "I'm calling Nagle later, and setting up the tennis match for Friday."

"I'm free Friday afternoon, I can meet you at his club," Nita said.

Steve sidestepped an oncoming jogger. "I can use all the support I can get."

"I might be able to get in a discreet interrogation or at least some insight into his character."

"The man's so shallow you won't have to dig far."

Steve had just completed a pile of insurance forms that had been gathering dust on his desk when Nancy buzzed him. "Agatha's, on line one."

Steve grabbed the receiver. "Is Captain Bill all right?"

"Jesus, Landau. You have a one-track mind. He's fine. It's me. I have a serious problem."

"Toothache?"

"No, and I'd never trust you with a drill in my mouth. Have you seen Lydia recently?"

"Who?"

"Lydia, the firewoman who was a guest on my boat."

"Why the hell would I see her?"

"I saw the way you were looking at her boobs."

"Agatha, I am totally involved with a very special lady now, and I probably wouldn't recognize your friend if I fell over her. Why don't you tell me what's wrong?"

"Lydia's disappeared."

"Come on, Agatha. She's probably taken a few days off. Have you called her at home?"

"Of course, you turkey. A couple of times a day, but she's not there, and she doesn't answer her cell either. She's been apartment sitting for her ex-husband."

"And she doesn't answer there?"

"I don't have his number."

"As I recall, you were an experiment in her quest for sexual identity. She's probably shacked up with some guy and doesn't want to be bothered."

"Goddamn it, Steve. You must have a screw loose in your gray matter. It's more serious than that. We've developed a relationship and have been speaking to each other three or four times a day. What's really worrying me is she's missed her last two tours at the firehouse, and she's never done that before."

"Okay, Agatha. I hear you. I'll call Dean Santisorio at Missing Persons and tell him you're family. He'll roll out the red carpet when you call. Give me a half hour, and keep me posted." Steve recited the department of Missing Person's number.

Steve doodled a chesty female figure while he spoke to Santisorio and made a notation under it to call him back in two days. Then he dialed Nagle's number.

"This is the office of Dr. H. Hugh Nagle."

I don't have patience for this bitch today, Steve thought. "Ms. Rauscher, this is Dr. Landau, returning Dr. Nagle's call," he fibbed.

"Please hold!"

"Hello, my good man," Nagle said, so promptly Steve didn't have to listen to his corny recorded message. "I didn't realize what a celebrity you are. I saw you last night on Court TV."

"Oh, you were the one."

"What can I do for you?"

"If your offer to play tennis is still open, I'd like to take you up on it."

"Of course—it will be a feather in my cap to invite the noted and now famous forensic dentist to my club."

My thirty seconds of fame. "Friday's good for me."

131

"Friday it is. Ten o'clock, loser buys lunch."

"You're on. Speaking of lunch, I'd like to invite my lady friend."

"Of course. I'll leave her name at the front gate. It's Nita, isn't it?"

"Yes, but how did—"

"Sorry, Rauscher's calling. See you Friday. Ciao."

Steve was still mumbling to himself when Nancy paged him on the intercom. "Insurance attorney in the arson case, Señor Doctor. Line dos."

"The Zorn babe broke down and confessed to fraud," said Piergrossi.

"No shit! What happened?"

"She and her husband bribed an assistant in a funeral home to remove a body from a closed coffin and deliver it to their mansion before they torched it. Her old man is living in a villa on the Greek island of Mykinos under an assumed identity. She was going to join him later. Cops are holding her, and the D.A.'s applying to extradite him."

"That's one for the good guys," Steve said,

"I couldn't have done it without your testimony. Thanks, Dr. Landau."

"Just doing my job my good man. Thanks for keeping me posted." *Jesus, I'm starting to sound like Nagle.*

17

The Tennis Match

Steve left City Island early Friday morning and sailed north to Orienta Point in Rye. He picked up a guest mooring and took the club launch to the dock. "Which way to the tennis courts?" he asked the launch operator.

"Today's ladies day," she replied.

"I was supposed to play a match with Dr. Nagle today."

"Oh, you're the one."

"The one what?"

"Dr. Nagle's the club champ. He told everyone he had a match with another ranked player. All the members will be there. You're on court one. Just follow the path past the main house and the pool. You can't miss it."

Fucking terrific, thought Steve. I'm playing the goddamn club champ, and I haven't held a racket in three months. That prick Nagle invites his entire club to watch me make an ass of myself. I'm going to have fun explaining this to Gagliardi. Steve walked past the sunning Westchester matrons as if he were going to his own execution.

Nagle was holding court in the front of the clubhouse surrounded by a group of admiring members. He affected surprise when he saw Steve coming up the walk. "Bonjour, my good man. I was expecting you to come in from the parking lot."

"It was easier to come by boat."

"Yes, of course, how forgetful of me. You live on board. How's your lady friend Nita getting here?"

"She's taking the train to Rye and a cab from the station."

"Excellent. Are you ready to warm up? I reserved the court for two hours."

"Sure, but I'll need some time. I haven't played for a few months."

"Certainly. I'm sure you'll do admirably. How quaint! You still play with an aluminum racket. You ought to get one of these graphite models. It gives you much more power."

I'd like to shove this metal racket up your smug ass, Steve thought as they walked to the court. A gaggle of teenage girls giggled at their obvious difference in style. Nagle was resplendent in the latest tennis fashion— white shorts with a rainbow outline on the left side that extended to a crisp, form fitting white polo shirt. His tennis shoes had the built in pump advertised on billboards.

Steve wore his usual white jeans cutoffs, Nelson Mandela T-shirt, and scuffed running shoes.

As soon as the warm up started, Steve knew he was in trouble when Nagle, with superb classic form, blasted the ball inches over the net into Steve's court. He barely had time to get his racket on it. The rest of the warm up followed the same pattern. Nagle punished the ball while Steve could only block the return, rather than taking his full swing.

After ten minutes, Nagle cheerfully called, "Ready to play?"

"I need five more minutes."

Nagle agreed with obvious reluctance. When it appeared Steve's timing was improving, Nagle impatiently declared, "Time to begin! We're losing the gallery."

Steve looked questioningly at Nagle as the last of the club members settled in the seats around the court. Steve felt like a Christian in the coliseum with the Romans betting their togas on how fast their gladiator would grind him into submission. The spectators weren't disappointed.

134

After a half hour of play, Nagle led four games to love. Steve couldn't get a handle on Nagle's ferocious serve and powerful volleys. The balls came in with enormous top spin and, because Nagle was left-handed, broke in toward Steve. Nagle was always in position to put the ball away. Finally, with the score five-love, Steve concentrated on pinpoint serves and won his first game. Nagle came back with a vengeance and won the next game and set with a blistering overhead.

The second set started out as a repeat of the first, and before Steve realized it, the score was two-love in favor of Nagle. Steve asked for a break and slowly walked to the water fountain. *I must look like the chump of the year, letting myself get suckered into a no-win game like this,* he told himself. *I ought to challenge Nagle to a one-on-one basketball game and salvage my dignity.* He swallowed a mouthful of water and stood at the fountain staring angrily at his relaxed opponent who was joking with the courtside members. *The shit-head isn't even sweating. Of course he isn't, I've done nothing to make him exert himself.* Steve became painfully aware of the obvious. *Schmuck,* he told himself. *I'm playing right into his strength. There's no way I can out power him.* He nodded in agreement with himself. *I have to change the rhythm and play at my own pace.*

Steve took another long drink of water and eagerly returned to the court. The club members were getting restless and many of them, thinking the rest of the set would follow the same pattern, started to drift away.

Nagle zipped in his overpowering serve. Instead of trying to power it back, Steve came in under the ball and sliced it back with under spin. As Nagle rushed the net, ready to put away another volley, the ball sailed over his head and landed six inches inside the baseline. The next serve produced the same result. Nagle, catching on, stayed back on his next serve, but Steve returned a drop shot that landed untouched. The crowd, sensing a change, returned to their seats. Steve took the serve to the deuce court and calmly placed it down the line while Nagle helplessly watched it pass him by. On Steve's serve, he kept the ball to the outside of the serving box, forcing Nagle wide, and then hit the return to the opposite side of the court. When Nagle rushed the net, Steve lobbed. When Nagle stayed back, he faced drop shots. The game took on a ferocious aspect, and the crowd responded.

During a change-over, Nagle, toweling off the sweat that now flowed freely down his face, snarled at Steve, "Why don't you play like a man, pansy?"

135

At another exchange at the net, Nagle screamed, "Wimp!"

Finally, with the score tied at six all, the pair had to play a tiebreaker. Nagle, breathing heavily and drenched in sweat, had lost much of his original zip. Steve was serving, the score seven-six in his favor. Nagle pounced on the serve and hit a scorcher down the line. Steve saw he would never reach it with his backhand, so on the run, he switched the racket to his left hand and dived for the ball. He barely got his racket under the ball, and sent a lob to Nagle's backcourt.

Nagle raced back to slam another forehand down the line and, with what seemed like his last bit of strength, stormed the net.

Steve saw his chance. He positioned himself for the inside break and hammered the ball cross-court past Nagle. He savored the moment as he saw it land just inside the sideline.

"Out," called Nagle.

Steve stood dumbfounded.

The crowd roared with glee, "Fair ball!"

The new kid on the block, the new favorite, walked to the spot where the ball bounced on the Har-Tru surface and pointed out the imprint with a glance of inquiry at his opponent.

Furious, Nagle stormed off the court without a word.

Nita had arrived courtside half way through the set. She sat in the back row, and with a practiced eye, observed Nagle's erratic behavior.

Steve spotted her in the crowd and gave her a thumbs-up gesture. He inched his way to her, through the well-wishers and backslappers, and whispered in her ear, "You look gorgeous. It looks like it's you and me for lunch. I don't think shit head will show his face."

Steve was wrong. As he and Nita sat at a dining table on the veranda, waiting for service, Nagle walked up, pulled out a chair, and joined them. He had freshened up and wore a white sport shirt tucked into a pair of tan slacks and white loafers without socks.

"That was fun," he said. "You must be the beautiful Nita. Welcome to my club." He took her hand and kissed it. "The food here is delicious. I recommend the Maryland crab cakes or the cold poached salmon. Garçon!

May we have some service?" He made no mention or apology for his outrageous behavior on the court.

They ordered drinks, and Steve soon learned that Nagle was right. The food was excellent.

Nagle couldn't keep his eyes off Nita and directed all his conversation to her, ignoring Steve. "You must look fetching in a tennis outfit," Nagle said to Nita, "do you play?"

If the putz had a mustache, he'd probably be twirling it now, Steve thought.

"Just a hacker," she said demurely. "I'm not anywhere in the league with you and Steve."

"Yes, I see," Nagle said. He inched his chair away from Steve and closer to Nita. "You should practice more—play mixed doubles. Your blonde locks would distract any male opponent."

Steve bit his lip, remembering why they were here.

"Is blonde your natural color?" Nagle continued.

"Yes, I inherited it from my mother, although I do touch it up now and then." She flashed her brilliant smile.

"My mother's a blonde," said Nagle. "She loves to show people, men in particular, that it was never bleached. Unfortunately, I inherited my father's dark hair."

"It seems to suit you. Did I detect a note of resentment about your mother?" Nita asked.

"What a strange question. Ah, yes, I forgot you're a psychologist. Actually, my father left when I was three, and my mother brought me up. We've had our ups and downs. Right now our relationship is nonexistent. I haven't spoken to her in years."

Nita knitted her brow. "That's too bad."

"Yes, I suppose it is. Do you ski?"

Nita, surprised by the sudden segue, could only nod.

Steve sat stone-faced.

"Excellent. Why don't you come up to my house in the Berkshires this winter — with Steve, of course. I have a wonderful weekend home on a lake and it's only minutes from the Jiminy Peak ski area."

"That would be nice," Nita rewarded Nagle with a demure smile.

Steve smiled, too, as he watched Nita draw Nagle out. "Excuse me, nature calls." He winked at Nita over Nagle's head, and as Nagle stared at Nita, Steve slipped the charmer's spoon into his pocket and left the table.

Steve stood in the shadows of the main house, watching Nita ply her profession, until he saw a veiled look cross her face. He hurried back, and she signaled it was time to leave. Nagle, the true sport, suggested they split the bill three ways.

"He told me where his country home is," Nita said, on the sail back to City Island. "The slimy bastard came on to me with his phony charm. I can't imagine how any woman would fall for his egotistical line. I know it's unfair to make a snap diagnosis, but he's obviously been severely damaged by the early loss of his father and appalling relationship with his mother. I'd be nervous if I had to spend any time alone with him."

The thought did not thrill Steve either. He clenched his jaws until they hurt while Nita told him about Nagle's futile attempt at seduction.

"We have to make sure we never put you in that situation," he said.

"Not to worry, my darling. I can take care of myself. He just gives me the creeps."

"You asked a couple of probing questions. Do you think he suspected anything?"

"If he did, he's a good actor. I think he was getting off on the attention."

"You're the shrink."

"Thanks, my tennis hero. By the way, he drives a Mercedes, and he said he felt so embarrassed for dominating the match, he let you win the second set."

Steve guffawed. The rest of the trip did not include any further conversation about Dr. H. Hugh Nagle.

Agatha, rushed out of her cabin, zipping up her jeans, immediately after Steve steered Impressions into his slip. "God! Am I glad to see you," she said. She caught the bowline Steve tossed to her. "You have to help me—I'm going out of my mind."

"Agatha, meet Nita. What's the problem?"

Agatha nodded at Nita and turned back to Steve. "I found out where Lydia's ex worked before he took off. I called your friend Detective Santisorio, but he's off today. Can you come downtown with me? Maybe we can get his address."

"Give me a few minutes, I have to shower."

While Steve soaped up, Agatha gave Nita a brief version of Lydia's disappearance.

"So the last time you spoke to her, she was calling from a singles bar?" Nita asked.

"Yes," Agatha said, "She said she was fed up with the rat race and wanted to resume our relationship. We had made a date for the following night. When she didn't show, I thought she had changed her mind."

"Sounds like your feelings for her are more than casual."

"We really hadn't spent too much time together, and I haven't exactly been leading a nun's life, but I thought there was something special between us."

"Then, why was she in a singles bar?"

"She wanted to give it one last try before making any commitment." Agatha was on the verge of tears.

Nita put her arm around Agatha's shoulder. "Don't worry, we'll find her."

Steve emerged from the main hatch, dressed in chinos and a Bronx Zoo T-shirt.

"I'm primed and pumped, let's go. We better take my car."

Agatha shook her head. "I'd have to be a pretzel to fit in your back seat. I'll take you guys in mine. I have more room."

"I can't handle traveling in the right lane all the way downtown," Steve said.

"Steve!" Both women chided him.

He tossed his keys in the air. "I only meant we'll make better time in the Porsche."

Steve lead-footed it over the City Island bridge. "Where to, Aggie?"

"Damn it, Landau. You know I hate being called that." Agatha's voice was barely under control.

Steve looked at her in the rear view mirror and held up his free hand. "Truce neighbor, I'll behave."

"Sweet Basil." She blew her nose. "Do you know where it is?"

"Are you kidding? It's my favorite jazz club and right around the corner from my office. What does Lydia's ex do there?"

"She said he's a part-time bartender and part-time musician."

"They must still be friendly, if she apartment sits for him. My ex would have a stroke, if I asked her."

"They have an arrangement. If he goes out of town for a long gig, he pays her," Agatha said.

The group was quiet for the rest of the trip downtown until Steve parked at a Seventh Avenue meter in front of Sweet Basil.

Steve turned around. "Zeke, the manager, is a patient. Do you want me to get the address?"

Agatha nodded.

"What's the dude's name?"

"Lydia never told me."

"I'll be right back."

"I'll stay with Agatha," Nita said.

Ten minutes later Steve rushed back to the car. "We're all set. He lives on Gansfort Street, over a wholesale butcher. It's a few blocks from here, in the meat-packing district."

Steve turned right on Morton and again on Greenwich Street. "His name's Miles David. I couldn't make up a better moniker for a jazz musician. He's on tour with Ray Charles and won't be back for a few weeks. You know why they split up?"

Steve watched Agatha shake her head in the rear view mirror.

"Zeke told me, the guy decided he likes buoys better than gulls."

"It figures, with my luck." Agatha sniffled and rummaged through her bag.

Nita handed her a package of tissues. "It happens more often than you think."

Steve parked in front of the restaurant Florent, and they scrambled out of the car. Agatha rubbed her sore backside while they crossed the cobblestone street that had been worn smooth by two centuries of use. Streams of metallic red stained water ran down each side emanating a mixed odor of meat, blood, and hot tar. The group stopped in front of an iron door of a two-story building. The number 71 was painted haphazardly in white at the top. Next to the door was a loading platform with an overhead circular armature through which a steel cable moved with a series of mean looking meat hooks. Two workmen wearing white coats and backward baseball caps were unloading the carcass of an entire cow from an eighteen-wheeler parked at the curb. A rusted sign with faded lettering proclaiming, *Louis Falco, Abattoir, Master Purveyor of Choice Meats,* jutted precariously overhead. Large strips of heavy plastic guarded the broad entrance. A large cloud of water vapor streamed out as the two men passed through with their bovine cargo.

Steve tried the thick handle in the middle of the iron door. "Locked," he pounded against the metal loudly, but only got a sore fist for his trouble. "Did your friend mention a spare key?"

Agatha, staring intently at the shaded upstairs windows, shook her head.

"If Mr. Falco's the landlord, he might have one," Nita said.

141

A short, swarthy man with a pocked face, slipped through the plastic strips followed by one of the white-coated workers. "Hey asshole," the swarthy man said to the worker. "You forgot to hose off the loadin dock." He turned to Steve and his entourage.

"Whadda you guys want?" His gaze zeroed in on Nita's cleavage. "We don't sell retail."

Nita put her hand on Steve's arm. "Let me handle this." She smiled sweetly at the pocked faced man. "You must be Mr. Falco."

"Who wants to know?" he said, displaying a mouth of uneven yellow teeth.

"I've heard so much about you," she said. "Can we have some privacy?"

"Sure, come on in." They disappeared into the swirl of man-made vapor.

Steve paced around the platform, occasionally kicking the door, while Agatha fidgeted in her bag for a cigarette.

"I thought you stopped," he said.

She smiled forlornly, lit it and took a deep drag as Nita emerged through the plastic strips brandishing a black key.

"What'd you have to do to get it?" Steve asked sullenly.

"I promised him we'd come back and take the guided tour. Do I detect a trace of jealousy?"

Steve mumbled under his breath as he turned the key and leaned on the door handle. The hinges, not oiled for years, groaned as Steve muscled it open with Agatha glued to his back. A dank, musty smell filled the tight space as Steve fumbled for an electric switch. "Light a match, Agatha. I can't see squat."

Agatha did as instructed. Steve pulled a chain hanging from a fixture and a grimy twenty-five watt bulb barely lit a metal staircase. The organic scents from Falco's abattoir were even stronger in the confined hallway and increased in intensity as Steve led Agatha and Nita up the staircase. Nita's heels echoed loudly on the steel steps. Halfway up, Steve stopped short. A new odor assailed him, one with which he was all too familiar. His skin crawled. He turned and held up his hand. "Listen up, ladies. I want you

142

both to go back downstairs. Nita, call Lonnie and have him send a squad car, wait for them."

"Go to hell, Landau." Agatha said. "I'm coming with you."

"This is not up for a goddamn debate, Aggie. Get the fuck out of here, or I'll throw you down the stairs, if I have to."

Both women had never seen Steve react so strongly. They started to back down the stairwell. "C'mon, Agatha," Nita said. "Let's see if we can wrangle a couple of steaks from the slime ball downstairs."

With sweat dripping down his chin, Steve continued up to a door at the top of the stairs. The stench, more fetid, forced him to breathe through his mouth. He tried the door handle, and it swung open easily. The rank effluvium overcame him, and he almost lost the lunch he had so recently enjoyed at Nagle's club. He covered his nose with a hankie and yelled through the door. "Lydia? Is anyone here?" After a few seconds of silence, he cautiously took a tentative step into the room. He stood for a moment in the entranceway of a huge loft that any developer could have easily converted into three separate apartments. The shiny modernistic glass, leather, and chrome furniture seemed lost in the cavernous space. Aside from a half bottle of wine and two red, stained glasses on an oval cocktail table, the silent room appeared empty and uninhabited. A room constructed of opaque glass squares in the far corner was the only structural break in the brick walls. Steve guessed it was the bathroom and started to walk toward it. He stopped midway to catch his breath. The stench, stronger now, made it difficult for him to breathe. He gagged before continuing.

"Lydia?" he called again, but his voice echoed off the walls. *What I wouldn't give for a swab of Vicks,* he thought as he reached for the chrome lever of the bathroom door. He pushed against it, and although he felt resistance, it swung open. He hesitated in the doorway to examine the interior. A large Jacuzzi bathtub stood before him with droplets of dried blood on the rim. A commode with a closed cover stood next to it. He edged into the bathroom to see a red stain leading into the bathtub drain. Suddenly, the door slammed shut behind him. Adrenaline pumping, he whirled, and for a split second, could not compute what his shocked eyes were seeing. He was unaware of the gut-wrenching scream that escaped his lips. He reflexively stepped back into the rim of the tub, lost his footing, fell in and banged his head on the wall behind. He lay in a crumpled heap, stunned.

143

Nita and Agatha heard the shrill wail down in the street, and they scrambled through the front door. Taking two steps at a time, Nita stopped at the opened apartment door, sucking in air and gasping from the odor. "Steve!" she screamed, "Are you all right?"

No answer.

Agatha came wheezing up the stairs as Nita was preparing to rush into the apartment. "Steve," she yelled again. "I'm coming in."

"Don't," Steve said in an unsteady voice. "I'm all right. Go back downstairs and call back Lonnie. Tell him we have a crime scene." He had never felt sicker. He sat immobilized where he had fallen, trying to steady his breathing and not hyperventilate. He kept blinking, in an attempt to focus his eyes on the blurry figure in front of him. Finally he locked onto Lydia's slack, naked body hanging on the back of the bathroom door like a landed marlin, held by a meat hook that jutted out through an open wound in her extremely lacerated lower jaw.

18

The Interrogation

Minutes went by before Steve could test his shaky limbs and lift himself from the bathtub. He had to sit on the edge for a few more minutes until the room stopped spinning and his run-away heart decreased to a trot. His legs shook as he slowly stood up, then bent over immediately and threw up in the commode. He weaved unsteadily through the loft, but the dizziness returned when he gazed down the narrow, poorly lit staircase. "Feets don't fail me now," he murmured as he placed an unsteady foot on the first step and clamped a death grip on the banister, but still almost fell twice while tentatively descending the metal stairs to the street. Once outside, he leaned heavily against the platform adjoining the exit, sucking in large gulps of air in an attempt to control the waves of nausea that rolled over him.

Nita broke away from the uniformed cops interviewing her and ran to him. "Darling, are you all right?"

Lonnie's unmarked Buick braked at the curb. He bolted out the door and after spotting Steve and Nita, rushed to them. "What's going on, little Brother? You look like a turkey on Thanksgiving morning."

"Whoa, one at a time! It's hard enough just staying erect. I'm okay," Steve told Nita, "I just have a nasty bump on the back of my head." He turned to Lonnie. "I never thought I'd be calling you to investigate a homicide."

"Homicide?" Agatha cried out as she joined them. "Lydia?"

"Sorry, Aggie," Steve extended his hands.

"Damn it Steve, I told you not to call me..." Agatha burst into tears and couldn't continue.

Steve and Nita tried to console her while Lonnie ran down a list of instructions for the patrol cops. "I need more blue and whites. Cordon off both ends of the block. Only workers and tenants get through — no rubber-neckers or reporters. Run your yellow tape from the loading platform here to the building next door. I'll call in a crime scene team before I go up. Now listen up. I want you men to round up all the transvestite hookers who work this area, and don't let any of the meat-packing workers or the restaurant employees go until they've been questioned by a gold shield."

Lonnie spoke to Gagliardi from his car radio before he moved back to Steve. "Sorry Bro — I know you're not feeling too swift but I need your input before I go up."

Steve nodded wanly and filled Lonnie in.

"Look like it's our guy?" Lonnie asked.

"If it isn't, he's a terrific copycat. I can't imagine more than one sicko who's this crazy."

"I hear you Brother. You touch anything?"

"Nothing in the loft, except of course, the door handle. I fucked up in the John. I left my lunch in the toilet and a few dozen prints in and around the tub."

"Hey, you did what you had to do."

"I don't have my forensic kit, and I'm too shook up to do a good job. Call my associate, Dick Marmor in Queens. Tell him it's at my request."

"I'll take care of it. You and Nita go on home, now. You've had enough excitement for the day, and you'll need your energy for tomorrow. Gagliardi's set up an interrogation at ten in the morning, with the primo dentist you picked out from his list. He'll need your help."

"I'll be there. Where's Agatha?" Steve asked Nita.

"Behind you." Nita pointed to her sitting on the curb, blowing her nose. "Perez just finished questioning her."

"C'mon, Agatha, We'll take you home," Steve said.

"I'm staying right here," she sniffled.

"It'll be hours before they finish the investigation and bring her down. You don't want to be in this neck of the woods at night with all the wackos they've got roaming the streets."

"I'll get a cab."

"Are you kidding? No cabbie in his right mind would cruise these streets after dark."

"Then I'll stay at the Lesbian and Gay Men's Alliance on the next block. They have extra cots."

"C'mon, neighbor. There's nothing else you can do here. Trust me. I'll keep you posted on every step of the investigation."

Agatha let Nita guide her to the Porsche and didn't object when Nita crawled into the back and gave her the front seat.

Steve dropped Nita off at her apartment the next morning and continued to One Police Plaza. He found Lonnie in a hallway giving instructions to Stone and Perez. They had brought in the suspect dentist and were setting up to interrogate him in a room with a one-way mirror.

Lonnie turned to Steve. "How're you doing, good buddy. Yesterday had to be rough on you."

"I'm coping. Any word on the investigation?"

"It was our guy, for sure."

Steve grimaced. "I have a present for you. With all the excitement yesterday, I forgot to give you this silver spoon hot off the hands of our number-one suspect."

Lonnie gingerly took the still-wrapped spoon and sent it down to the fingerprint lab. "Hey, Steve you still look like your cable's stretched as far as it'll go," Lonnie said while they waited for the suspect to be brought in.

147

"Maybe this'll loosen you up. I overheard a conversation in the elevator between two dentists. One said he was treating a patient with TB, rabies, and bubonic plague. The other dentist asked him what procedures he was using with a patient with all those diseases. The first dentist said, 'Special diet—fried eggs, matzo, and flat bread.' 'Why such a crazy diet?' The other guy says. 'Those are the only things I can pass under the door!'"

Steve snorted, as two cops led the suspect, Fred Bogan, into the interrogation room. Steve and Lonnie stood behind the one-way mirror to monitor the questioning.

Bogan was a middle-aged, meek-looking man. His height, weight, and shoe size fit the description of the serial killer, but his amorphous, egg-shaped figure negated any illusion of strength. He had a ring of muddy-brown hair surrounding a mottled bald head.

Lonnie whispered as he read off the salient points on the suspect's rap sheet. "Dirt bag was convicted of molesting a coupl'a teenage girls and raping one of them in his dental chair while they were under sedation. We nailed him with an undercover policewoman who was wired and had radio-opaque powder placed on her inner thigh.

"Another black eye for my profession."

"I hear you, Steve. We have our share of crooked cops."

Stone led the suspect through the preliminaries by reviewing his record in a monotone voice. Perez, a fierce-looking Latino with a Zapata mustache stood at the far end of the table, dragging on a black cigarillo while he glared at the beleaguered dentist through a column of foul smoke. He broke in and demanded, "Let's cut through the bullshit! Tell us where you were on Saturday night, June 12th, Wednesday night, June 15th, Friday night, July 6th, and Friday night July 23rd."

Bogan blinked at Perez, confused. Perez stared back, a malicious look on his face.

"That was over a month ago." Bogan quivered. "I was probably at home watching TV That's all I do, these days." His watery eyes shifted to Stone with a look that begged for help.

Stone interceded, "Maybe your wife or children would remember."

"My wife left me and took my two sons with her, after the incident."

Perez barked, "Incident? What incident?"

"The one that landed me in prison. The one that's brought me here to answer your questions."

"Refresh our memory."

"I was convicted for molestation and rape," he whispered.

Steve shook his head in disgust behind the mirror.

"I can't hear you—speak louder," shouted Perez.

"I was—"

Stone interrupted, "I'm sure you can remember where you were this past Wednesday evening."

"Wednesday?" Bogan's face lit up. "Yes, of course. The Red Sox were in town. I watched the entire game on TV"

"Terrific!" Perez sneered. "I don't suppose you had any visitors?"

Bogan dropped his head. "No."

"Who won, and who was the starting pitcher?" Perez shot out.

"The Yanks, three-two, and El Duque pitched a complete game."

"Big deal! You could have read that in any paper," Perez said.

"I saw the whole game. I swear on—"

Stone interrupted again. "Never mind. Do you know what a Vee Hee carver is?"

"A Vee Hee? Yes, of course. Any dentist would know about Vee Hee carvers. We all use them in our work. I mean I used to use one."

"Have you ever used a larger-sized carver?"

"Yes, of course, for denture wax-ups. Why are you asking me about..."

"We ask the questions here," Perez snapped. "Do you own a 1979 blue Chevrolet?"

"Yes, I do. It's all I can afford. I used up all my assets to pay for the lawyers."

Gagliardi joined Steve and Lonnie in the observation room and studied the sweating dentist.

"Have Perez ask him if he did his own lab work," Steve told Lonnie.

Lonnie pressed a button, and a light lit up behind Bogan. Perez abruptly left the room without a word.

Stone continued without missing a beat. "It might help, if you could remember what you had seen on TV on any of the other nights."

"I can't remember. If the Mets or Yanks were playing, I would have been watching the game. If not, I usually watch nature shows."

Perez came back into the room. "You wear a piece?"

"A piece? Oh, you mean a toupee'? Well, yes I do, but only for social occasions."

"Such as?"

"Weddings, bar mitzvahs, things like that."

"Do you ever put it on before going out boogying in singles bars?"

"Officer, I am not the boogying type, and I certainly do not go to singles bars."

Perez continued. "Okay, Doctor, we're almost through. Did you do your own lab work?"

"No, I used to send it to a commercial lab."

"Tell us the name."

"Ceramco Dental Labs, Mount Vernon."

"Thank you, Doctor, that will be all." Stone said.

Bogan exhaled loudly and scuttled out of the room, past the scowling Perez.

"Whadda ya think?" asked Gagliardi.

Steve and Lonnie shook their heads. "No way," said Lonnie.

"If any of our victims had ever come on to him, he'd would've wet his pants," Steve said.

Perez and Stone joined them in the viewing room. "You'd of thought we threatened to cut the wimp's dick off. He's not the one," Perez said.

150

"Okay, we all agree on that," Gagliardi grunted. "Anything on your guy, Doc?"

Steve reviewed the tennis match for them, including Nagle's outburst and his emotional about-face at lunch.

"Nita was terrific," he said. "She got him to tell her about the terrible relationship he had with his blonde mother. Fucker practically drooled over Nita. Thought I'd have to get extra napkins for the table."

"Can't blame him for that," Lonnie said.

"If you weren't so freaking big, I'd challenge you to a duel," Steve said. "But there's more: Nagle's left-handed. He's a clotheshorse, who dresses in the latest fashions. He drives a new Mercedes and owns a house in the Berkshires — Hancock, Massachusetts. I'd have to guess, but it looked like his shoe size is eleven. And finally, I got a thumbprint that's being processed as we speak."

Gagliardi was effusive. "Great work, Doc — you'll get that gold shield yet. Did you find out where he buys his clothes?"

"No, but I think I can get that information from his Nazi nurse."

"I have a buddy who's a state trooper in the Berkshires," Stone said. "I'll call and see what I can find out about Nagle's country place."

"Doc, I know it's a lot to ask, but do you think you or Nita could find out where your Prince Charming was the night your neighbor's friend bought it?" Gagliardi asked.

Steve shook his head. "I think Perez or someone from our investigating team would do a better job."

"Lonnie, see what you can do without alerting him," Gagliardi said.

Lonnie penned an entry into his notebook. "We don't have a hell of a lot to add with the latest homicide," he said. "Except it's definitely our guy. Transvestite hooker was doing a John a few doors down, around midnight, when Lydia and Dracula went upstairs, but was too busy to get a good look. He/she did notice the man was wearing a tie. Waitress from the restaurant across the street on a nicotine break saw him leave alone about two o'clock and drive away in an old blue car. She says she didn't see his face, but remembers he wasn't wearing a tie, and he was wiping something with what she thought was a rag. We got guys going through the trash in the neighborhood, looking for bloody neck ware."

Len Frank came up from the fingerprint lab, but said nothing. He frowned as he scanned the computer readout in his hand.

The suspense got to Gagliardi, and he exploded. "Well?"

"Hold your horses, Loo, I don't have too much for you."

"Why dont'cha just tell us what'cha got?"

"The print was smudged in a few critical areas. We were able to get three, maybe three and a half points of match-up. Not enough for a warrant, much less a conviction."

"But enough to tell us if he's the perp?" asked the frustrated Gagliardi.

"Maybe. We can't be definite."

"Thanks for the rush job, Len." Gagliardi turned to Lonnie. "It might be enough to get a phone tap. See if you can wrangle a court order from a friendly night judge. Stone, check your contact with the Massachusetts State Police. Steve, get us the name of the men's store where Nagle shops from his nurse. Let's get this turd before he does another one."

19

The Visitor

Steve stopped by the office to pick up his messages. Nita's throaty voice came through the speaker. "Hi darling. I have to see an unstable lady this evening who's threatening to commit suicide. I don't know how long I'll be so we better skip tonight. I'll call you tomorrow."

A frantic message from Art Powers begged Steve to provide moral support at his first rehearsal with the new Dracula teeth. The next call, even more urgent, was from Sam. Steve immediately punched in her number.

She picked up on the first ring, sniffling. "Dad, I've been biting my nails down to the knuckles waiting for your call."

"What's wrong?" Steve tried to keep his voice level.

"Mom and Nick got married today."

Steve slumped into his desk chair. "Didn't they give you any notice?"

"No. It was a spur-of-the-moment kind of thing. I'm really bummed."

"I understand, kitten. You want to stay with me tonight?"

"I can't, Dad. They're inviting people to the house, and I think I should be here. Otherwise we'll really get off on the wrong foot."

"That's wise, Sam. I'll be home tonight if you need me."

"Thanks, Dad. I love you."

As Steve slowly hung up the phone an overwhelming sense of grief gripped him. He couldn't shake it during the drive to the boat, and by the time he reached City Island, his depression deepened. He couldn't understand it—he had been cut off emotionally from Carol Ann for more than five years. Their only contact involved Sam, and those occasions were usually acrimonious.

While he prepared Captain Bill's dinner, he went over his usual mental litany on how really different they were. She's the ultimate Breck girl for Christ's sake. Blonde hair, freckles, the whole bit, while I could be a poster boy for Sadaam Hussein's basketball team. And the way she dressed every day, like she was going to a party, while shlump-city me looked like a Salvation Army reject. What about six-four me to five-one her? We were the Mutt and Jeff of Biloxi. I should have listened to my mother, "Southern drawls and Brooklyn accents don't have a good future."

He glanced up and caught his reflection in the large plexiglass window of the main salon. "Leave my son's aquiline schnoz alone—it's part of his semitic character," was another of mom's beauts, after Carol Ann had suggested I get a nose job.

He had always felt guilt about the divorce, and constantly fantasized that Carol Ann would find someone to clear his conscience. Now that it finally happened, he felt only remorse. He needed Nita more than ever but she was unavailable.

Depressed and unable to face the evening alone, he locked up and walked to Scotty's for a drink.

After Steve's third martini, Scotty joined him at the bar. "Go easy on that stuff, Steverino, or you'll be hearing bagpipes inside your head."

"Blow it out your ass, Mon. I could drink you under the table."

"Hah!" Scotty ordered a double martini.

By the time the last diner left, they were both roaring drunk and maudlin. "Bert, give my bestest and most closest friend here, another drink," Scotty ordered his bartender.

"Sorry, Boss. It's two o'clock and I'm cutting you bozo's off."

"Jus-a-sec. This here's my joint, an' we wan' one more for the road. Don't we, Steverino?" He slapped Steve on the shoulder.

Steve tried to answer, but his lips were too numb to form any vowels. "Bsgrgh!" was all he managed.

"See?" Scotty said. "Now give us a nightcap"

"In a pig's eye," Bert said. "I'm taking you drunks home, as soon as I lock up."

"You and I," Scotty sang loudly.

"Will die," Steve sang even louder.

"In a pig's eye," Scotty sang at the top of his lungs as Bert loaded them into his car.

Bert walked Steve to the marina entrance, then returned to the car to drive Scotty home. Steve heard the receding refrain, "Even educated pigs do it, let's fall in love," as Bert U-turned, and sped away.

Steve weaved his way down the pier to Impressions. As he climbed, fell, and then struggled up the ladder aboard, he heard his cat complaining.

"Hold on, Cap'n Bill, I'll have you fed in a minute," he mumbled.

After a struggle with the lock on the hatch, he stumbled below. But Captain Bill was not on board. Steve crawled back on deck, whistled, and while he waited for the Captain to return an uncontrollable urge to void his bladder gripped him. He relieved himself off the stern, willing himself not to fall overboard. "Shh! Better not wake Aggie, she hates when I do this," he muttered, trying desperately to clear his head. Captain Bill's indignant meows grew louder, but Steve still couldn't focus enough to see him. When he slid down the boarding ladder to the dock, the yowls became even more furious. Oddly enough, they seemed to be coming from under his feet. Befuddled, he looked down, and there, between the planks of the deck, crouched a very wet and chagrined cat. He steadied himself, pried a board loose, and extricated a shivering Captain Bill from his precarious roost.

"You poor baby, you look more like a drowned rat than a cat." He giggled at his own joke. "How the hell'd you end up unner the deck? You never fell overboard before."

Steve carried his shivering pet down to the galley, where Steve struggled to hold him steady while he washed the salt water from his coat with warm tap water and dried him off with a big bath towel. He filled his bowl with his favorite cat food and after setting it down, looked around and came to the slow realization that the boat looked different. A drawer that should have been shut stood half-open. Personal items on his desk didn't seem to be exactly where he had left them. He tried to clear his head by shaking it, but still couldn't fully concentrate. One thing was sure, someone had come aboard and had probably kicked or thrown Captain Bill overboard.

He was too tired and drunk to take any action other than check the hatches and throw the bolt on the companionway door. The effort exhausted him. He loaded his shotgun, flopped into bed, and fell asleep.

When the alarm went off at seven the next morning, Steve felt like he had just dropped off. "Jesus, it's not fair that a good person like me should feel this shitty," he muttered, when he tried to lift his head off the pillow. Captain Bill, who had joined Steve during the night, got a whiff of his breath and took off for the forward cabin.

"My mouth feels like it's stuffed with gauze pads," he groused. He massaged his temples, but they throbbed no matter which way he turned.

"A glass of water is about all I can handle," he confided to the returning Captain Bill. "How're you doing, buddy? Wish you could talk, tell me who the dirtbag was who evicted you last night."

Captain Bill craved food over conversation and rubbed vigorously against Steve's leg.

Steve examined the boat more closely after feeding his cat. The only thing missing was a photo that Lonnie had taken on their boat trip of Nita, Sam, and Steve. He had a bad feeling, but attributed it to his hangover.

I have some serious thinking to do. I know I'm going to hate it, but I better go for a run to clear my head, he thought and painfully laced on his running shoes.

Agatha emerged from her cabin while he was stretching against his dock locker. Her hair hung limply and her clothes looked slept in.

"How're you holding up, Neighbor?" Steve asked.

"Barely coping." She stared at Steve through swollen eyes. "You look like yuck city."

"Go easy on me, Aggie. Had a rough night."

"Did Nita finally come to her senses?"

Steve smiled. "Glad you're feeling well enough to insult me. See any strangers around last night?"

"No. Why?"

Steve thumbed toward Impressions. "My humble abode was tossed, as was Captain Bill. He ended up in the drink."

"I thought I heard him crying, but I heard you banging around last night and figured you had everything under control."

"Damn! I had hoped you didn't hear me pee off the stern."

Agatha grimaced. "You're lucky I didn't. You are a male pig, and a chauvinist to boot."

"You're just jealous because you can't do it like us guys. Wait a sec! What time was that?"

"About ten."

"That wasn't me."

"My God! A fucking intruder was mucking about next door." Agatha snapped her fingers. "Does this have anything to do with Lydia's murder?"

"Let's not jump to any conclusions. I'll phone Lonnie as soon as I get back from my run." Steve trotted down the dock.

He could manage only half his usual distance and took twice the time to return to the boat, drenched in gin-tinged sweat. He gasped and moaned through an ice-cold shower, had a light breakfast, and called Lonnie at home, but the line was busy. He tried Nita, with the same result. He lumbered around the boat, then slapped his head and dialed the number for his parents' condominium in Fort Lauderdale.

"Hi, Mom! Happy birthday!"

"Who's this?"

"How many sons do you have?"

"I used to have one who called me every week. Now, I know this stranger in New York who calls me whenever he feels like it."

"Mom, I just spoke to you last week."

"It was three weeks ago. But who's counting?"

"I'm sorry. It's been kind of hectic here. I promise to keep in touch more often. Anyway, happy birthday!"

"Thank you. How's my gorgeous granddaughter?"

"She's not a happy camper right now. Carol Ann got married yesterday."

"Good for her. I wish you would find someone and settle down too. Your father and I want more grandchildren."

"That's my present for you today. I met someone and I'm head over heels."

"*Mazel tov!* That's a wonderful gift. How long have you been seeing her? What's her name, and by the way, what does she do?"

"Her name's Nita Lazar. She's a forensic psychologist, and I met her about a month ago."

"A month! Wait until your father comes back from his walk and finds out you waited this long to tell us."

Steve smiled, remembering how often his mother used to tell him, 'Wait until your father comes home.' Then his father would walk him outside and berate him for about thirty seconds before taking him to the neighborhood ice cream shop for a hot fudge sundae.

"Just a second! You can tell him yourself," his mother said. "He just came in. Lou, come here. Your wayward son's on the phone, and he has a girlfriend. A forensic something or other."

"Hello, stranger!"

"Dad, not you too."

"Don't be such a wise guy. I can still put you over my knee."

Steve smiled again, picturing his five-foot-four father trying to fit Steve over his knees.

"So what's your new girl like? Is she a dish?"

"Absolutely, and she has the brains to match."

"Maybe she has a friend. Your mother's been driving me crazy."

Steve heard his mother in the background. "Big shot! You wouldn't know what to do with a young one. My friends were right; I never should have married you."

"So how come you begged me after our first date," Lou Landau jibed.

"Hah! You forget, you had to ask me five times before I said yes," Ann Landau retorted.

"Hey, Dad! I'm still here. You and Mom should take your act on the road. You'd be a big hit on the condo circuit."

"So how did you and this forensic dish meet?"

"We're working on a case together for the NYPD."

"You're still fooling around with that stuff?"

"You could say that."

"Wait a second! Is it the Dracula Killer we've been reading about in the papers down here?"

"Yes, but don't tell Mom. She'll have a fit."

"It's all right! She just went into the living room to watch Regis. I think she has a crush on him. You'll let me know when you catch the perp?"

"You've been watching too many detective shows."

"I'm addicted. Be careful, the both of you. Bring her down to meet us as soon as you can."

"Will do. I love you, and I promise to call you next week."

"You better, or my ass is grass."

Steve hung up feeling much better than he did before his call. His parents' banter always raised his spirits, except now, the image of Lydia harpooned to the bathroom door intruded on his pleasant thoughts. He dialed Lonnie's number again.

"What's up, Steve?"

"My aching head, for one thing. I had an unannounced visitor on the boat yesterday."

"You sure?"

"Positive, and Captain Bill took an unscheduled swim."

159

"Maybe he fell in."

"No way! He's too surefooted. He hasn't slipped overboard since I brought him aboard as a kitten."

"Okay, Bro, I hear you. I'll call the local precinct and have them check your dock. routinely. You have any firearms?"

"I keep a shotgun on board for skeet shooting."

"Good, get double-zero pellets and keep the gun available, and change your locks."

"Will do, thanks, Lonnie."

Steve called Nita next, but after five rings, her answering machine came on. He left a message that he would pick her up after her karate class that evening. He replaced the hatch door hinge with a reinforced one and found a strong combination lock in his utility box. He heard a satisfactory click after securing the lock, took Captain Bill over to Agatha, advised her to do the same with her hatch, and left for his office.

20

The Rehearsal

Steve had scheduled only Art Powers later that day, in order to insert and adjust the set of Dracula teeth, then accompany Powers to the theater to check the acoustics. To Steve's surprise, Art came on time and was reasonably calm.

Steve removed the finished overdenture from Hans Dieter's lab box and inserted it over Art's teeth.

"Wow! They feel exthremely comfortable," Art said. "How do they look?"

"Imposing!" Steve handed Art a hand mirror. "You make a menacing Dracula."

"Yeth," Art said, studying his image while he practiced curling his lip. "You promith the lithp will go away?"

"Trust me. You just have to work with them awhile."

"You're the doctor," Art said.

But, as the pair neared the theater, Art's resolve dwindled. By the time they reached the stage door, he was hysterical with apprehension.

"Thteve, I have to take them off, or everyone ith going to laugh at me."

"Be patient, I'll explain it to everyone before rehearsal starts. You'll see, they'll all be pulling for you."

"Do you have to yooth a dental metaphor? I with I had your confidenth."

The stage manager let them in. "Holy cow! Mr. Powers, you'll have the Wednesday matinee ladies screaming in terror."

Art nodded graciously, a bit more confident as they walked down the aisle of the dark theatre to the second row, where the director sat.

"Hal," Steve announced, "I give you Dracula."

Hal studied Art with a professional eye. "God dammit," he said. "You look sensational, Art. Are you ready to go over the scene?"

"Yeth," said Art.

"Excuse me?" Hal looked puzzled.

Steve took his cue. "Art wants me to address the cast and crew before you start, so they'll know what to expect."

Hal nodded and rose. "Listen up, everyone," he projected in a deep bass voice. "Cast and crew, stage center right now for a powwow."

It took three minutes for all the actors, stagehands, and the production staff to congregate. The houselights were turned on, and Steve stared in amazement at the amount of people required to produce a Broadway musical. He stood at the base of the proscenium and waited for quiet, before he addressed the crowd of more than seventy people.

He cleared his throat and said, "My name's Steven Landau, and I'm the dentist who made the set of teeth Art Powers will wear as Dracula in your play. There's going to be a very difficult breaking-in period for Mr. Powers during the next few weeks. He'll have to rehearse with the teeth in place, so he'll be comfortable with them by opening night. Initially he'll have trouble with his speech and will lisp. There'll be a few other minor difficulties, but the speech pattern will be the most obvious. On behalf of Mr. Powers, I'm asking for your indulgence and support. It will be a very trying time for him, and he needs all the help you can give him to get through this period. Thank you and good luck on your production."

"All right everyone. Set up for act one, scene five," Hal barked.

The crowd dispersed in all directions. Stagehands wheeled out a four-poster bed to the right side of the stage, and lowered a large flat containing a window to stage center. The lighting staff doused the house lights and switched on the stage lights, creating an eerie blue effect on the set. The actress, Elayna Holtz, looked stunning in a silver nightgown, as she got into the bed, pulled up the cover and pretended to sleep.

"Hold down the noise backstage," bellowed Hal from the second row, where Steve had joined him. "Places!"

The window opened, and Art Powers, with his hair slicked back and wearing a black cape, and Steve's teeth moved stealthily into the bedroom.

Elayna called out, "Who's there?"

Art answered, "Count Dracula."

Elayna, cowering, got out of bed and faced Art. "What do you want?"

"To thuck your blood, Thuthan."

Elayna stared wide-eyed at Art then fell back on the bed convulsed in laughter. Pandemonium followed as the rest of the cast, crew, musicians, and even Hal broke up.

Art stood, legs apart, hands on hips. "You call thith thupport?"

He ripped the teeth from his mouth, flung them at Steve, and stormed off the stage. Steve and Hal bounded after him and caught up to him in his dressing room. After thirty minutes of massaging his ego, Art finally calmed down and agreed to attempt the scene again.

His leading lady could not get over the giggles though and broke up during the next five run-throughs. Finally, all Art had to do was climb in through the window, and the blanket under which Elayna was supposedly sleeping heaved and shook until she threw it off in a hysterical outburst.

"I'm splitting," Steve whispered to Hal, "before I become a witness to murder."

He called his office from the lobby phone and caught Nancy as she was getting ready to leave.

"Hey, boss, how'd my heartthrob make out?"

"Don't ask."

"That bad, huh? If he needs any help with the love scenes, just let me know."

"I'm sure he's anxiously awaiting your call. Any messages?"

"Two that need your attention. I took care of the rest. An enormous black dude, named Lonnie, stopped by, told me some dumb dentist jokes and left word for you to call him. He says you have his number. The D.A. called. They arrested a creep who beat up and killed his three-year-old daughter. Besides the hematomas and fractures, she was also bitten. The suspect refused to have impressions taken so The D.A. got a court order to sedate him and have you do your thing."

"Don't tell me—he's at Riker's."

"Nope, you drew the right straw on this one. They're holding him at Bellevue. An assistant D.A. will meet you on the seventh floor, at ten o'clock tomorrow."

"Thanks, Nance. Pack an impression kit and meet me there."

"It's already done."

"I should have known. Have a good night." Steve punched in Lonnie's number.

"Hey Steve, we got a big break. Any chance I can see you tonight?"

"I was just going downtown to play basketball. You're welcome to join me."

"Where are you?"

"The theater district. I'm calling from the lobby of The Music Box."

"Have a beer in the Mexican joint across the street. I'll be there by the time you finish."

Lonnie, gym bag in hand, walked through the stained glass doors as Steve placed an empty bottle on the bar. Lonnie ordered a Corona and sat down with a big grin on his face. "How's that for timing?"

"Flawless. What's the big break? I've been sitting here on pins and needles."

"First, I have to tell you about this little old bubby who grabbed her dentist by the balls and said, 'We're not going to hurt each other, are we?'"

Steve banged his empty bottle on the bar "Lonnie, goddammit, I'm sitting here dying of curiosity, and you're telling me lousy dental jokes?!"

"Chill out, man, thought I'd slip one in. Here we go: On a hunch, I checked with the Massachusetts Motor Vehicle Bureau, and guess what? Never mind, I'll tell you. Your friend, Dr. Nagle, owns a blue 1967 Ford registered at his house in the Berkshires. I spoke to Stone's buddy, Trooper Oates. He knows Nagle. Says he gave him a warning, then a ticket for hotrodding around the Tanglewood area. Nagle suped up and customized the old muscle car and likes to show off for the locals. Oates distinctly remembers Nagle's passenger, said she was hard to forget. A blonde with more cleavage than the Taconic Valley."

Steve smirked, "The thick plottens."

"You can bet your last shekel on it. Anything turn up with your night visitor?"

"Not a thing, except I'm getting paranoid about security."

"Cool it, boychick. There's too many mischugynas roaming our fair city, and one of them knows your address."

Steve laughed. "You break me up, every time you use Yiddish to make a point."

"You can thank the leader of my Klezmer band, Williamsburg Willy."

"Okay, Bro. I be watchin' fo' trouble." Steve said.

"Y'all needs work on yo ebonics, honkie man." Lonnie scooped up his gym bag and headed out the door. At his car, he removed the police department card from the dashboard and opened the passenger door for Steve. "I'm heading up north tomorrow to poke around. I can use company…"

"Sorry, man. I have a date with a sadistic father at Bellevue. If you can wait until Friday, Nita and I can join you."

"No problemo, I can use the time to tie up a few loose ends. Make sure you check Nagle's whereabouts. We don't want to get caught red-handed. Oates told me he can get a general search warrant and the house keys. We caught a break, Nagle's alarm system is wired into the sheriff's office."

"Too bad. I thought I'd finally get the chance to watch a real pro pick a lock."

"Sure, and screw up any case we can make against Nagle. I'll see you at Nita's, Friday at nine," Lonnie said. He parked next to a hydrant on 6th Avenue in front of the basketball court in Greenwich Village and placed his police card back on the dashboard.

They threaded their way through the crowd watching the game in progress through the chain link fence that surrounded the court, and went to the sidelines reserved for the next in line to challenge the winners.

"Shit, Luis is here," Steve muttered as he laced on his sneakers.

"The dude under the basket with the flying elbows?" Lonnie asked.

"Yup. The fucker's one tough hombre, and the dirtiest player in the neighborhood."

"I better take him."

"Leave him to me, I know all his moves. You can take King Kong, the guy who just rebounded, he's not exactly a pussy."

Steve and Lonnie high-fived with the three other players on the next game line, and then jogged onto the court to shoot warm-up baskets. Luis glared at Steve and gathered his team around the water fountain to discuss strategy.

Steve took the first shot of the game and missed, but Lonnie outmuscled his man, rebounded, and sank an easy lay-up. Luis took Steve in low and scored next with a jump hook. Steve found the range with his next two jump shots, but paid the price each time with an elbow in the ribs. The score see sawed back and forth but was tied at sixteen as they got closer to the twenty baskets needed to win. After Luis almost took Steve's head off on a driving slam dunk, Lonnie said, "Take my man — that fucker is mine!"

The next time down the court, Luis faked to the right and left Lonnie flat-footed as he went in for an easy lay-up. When he did it a second time, Steve backpedaled in front of Lonnie and said, "He always fakes right and goes left."

"Not anymore," Lonnie set a solid pick that Luis tried to fight through as Steve sank a fifteen-footer. The next time down, Luis faked right again, but this time dribbled into a solid black wall. Lonnie stripped the ball and zipped a long pass to Steve on a fast break. Luis, infuriated, took off down the court and charged into Steve as he went up for the lay-up slamming him into the fence behind the basket. As Steve lay stunned, Lonnie stormed

166

down the court and body slammed Luis into the fence. "That's an automatic forfeit, shithead," Lonnie raged. "Get off the court."

"Sez who, mothafucker? Maybe where you homeboys be playin', but down here, he jus' take the ball out again. An don't be bangin' into me again."

"Says who?" Lonnie's BB eyes fastened on Luis.

"Sez me an' my gang."

Steve was on his feet by the time Lonnie grabbed Luis and flung him into his charging gang. The blow scattered them, but they regrouped and swarmed over Steve and Lonnie. The rubber-neckers lined along 6th Avenue rushed in to join what looked like a good brawl. Two blue and whites, called by the beat cop, screeched to a halt in front of the court entrance.

"I'm on the job," Lonnie shouted as the precinct cops rushed in and tried to peel him off the unrepentant Luis.

Lonnie produced his gold shield, after order was restored. Houlihan, the beat cop asked, "What do you want to do with these gang bangers, Sarge?"

"Kick the mutts off the court. They show their ugly mugs here the next few days, lock 'em up."

"You must've been a barrel of laughs on the football field," Steve said to Lonnie as they were leaving. "Are my ears still buzzing, or is that your beeper?"

Lonnie read the number. "It's Gagliardi." He walked over to the squad car. "Officer Houlihan I need your radio for a minute, "

Lonnie listened intently for a few minutes, then returned the walkie-talkie to Houlihan. "We got a live one," Lonnie beamed at Steve. "Dental supply man. Right up your alley. I could use your help, Brother."

"After what you just did for me? Let's roll."

Lonnie clapped a red flashing light on top of the car and squealed out of the parking space. "Bartender in the financial district, called us after observing a bad-ass who fit our description putting moves on a blonde regular."

"Must happen a couple hundred times every day," Steve said. "What makes this guy special?"

"The blonde — a dental hygienist, by the way — wanted no part of the jerk, and he got aggressive."

"Physically or verbally?"

"Both. The bartender called it in. Kelly and Magnin, from our team, responded. They found out the skel sells dental supplies for a living and has a pink sheet for beating on a few girlfriends. They read him his rights, and brought him downtown to cool his heels for a while." Lonnie swerved around a bus. "Gagliardi arranged a line-up with a coupla witnesses."

Steve followed Lonnie into a darkened room where Gagliardi was talking to three detectives in the back row of a small amphitheater facing a glass wall. "Who're our shills?" Gagliardi asked.

"Three of our undercover guys, and Angelo the waiter from the Blackjack. They all fit the general description," Magnin said.

"What'd you guys do to get skinflint Charlie to let Angelo off for a lineup?"

"We told him we'd stop using his joint as a cop hangout."

The lieutenant nodded appreciatively. "The witnesses ready?"

Steve shot an inquisitive look at Lonnie. "The hooker, bartenders, doormen, waitresses and friends of the first victims who caught a glimpse of our man," Lonnie said.

"They're waiting outside." Magnin opened the door and motioned a group of people in. He had them sit in the back of the amphitheater and issued instructions to each one.

"Bring in the suspects," Gagliardi bellowed.

The wall of glass lit up to reveal a small stage in the room beyond the glass. Horizontal lines of measurement painted on the back wall showed the height of the five men who shuffled into the room and lined up, squinting in the glare of the lights.

"Jesus, I know the guy on the end," Steve said.

"That's our man," said Gagliardi. He spoke into a microphone: "Number five! Step forward." Gagliardi switched off the microphone. "What can you tell us about him, Doc?"

"I saw him trying to con my friend Herm Bressack in his office. He probably doesn't remember me."

Lonnie stared at the man with the cold passionless eyes who kept clenching and unclenching his fists. "He's one mean-looking fucker. How'd his con work?"

"His name is Vincent Andrews. He owns a company that distributes dental supplies, and he suckers in dentists with ridiculously low prices. After they sign a contract with him, he raises his rates sky-high. When the dentists balk, he has an ambulance chaser threaten them with a lawsuit, and then offers to settle out of court. Most dentists pay him off, rather than lose a week stuck in court."

"Nice scam," Gagliardi said, "but that don't make him a killer."

"I'd still like to see you throw his larcenous ass in the slammer."

"We'll see what we can do. Have the first witness come down," Gagliardi commanded.

Doris Walker's doorman was escorted down the steps for a look through the glass wall.

"Frank, take all the time you want," Gagliardi said. "Any of those men look like the man who brought Doris Walker home the night she was murdered?"

The doorman's brows knitted as he stared through the glass. "Number five looks vaguely familiar."

"You certain?"

"No, sorta, though. The perp I saw had longer and wavier hair."

Lonnie whispered to Steve. "We gotta find witnesses that don't read detective novels."

The transvestite, dressed in a black leather mini skirt and an off-the-shoulder pink blouse—with enough cleavage to make the detectives wonder—ambled down on five-inch stiletto heels, accompanied by a beat cop. She waved a painted nailed hand in front of her face. "Gawd! Is it hot in here, or is it my raging hormones? Oh hi, Lieutenant." Dolly fluttered her eyelashes at Gagliardi. "So nice to see you again."

All eyes in the room turned to Gagliardi, he cleared his throat, "Dolly helped us put away the dirtbag who killed her best friend for a long stretch. Check the bunch we have behind the mirror, Dolly, and see if you can identify the man you saw on Gansfort Street the other night."

The transvestite's lips puckered up in concentration as she intently studied the men in the lineup and stopped at number five. "Uh oh!" she said, eyes glued on Vincent Andrews. "The man I saw was wearing a tie. Can we..."

Gagliardi stripped off his neck ware and gave it to the cop with instructions. The cop walked into the lineup room, and after a heated discussion, Andrews put the tie on with a big Windsor knot.

Dolly, busy straightening her mesh black stockings, missed the exchange. After some gentle prodding by Gagliardi, she turned her attention back to number five and exclaimed, "Oh, No!"

"What is it?" Gagliardi asked, unable to keep the excitement out of his voice. "Do you recognize him?"

"The tie! It's just terminally atrocious. The one I saw was a lavender, silk Cardin."

"Can't you use your imagination?"

"I'm sorry Lieutenant. I just can't be positive,, I was kind of busy at the time."

Of the remaining six witnesses, two picked Angelo the waiter, one an undercover cop, and the rest chose number five, but like Frank and Dolly, none of them was willing to positively finger their choice.

"What now?" Steve asked.

"We'll check Andrew's alibis for the nights of the murders," Lonnie said.

"Does he stay locked up?"

"No way! His shyster's waiting in the hall with a release. If his story doesn't hold up, we'll get a warrant," Gagliardi said.

Steve nodded. "I'm out of here. I have to pick up Nita at her karate studio."

"Remind her of the trip north on Friday," Lonnie said.

"You still think it's necessary?"

"Hey, man, it ain't over till a fat suspect sings. All we got is another possible. We nail one for sure — the other gets kicked loose."

As Steve left the room, Vincent Andrews, suspect number five, was exiting the lineup room. Before he turned the corner, he spotted Steve. The intensity of Andrews' icy stare sent shivers down Steve's spine.

21

The Kada

Steve hailed a cab and gave an uptown address. He was so deep in thought, he paid no attention as his turbaned driver weaved demolition-derby style through Manhattan traffic. Finally, the cabbie slammed on the brakes in front of a dojo on Lexington Avenue. Steve paid the tab, told the cabbie to keep the change, and almost got his hand ripped off as the driver zipped off toward another innocent fare.

A Japanese receptionist typing on a computer keyboard with festooned fingernails looked up.

"Good evening, may I help you?" she asked.

"Yes, I'm here to meet Nita Lazar."

"Ah, yes. She's in the main room."

"Can I go in?"

"Oh, no. Sensei does not allow distractions during his master class. Besides, Nita is scheduled for a kada tonight."

"A kada?"

"Yes, a mock battle. You may observe through the windows in the door."

Steve peeked in tentatively and saw ten students — Nita was one of two women in a large mirrored room. All were dressed in white pajama-like gis with black obis tied around their waists. Steve's attention was diverted to the black-belted sensei, a squat Japanese man in his late forties who stood in front of the group. His back was reflected in a full-length mirror. Through the door, Steve heard him bark orders and the students' response of gut yells, or kiyis as they performed their karate moves. They stopped abruptly following a shout from the sensei, and then formed a circle around a large mat in the center of the room. Nita toed one of the two parallel lines, drawn six feet apart on the mat. A lean, Asian man stood alertly at the other. Steve couldn't hear the instructions the sensei was giving to Nita and her opponent. He stood transfixed by Nita's beauty and serenity as she stood waiting for the kada to start. She and her opponent bowed to each other and came up into a karate stance.

The transformation of Nita's calm demeanor into an intense and forbidding stance took Steve by surprise. He suppressed a cheer of *bravo* as he watched an artistically choreographed, imaginary battle progress. He stood awestruck as Nita and her opponent, with precision and a fierce concentrated energy, performed upper and lower jabs and blocks, front and side elbow thrusts, augmented with spins and jump kicks. The bout progressed into a highly stylized, ritualistic dance that was almost balletic in form.

After eight intense minutes, the sensei clapped his hands to end the match. Perspiration flowed freely from under the combatants' headbands as they smiled benignly and bowed to each other.

After her shower, Nita came into the lobby and hugged Steve like she hadn't seen him for a month.

"Hey," Steve said, "you were great in there. How come the guy in charge didn't raise your hand as the clear winner?"

Nita's cheeks flushed. "I didn't know you were watching. I'm not ready to have you observe my karate sessions."

"What're you talking about? I enjoyed every minute of it."

"It's not exactly the image I'd like to project to my lover."

"What, you think I want my woman more demure and ladylike?"

"Well, don't you?"

"Occasionally, yes, but that's the point. You are, in my eyes, the queen of femininity. But now, I feel safer walking the streets of New York with you to protect me."

Nita gave Steve a mock karate chop as he raised his arm to hail a cab. When his first attempt failed, Nita put two fingers in her mouth and with a shrill whistle got two cabs to fight for their fare. Steve could only shake his head.

During the ride up First Avenue to Nita's place, Steve filled her in on the new developments in the Dracula case.

Nita said, "I'll get a better handle on Nagle if I help you and Lonnie investigate his country house."

"It's a done deal. Lonnie's picking us up Friday morning. Are you making any progress getting your patient to talk to us?"

"I'm working on it. He's starting to come around."

"Let's hope it's soon. He could crack the case."

They inched forward amid a sea of red blinking lights, stuck in the Queens Borough Bridge gridlock. "It's only ten more blocks, we'll make better time if we walk," Steve over tipped the cabby to compensate for shortening the trip.

After strolling a while in silence, Nita said, "You must promise, not to watch another of my karate matches, until I'm ready."

"How come? You saw me getting creamed on the tennis court."

"That was different."

"Aren't you being overly sensitive?"

"You can't tell me how to feel."

"How do you feel?"

"I become a different person and let out all my aggression. I'd feel funny, if you're watching the other me."

Steve tweaked Nita's nose. "Nita, you're being silly."

"Fuck off, Steve."

174

"Are we having our first argument?"

Nita scowled. "Not if you promise *not* to be a spectator until I say it's okay. It makes me too nervous."

"Funny you should mention that. I'm feeling a little uneasy right now."

"Is that how disagreements affect you?"

Steve snorted. "No! I've had enough with my ex to make it a way of life. It's hard to explain. My palms are sweating and the hair on the back of my neck is standing up. It's like the feeling I get while sailing through a storm or getting lost in fog."

Nita reflected a moment. "I do also. I feel like we're two goldfish in a small bowl being circled by a hungry kitty.

Their relaxed walk through a familiar neighborhood became a tense retreat. They stopped in front of an antique shop, but none of the objects d'art registered as Steve and Nita scoured the reflections in the window searching for any questionable movement on the street behind them. They started to walk again taking turns scrutinizing the surrounding crowds, but came up empty on any suspicious looking characters.

A few blocks down, Nita asked, "How about that guy in front of the pizza joint?"

They paused for a few minutes as if to peruse the headlines at a news kiosk, and occasionally glanced at the man. A young girl joined him. When the couple embraced and went into the restaurant Steve and Nita let out their held-in breaths. He took Nita's hand and they continued on, frequently looking over their shoulders, until they reached Nita's block and turned the corner. The street was eerily quiet. Their uneasy feeling reached a new height.

"C'mon, I'll race you to your building," Steve said with an earnestness that belied his smile.

The doorman held the door for the breathless pair, admitting them into the lobby. They moved quickly to the elevator and exhaled theatrical sighs of relief as the doors closed. They took one last look down the empty corridor before entering Nita's apartment, then double-locked the door.

Steve left by the same door early the next morning and walked down First Avenue to Bellevue. Still haunted by the uneasy feeling of being followed, he occasionally checked the street behind him. He picked his way through the new hospital construction and finally located the bank of elevators that went to the seventh-floor prison ward.

Nancy looked up as he entered into the anteroom. "Hey boss, you okay?"

"Sure, why?"

"You have the manic look of a fugitive from the chain gang." She handed him his bag of sterilized instruments.

"Your powers of observation always amaze me. Are you going to gab all day or assist me taking impressions of our father of the year?"

A beefy guard led them through a series of locked doors into an interrogation room where the prisoner, Pablo Simon, was strapped in a chair. A rookie female A.D.A. was reading the court order to him. "The state has the right to take your impression, even if general anesthesia has to be used. Do you understand?"

Simon glared at the woman and spit in her face. She took a handkerchief from her handbag with a trembling hand and scrubbed at her cheek. In a barely controlled voice, she said, "I take that to mean you do."

She turned to the anesthetist, "Stick the fucker."

The guard roughly stuck a piece of duct tape over the prisoner's mouth. "You can remove it, Miss, when we're through," he said with a sly smile, and then tied a rubber strap tightly over the prisoner's upper right arm. The anesthetist injected sodium pentothal into a vein, and in five seconds the suspect was asleep. The A.D.A. ripped the gag off, taking some of Simon's mustache with it. Steve inserted a mouth guard, and after Nancy mixed the alginate impression material, he took the upper and lower impressions without incident.

"Nancy, you don't have to go to the morgue with us," Steve said, after he was finished. "Pour up the impressions in the washroom and wait for me in the lobby."

Nancy gave Steve a grateful nod and he and the shaken A.D.A. entered the elevator. Steve assessed the pale woman on the ride down to the basement,. "I'm sorry, I don't know your name. Are you all right?"

"It's Alice, and no, I'm not. That son of a bitch! That goddamn son of a bitch! Wait till you see what he did to his daughter."

"Easy, Alice. Don't let it get to you. You handled the situation remarkably well. We'll put the shithead away for a long time."

Alice gave the morgue attendant the court papers. He led them into a frosty, stainless steel room. He consulted his list, and then rolled out one of the refrigerated units, a metal slab with a tiny blue figure on it. Alice stared at the dead child. Tears streamed down her face. "If I had my way, I'd string the bastard up right here." Vapor framed her words.

Steve led her out to the hallway and waited until she regained control. "I'll finish up here and send you a full report," he said.

Alice blew her nose, and whispered, "Thanks." She rang for the elevator.

After Alice left, Steve examined the tiny cold body of the girl. He picked up her broken leg tenderly and noted it in his log. He closely examined the contusions and bruises covering her body and, finally, her fractured skull. *I should be immune to this by now,* he thought, *but I'm as outraged as Alice.* Gently, he turned her over and noted a clear bite-mark on her right buttock. After he inspected the discoloration around the mark, Steve concluded she was bitten ante mortem. He cursed under his breath as he outlined each indentation with a soft carbon marker. He heated up an acetate sheet with a portable butane burner and placed it lightly on the bite area. The carbon marks transferred to the acetate as it cooled. He laid his millimeter ruler next to the marks, and clicked off a series of photographs some with the marked acetate laying over the bruised bite marks, and noted it in the chain of evidence.

A few minutes later, the morgue attendant brought in the stone models of the prisoner's mouth. Steve lined up the teeth on the models with the acetate carbon marks.

"Gotcha, you bastard," he exclaimed. The match was perfect. He labeled the models with Simon's name, placed his millimeter ruler next to the grouping, took a few more shots from various angles, and made another entry into his notebook. When he was through, he rolled the morgue slab back into its refrigerated space, careful not to bump it against the sides.

He typed the report on the morgue computer and faxed a copy to Alice at the D.A.'s office. He looked forward to being deposed by the A.D.A. and to testify at Simon's trial.

Steve took Nancy to Emilios, her favorite Italian restaurant, as compensation for having to trudge cross-town to Bellevue and work in the confines of the prison ward.

"Dr. Nagle called a few times yesterday and tried to track you down," she said, during the antipasto. "Also, Hans Dieter wants to know how many sets of Dracula teeth you want duplicated. I told him you would be at the morgue all morning and would call him back as soon as you were through.

Nancy dabbed her lips with a napkin. "Your monster friend, Lonnie, called to confirm your appointment for tomorrow. I don't know how to tell you this boss, but, your sorry attempts at eating pasta needs mucho work," Nancy said after the linguini and clam sauce was served. "You have to roll it around your fork, while holding it against the spoon."

"Guess I need more practice. Excuse me, while I make those calls."

Steve dialed Nagle first. "This is the office of Dr. H. Hugh Nagle."

"Ms. Rauscher, it's Dr. Landau. Dr. Nagle has been trying to reach me. Is he in?"

"He's out to lunch. He can call you when he gets back."

"I'm not in my office. Do you know what he called about?"

"He didn't say."

"Will he be in tomorrow?"

"Yes, the Doctor has a full schedule."

"Thank you. By the way, I was admiring his sports coat. Do you know where he shops?"

"That would be Howard's Haberdashery on Madison Avenue and 58th Street."

"Thank you, Ms. Rauscher, you've been very helpful."

Steve called Lonnie and left a message on his answering machine. "We're on for tomorrow."

The phone rang for a long time at Hans Dieter's lab, and Steve was about to hang up, when a breathless Dieter answered. "Hope I'm not interrupting anything important," Steve said.

"No, I was in the middle of a workout and had to replace the weights."

"You're able to work out at your lab?"

"Yes, I have a large loft with sufficient room for my lab, living quarters, and a fully equipped gym."

"Sounds like a great way to stay in shape. Nancy told me you called. I can use ten more sets of Dracula teeth. They're expecting a long run."

"I will have them in your office early next week. I don't mean to pry, Doctor, but your receptionist said you were in the morgue. I hope your dental work on a patient isn't what brought you there."

This guy's a laugh a minute, Steve thought. "I'm a forensic dentist and every so often, I have to work out of the office."

"How interesting. We should get together. You must have dozens of interesting stories to tell."

Sure, just what I need, another lunch with an egotistical Prima Donna. "I'll be in touch."

Steve rejoined Nancy as she bit into her second cannoli.

Lonnie was waiting in his unmarked Buick in front of Nita's building, when she and Steve emerged at nine the next morning. They drove north for two hours, up the Taconic Parkway to the final exit, then, headed east to Hancock, Massachusetts, and the Jiminy Peak ski area. A state police car was parked in front of the main lodge.

Lonnie pulled alongside the blue and gray. A trooper unfurled his six-foot-four inch frame from the front seat and approached their car. He opened the back door and extended his hand to Steve. "Sergeant Wright, I'm Trooper Oates."

179

"Glad to meet you," Steve responded, "but you have the wrong man. I'm Dr. Landau, this is Dr. Lazar. The man driving the car is Detective Sergeant Lonnie Wright, NYPD."

Flustered, Oates stammered, "I'm sorry. It was a natural mistake. I mean you two were sitting in the back of the car. I thought he was your driver and—"

"Oates, forget it," Lonnie interrupted." You have the search warrant and keys for Nagle's house?"

"Warrant's here." Oates patted his shirt pocket. "We can pick up the keys at the sheriff's office. It's on the way."

"Let's get this show on the road. We've got a long ride back."

Oates led the way. He pulled into the town hall parking lot and invited Lonnie to join him inside and sign out the keys. When they came out, Lonnie had his arm around the state trooper's shoulders, and Oates was laughing. Lonnie took the wheel again and followed him out of the parking lot. "I hope you didn't tell him one of your lousy jokes," Steve said.

"Sure did. I had to loosen up his tight ass. There are people who appreciate my subtle wit."

Steve and Nita stuck their tongues out, looked at each other, and laughed.

They followed the blue and gray Crown Victoria for a few miles down a black tar country road, past acres of corn fields. A right turn onto a dirt road threatened the shock absorbers as they bumped up a driveway that was heavily wooded on either side. A final turn led to a clearing and an unobstructed view of the summit of the hill. A unique two-level round house with a pagoda roof, ringed by a full deck, filled the windshield. A tennis court and a two-car garage were behind the main house.

Oates bounced two steps at a time up to the upper deck and the front door. He paused before inserting the key. "Judge Flynn thought the probable cause was iffy, and only issued a warrant for a cursory search. What exactly are you looking for?"

"We have plaster casts to match to his tires, and we need samples of his fingerprints. Everything else is a fishing expedition. Our investigation is stalled, and we need a jump-start."

Steve and Nita stood for a few moments admiring the panorama of the lower range of the Berkshires. "How'd a loser like Nagle get lucky enough to have such a great view?" Steve asked.

"Wow!" said Nita as they crossed the threshold, and she craned her neck back to view the twenty-five-foot pagoda ceiling that covered the huge open space. "I feel like we're standing under a circus tent."

Steve walked around the circular fireplace with a suspended copper chimney that dominated the center of the great room. A white leather couch big enough to seat twenty surrounded the fireplace. The outer circumference of the room was separated into a TV/DVD theater, a professionally equipped country kitchen with a pine dining table, and a Jacuzzi for six.

Lonnie broke into their reverie. "Enough Architectural Digest fawning. We have work to do. Make sure you put everything you check back in the exact position you found it. Oates, you take this floor, we'll go downstairs."

Lonnie led his team down an antique spiral staircase to the lower level. The first room on their left was a sculpture studio that contained three armatures covered by damp cheesecloth's. Lonnie motioned them on. "We'll cover this later."

"Get a load of this," Nita said pointing into what was obviously the master bedroom. "It looks like it was decorated for a hyperactive sultan."

They entered the three-quarter round room, in which the walls and ceiling were mirrored. A circular water bed covered with red satin rested on a wall-to-wall white carpet. Facing the bed was another large-screen TV/DVD console. They found an extensive library of X-rated films in the cabinet below it.

Steve pointed to a bidet next to a Jacuzzi in the marbled master bathroom. "Now here's something I can use on the boat."

Nita pinched Steve. "Looks like a neat place to wash my hair," she said.

"I'm not going to touch that one," Lonnie said as he yanked open drawers in the dressing table. "You guys check the walk-in closets."

"Bingo!" Lonnie exclaimed and gingerly lifted a pearl-handled .38 with his pencil in the barrel. He recorded the registration number in his notebook, then dusted it for fingerprints.

"Any luck?" Steve asked.

"Nah, clean as my bank account," Lonnie said and continued to the next drawer. He withdrew a large manila envelope and opened it. "Double Bingo."

Steve and Nita peered over his shoulder. He spread out twenty eight-by-ten photographs of naked women lying on the water bed in garish erotic poses. All were blondes.

"He must have paid them." Nita said.

"That figures — I can't imagine a schmuck like Nagle getting this many women to pose for him for free," Steve added.

"Steve, you have enough film?" Lonnie asked.

Steve pulled out three rolls from his camera bag.

"Shoot each print and return all of them to the drawer," Lonnie said. "If any of these women are the victims in our investigation, I'm pulling Nagle in."

Steve screwed a micro lens onto his Nikon and snapped all of Nagle's photos.

Nita opened the second closet while Steve helped Lonnie put the pictures back into the envelope. A loud crack behind them snapped their heads back. Nita posed dramatically in front of a mirrored door in a black leather mask, brandishing a bull whip. "Triple Bingo, slaves," she said in her throaty voice, "come see what I've found."

She gestured to the interior of the walk-in closet. Hung neatly on evenly spaced hooks were panties, jockstraps, bandoliers, and masks all in black leather, bristling with silver studs. Shelves filled with dozens of neatly arrayed sado-masochistic devices stood behind them. Below the shelves were custom-built shoe racks that contained hip-high stiletto-heeled boots studded with silver tips and spurs.

Steve opened a closet dresser and found vibrators, lubricants, salves, and body oils. "Looks like the Pink Pussycat Sex Shop in the Village," he said.

Lonnie dusted a drinking glass in the bathroom for fingerprints, but drew another blank. He washed it carefully before replacing it.

The other two bedrooms were furnished more traditionally and yielded nothing of interest.

They returned to the studio, and Nita removed the damp cloths from three clay pieces to reveal more of Nagle's prurient interests. Lonnie gave a low whistle at the first clay model, a woman on her back, legs wide apart, and both hands lewdly spreading her intricately carved vaginal folds.

The remaining two were even more blatant versions of the first figure. All three faces were carved with grotesquely painful features reminiscent of Munch's The Scream.

"Nagle's a sex researcher's dream," Nita said.

"Or nightmare," Lonnie corrected.

"Ho, Ho, Ho! What do we have here?" Steve pointed to a large Vee Hee carver amid an array of sculptor's tools in front of the armatures. "Same company that made the one at the murder scene," he said.

Lonnie dusted it, lifted a print, noted it in his log then wiped the carver clean. They replaced the damp cloths and headed out to the garage.

Lonnie used the key Oates had given him to unlock the door. Inside they found a riding tractor mower and a restored 1967 Blue Ford. Lonnie got down on one knee to inspect the tires then muttered, "Goddamn it all to hell!"

Nita looked over his shoulder. "What's wrong?"

"They're all brand new. They still have a yellow stripe across the treads."

Steve found the car keys under the driver's floor mat and opened the trunk. A dark stain in the center of the trunk lining caught his attention.

"Could be blood," Lonnie said. He scraped a section from the center with his knife blade and placed it in an evidence bag. The rest of the car was clean. As Lonnie locked the garage door, Oates called from the upper deck. "Sergeant Wright, I found something you should see."

Lonnie, Steve, and Nita hurried up the deck stairs into the great room, where Oates was rewinding the DVD with a remote. He stopped it halfway through and hit the play button. The screen came alive with a naked man wearing a leather hood snapping a cat o' nine tails back and forth. A naked blonde crouched on her hands and knees on a table with her rear end raised. The room appeared to be a laboratory, and the tabletop a gray slab with channels running down either side to a drain, similar to a morgue counter. The hooded man grunted as he whipped the blonde with enthusiasm, turning her buttocks beet red. She groaned hoarsely after each blow and cried out in pain, begging him to stop. He replied in a fake German accent, "If you sink zat hurts, bitch, zen try zis."

He rammed his swollen penis into her anus, forcing a howl of pain from her lips. Her cries seemed to arouse him, and he rammed even harder. Her eyes widened in fear. When she tried to get away, he grabbed a handful of her hair, picked up a large scalpel, and jerked her head back. As he reached his climax, he ran the scalpel along her neck, drawing a thin line of blood. The film went blank for about fifteen seconds, and came on again with a shot of the drain with blood gushing into it from both channels. The image faded out.

The four viewers stared at the blank screen, feeling as if all the breathable air had been sucked out of the room. Finally Lonnie exploded, "A Goddamn snuff film. Nagle is one sick mother fucker."

"I've heard about them, but never dreamed they really existed," Steve said.

Lonnie spat, as if he had swallowed a fly. "The tapes are collected and passed along from one sicko pervert to another."

"Can we arrest Nagle?" Nita asked.

"We can get an indictment against the man in the film if we can identify him and prove the film isn't doctored," Lonnie said. "I don't know about the laws in Massachusetts, but you can't be prosecuted in New York for possession of the video. Besides, we're in here with a shaky warrant. It'd never hold up." Lonnie pressed the rewind button.

"Something's wrong with our system," Nita said.

"Tell me about it," replied Lonnie. "Be patient, Nita, we'll get the bastard."

Oates interrupted, "I found an address book by the phone, Sergeant."

"Good work. We'll make copies of everything we found, return the originals and get back to New York."

The team was too disturbed by the video to have much to say after they left Oates. Lonnie opened the windows, as if the incoming rush of air could cleanse the images from their minds.

As they approached the city, Lonnie said, "I'm too bummed out to go home. How about another go on the basketball court, Steve?"

"Great idea! A little sweat's what we need. You'll need sneakers and shorts."

Nita tapped her fingers on the dashboard. "Aren't you guys forgetting something?"

"Nope. Got everything in my locker," Lonnie replied

"How about me? I don't feel like going home, either."

"You play basketball?" Lonnie asked.

"Not in your league. I'll have to be content watching you jocks take out your aggression on the poor neighborhood delinquents."

"I think you have that backwards," Steve said.

Luis spotted the pair from the court as soon as they entered the next game line. "Hey! Didn't you guys have enough last time?"

Steve gave him the finger.

"I'll take Luis this time," Lonnie said on the sideline.

Steve didn't argue.

Luis was in rare form, hacking any opposing player that got in his way. Things got out of hand when Luis backed the opposing center down, and crashed an elbow into his face before spinning to score the winning basket. The center got up, blood streaming from his nose, and bounced the ball off the top of Luis's head. Luis stood stock still for a second in disbelief, then floored him with a wicked punch to his mid-section.

Lonnie made straight for Luis, yelling, "Ain't no call for that, asshole. It's a goddamn pick-up game, not the NHL."

Luis swung a left hook, but Lonnie slipped under it, grabbed his wrist, and whipped it behind Luis's back. The beat cop pushed through the crowd onto the court. Lonnie pushed Luis toward him. "Houlihan, what the hell took you so long?"

185

"Jesus, Mary and Joseph, it's you two again. Why can't you boys find something tamer to let off steam, like maybe bullfighting?" Houlihan cuffed Luis.

While Lonnie unlaced his sneakers, his cell phone rang. After he signed off, he turned to Houlihan. "Let this sucker cool his heels in the holding tank for a coupla hours. We're outta here." He beckoned Steve and Nita to him. "We got a live one in progress."

Lonnie slapped a blue light on the roof of his car and burned rubber swinging out onto the Avenue of Americas. "Bartender at Broadway Bobs called. Guy who fits our description to a T, bothering one of his blonde patrons at the bar."

Steve shook his head. "Feels like déjà vu."

Nita glanced at her watch. "Isn't it kind of early for bar hopping?"

"They keep moving up the happy hour," Lonnie said.

Two cops waited in their blue and white, as Lonnie pulled up in front of the restaurant. "He's still in there, Sarge. We'll stay here as backup."

"Steve, you and Nita go in first and get as close to him as you can. I'll join you in five minutes."

"It's been quite a day," Nita said as they pushed through the front door. "I thought watching you and Lonnie play would be all the excitement a girl could handle."

Steve motioned toward a man with his back to them. The man wore brown slacks and a tan sport jacket. He had long, wavy hair and was crowding an attractive blonde woman at the end of the bar. The man turned to the bartender. "Yo, another Martini."

"Jesus!" Steve said. "It's Vincent—I feel like I'm in the middle of Groundhog Day."

"Will he recognize you?" Nita asked.

"I'm not sure. He looks a little glassy-eyed, but I sure as hell know him."

"Let's find out." Nita boldly sat down on the bar stool next to the couple and ordered a white wine spritzer. Steve joined her. Vincent seemed to register a flicker of recognition, but it turned to disdain after he eyed Steve

186

in his shorts and sweaty Knicks T-shirt. Steve ordered a beer, and he and Nita sipped their drinks while eavesdropping on the patter next to them.

"That's quite a line you have, Vincent. But I don't trust salesmen," the blonde woman said.

"Hey, we're only talking dental supplies here."

Steve gave Nita a thumbs up.

"You still have to stretch the truth to make a sale," the blonde said.

"Nah! I don't have to lie. Dentists are real jerks."

"Hey, I'm a dentist." Steve said.

"I should have known," Vincent said, trying to focus on Steve's sweat-shirt. "Who the hell invited you into our conversation?"

"Just defending my profession," Steve said, as Lonnie joined them.

"Look at this — you fuckers come from a sweaty T-shirt convention?" Vincent said.

"Is this man bothering you, Miss?" Lonnie asked.

"Yes, I wasn't looking for company."

"Hey, why don't you bozos get lost, or I'll have the bartender call the cops."

"I am a cop." Lonnie produced his shield. "I want to ask you a few questions."

"You gotta be kiddin'."

The look on Lonnie's face told Vincent he wasn't.

"Not without a lawyer," Vincent said.

"That's your right. You can call him and tell him to meet us here."

"This is getting too heavy for me." The blonde woman eased off her bar stool and slipped out without finishing her drink. Nita followed her outside and spoke to her for a few minutes before returning.

"Ain't you supposed to read me my rights?" Vincent asked.

"Only if I place you under arrest," Lonnie said. "I just want to ask you a few questions."

"Hey, take a hike! I don't feel like answering any."

"You know how the system works. Ever done any time?" Lonnie asked.

"Nonna your business. If you gentlemen will excuse me."

"Let me spell it out for you, Vincent."

"How the fuck you know my name?"

"Either you talk to us now," Lonnie continued. "Or the woman you were just harassing will swear out a complaint, and we can talk downtown. Isn't that right, Nita?"

Nita nodded.

"You're bluffing."

Lonnie called in the precinct cops, and they escorted a belligerent Vincent to One Police Plaza. After they left, he called Gagliardi.

As the three walked out to Lonnie's car, Lonnie put his hands on Steve's shoulders. "You look like chopped liver. The last two days must've scrambled your brains."

"I'm okay. I want to hear what Vincent has to say."

"Nita, take this bag of bruises home. Gagliardi and I can handle it. I'll be in touch."

Nita whistled down a cab. Steve hesitated at the door, until Nita gave him a gentle push. "Come on, big guy. Nurse Nita will take care of all your black and blues."

"What about the soft and pinks?"

"Nurse Nita will use her special talents to turn those parts into something hard and red."

For the remainder of the weekend, Nita kept her promise.

22

The Bronx Zoo

Monday morning, Steve drove the Harley to the zoo to keep his appointment with Emil Dolensek and Amy the gorilla.

As they stood outside the cage, Steve commented, "Baby Annie, looks like she's gaining weight."

"Nothing like mother's milk, said Emil. "But as you can see, mama's jaw is swollen again."

"Looks like it's cold steel and sunshine time," Steve said.

Dolensek loaded up a syringe of ketamine and Valium, inserted it in a dart gun, and handed it to Steve, who shot the loaded mixture into Amy's rump. They waited for her to pass into a twilight sleep before they entered the cage to gently remove the screeching baby primate from her arms. Emil emptied a syringe of the stronger Telazor into Amy's ulnar vein. Thirty seconds later, she dropped into an unconscious state.

Steve examined the offending tooth and called Nick, "Let's get her into the operating room."

Nick and his team of attendants placed the massive gorilla on a gurney and wheeled her into the next building. "I'll have to split the tooth and remove each section separately," Steve said over his shoulder while he scrubbed up. "Nancy's stuck in the office today Emil, you'll have to assist me."

Dolensek nodded and snapped on a pair of latex gloves. Steve inserted a disc into the operating room CD player, donned a surgical gown, and slipped into his gloves. To the strains of Beethoven's Fifth Symphony, he split the tooth with a surgical drill, and elevated each root out of Amy's huge mandible while Dolensek suctioned. Steve stitched the socket closed with dissolvable sutures, gave Amy another injection of antibiotics, and summoned Nick to wheel her back to her restive infant. In a little while, Annie cradled contentedly back in her mother's arms.

"How about lunch?" Dolensek asked with a big smile.

"I'm pretty backed up today."

"I'm buying," Dolensek broke into an even wider grin

"Where are we going?"

"Antonio's on Arthur Avenue?"

"Like I said, lunch would be great."

After they were seated Dolensek got right to the point, "Remember our conversation last year about captive animals prematurely losing their teeth?"

"Sure, I told you they'd live longer if we could insert implants, so they could eat better. But that the cost would be prohibitive."

Dolensek handed the waiter his menu. "And I told you a government grant would help."

"Emil, you've been grinning like the Cheshire cat all day. Will you cut to the chase?"

"I've been bursting to tell you, but I wanted to wait until we could celebrate. I got a grant."

"Fantastic!" Steve leaned across the table and high-fived with Dolensek.

"Who do you think should be the first recipient of our new found largesse?" Dolensek had a sly look.

Without hesitation, Steve said, "Mr. Snow." The rare albino lion was one of two males that survived in captivity. By mating him with the few remaining unrelated females, the zoo could keep the gene pool alive.

"I'll set it up," Dolensek said. "You have to try this lasagna, it's worth every calorie."

After Steve and Dolensek finished a second cup of espresso, Steve excused himself and called Nancy on his cell phone

"*Hola*, boss," she answered, "*dos problemos*, Mrs. Austron needs an adjustment on her denture, and Mr. Casconi has a gum boil he wants you to look at. Oh, and Detective Wright wants to see you — are you into anything illegal?"

"You mean like making death threats to my nurse?" Steve waited for the usual guffaw, and then continued. "Tell the patients to come in. I'll be there in half an hour."

Steve motored down to his office, and after he attended to his two emergency patients headed over to One Police Plaza.

Lonnie had chalked a notation on the blackboard in Gagliardi's office, and the lieutenant had been concentrating so intently on the entry he barely acknowledged Steve's arrival.

Steve knocked on the doorjamb. "What's going on, gents?"

Lonnie smiled. "Good news, Brother. We got ourselves a photo finish for prime suspect."

"Vincent?"

"Yep. Scumbag used an alias. Computer picked it up and we have a lot of interesting items to add to his pink sheet like extortion, battery on his old lady, and, get this — attempted rape."

"Hah! His nice guy act didn't fool me for a second," Steve said. "Could he account for his time during the murders?"

"Perez and Stone are checking his alibis. So far, he's got all our votes."

"Can we get a blood sample to type, and DNA test?"

"His lawyer wouldn't let us touch him with a ten-foot pole until we charge him."

"What about my deviant colleague, Nagle?"

191

"A lot of stuff, but nothing conclusive. The fingerprint we lifted is real close, but still no cigar. The pistol's registered in Massachusetts, to Nagle. The stain in the trunk was blood, but not human. None of the pictures we found match any of the victims. But Doris Walker's name was in Nagle's address book. Before you get too excited, the phone number didn't match her home or office. We checked with AT&T, and their Doris Walker had a different address."

Lonnie picked up a sheaf of typewritten pages from Gagliardi's desk. "Figlerski questioned the three major dental supply companies in New York. She made a list of all the dentists and lab people who bought large S.S. White Vee Hee carvers in the last three years. Our boy Nagle's name was on the list. So was yours by the way."

"Guilty as charged, I bought one two years ago. Can I see the list?" Steve scanned the two hundred names. In addition to his and Nagle's names, he checked off the names of Norm Wagshul and Hans Dieter.

"This isn't going to be much help, it's too common an instrument."

"Yeah, I know," said Lonnie, "but every little bit helps. Who's Norm Wagshul?"

"An oral surgeon and a schoolmate."

Gagliardi's ears perked up. "An oral surgeon, huh? He's gotta be pretty handy with a scalpel."

Steve shook his head "Give me a break, Loo, he's a close friend. I've known him for years."

"Just the kinda guy you gotta watch out for. Like your other buddy, Nagle."

Steve waved his finger at the lieutenant. "You're talking apples and oranges."

"Some facts don't add up," Gagliardi moved back to the blackboard.

"How's that, Loo?" Lonnie asked.

"We almost got enough to book Nagle, but there's not one concrete piece of evidence to tie up all the loose ends."

Lonnie and Steve left Gagliardi still pondering the blackboard. In the hallway, Lonnie asked, "Any more incidents on the boat?"

"No, it's been quiet. Which reminds me, I better get back soon, Captain Bill must be starving."

"Take care, good brother."

Steve pulled into the marina parking lot as the afterglow of the sunset faded into darkness. A distant rumble of thunder threatened from the west. The wind increased, swirling loose debris into miniature tornadoes. The dock lights came on as he strode down the ramp toward Impressions, surprised that a voracious Captain Bill hadn't scurried up the slip to insist on dinner. He blew his bosun's whistle a few times and climbed on board. Cursing himself for forgetting the new combination to the hatch, he fumbled with the dial, but the hinge holding the lock fell onto the deck. The hair bristled on the back of his scalp. Steve grabbed a winch handle and opened the louvered doors. He peered into the interior as a flash of lightning lit the main salon. He climbed down the hatchway steps and flicked on the lights. A quick inspection revealed the main salon and galley were untouched. His pulse started to return to normal, when he saw that Captain Bill's breakfast had been only half-eaten. "Captain Bill," he shouted, and waited for the familiar "meow." "Jesus, don't tell me he fell overboard again," he muttered, and quickly climbed topside. Agatha's slip was empty. She had told him that morning that she would be going on a boating trip with a few friends, and he knew she never would have taken the Captain without notifying him.

"Captain Bill," he called again, and blew the shrill bosun's whistle as loud as he could. But the increasing fury of the wind drowned out the sound. He gazed hopefully around the docks as the first drops of rain splattered the wooden slats. He jumped down on the dock to look under the surrounding slips for a splotch of white, but found nothing. He was drenched when he returned to the boat to check his answering machine. One call, a dunning message from his credit card company. He left Captain Bill's hinged exit door in the main hatch unlatched.

He conjured up a vision of his cat lying under the protection of the marina overhang with his latest female friend "I hope she was worth me getting soaked," he mumbled.

He took off his wet shirt, and headed to the aft cabin to get a dry one. He nearly jumped out of his skin when a tremendous clap of thunder rumbled overhead. He had to scramble to regain his footing when a gale force gust violently rocked Impressions from side-to-side. Suddenly the lights went out. He extended both arms against the passageway walls to navigate the short distance to the aft cabin. The wind screaming through the rigging increased his disorientation. Sheet lightning lit up the aft cabin after Steve entered. He stopped and gasped. Captain Bill's little legs straight up, lay on his back on the bed, his face frozen in a macabre death mask. His throat had been cut from ear to ear.

23

The Funeral

Steve called Sam as soon as the last cop left his boat. "Hey dad, whassup? You never call this late." She sounded cheerful.

Steve clenched his jaws. "Terrible news Kitten. Captain Bill is dead."

"Oh my God! What happened?"

"I'll tell you tomorrow. Come to the boat in the morning. We'll bury him at sea."

"Oh, Dad," Sam sobbed. "I feel like I lost a brother."

Sam had been through so much, with the divorce, Carol Ann's remarriage, and now this, Steve thought, *this Dad job sucks sometimes.*

"I know how you feel, darlin'. Captain Bill was family, he filled a special role in our lives."

Steve hung up the phone wishing he could shelter Sam forever. When something bad happens to your kid, the hurt is magnified, he thought. He vowed with bitter determination that he would never rest until the cops arrested the sick bastard who killed Captain Bill. He poured a stiff bourbon on the rocks and made the rest of his phone calls.

He crawled out of bed early but bleary-eyed the next morning after a sleepless night. Following a quick cup of coffee, he fashioned a makeshift coffin out of a small metal toolbox. He washed the blood off Captain Bill's neck and arranged his fur to hide the ugly wound before his daughter arrived.

When Sam came aboard, she threw her arms around Steve and held on tight with a teary hug. She nodded approval of the coffin, and after she lined the box with Captain Bill's pillowcase, she placed his favorite toys around the edges. Steve gently laid Captain Bill in the coffin, inserted a few lead sinkers, closed the lid, and fastened the metal clips.

"How did my poor baby die?" Sam sniffled.

"First tell me your favorite Captain Bill story while we're waiting for the others to arrive," Steve said.

Sam blew her nose and said, "Remember, when you accidentally locked him in the foot locker?"

"He scared the hell out of me, when I opened the door an hour later."

"You almost fell off the dock."

"I'll never forget when you slept over," Steve said. "I came in to wake you, and he was sleeping on top of your head. It looked like a little girl's body with a small cat's head."

Sam put her hand over her mouth and burst into tears. "Why didn't God save Captain Bill?"

"I don't know Sweetheart. Maybe there's a different god for animals."

"But the Captain was so sweet and innocent."

"Let's just say he was in the wrong place at the wrong time."

"What do you mean?"

Lonnie's booming bass cut Sam off. "Anyone aboard?"

Steve and Sam went topside to see Nita climbing the boarding ladder while Lonnie and Candy waited their turn. They hugged Steve, then Sam, and offered their condolences. Steve hit the ignition switch as Cleveland rushed up, out of breath, and full of apologies.

The lingering aftermath of the previous night's storm sent dark gray clouds scudding across a low sky, as Steve backed Impressions out of her berth. A light drizzle started to fall when they reached deep water, now stained a Sicilian olive green. Steve let Impressions drift and asked everyone to congregate on the stern. Sam and Candy sobbed softly, as Steve said, "Good by old friend, you gave us nothing but devotion and happiness. Rest easy, knowing we'll catch the S.O.B. who did this. You'll be sorely missed." Steve used fishing line to slowly lower the coffin into the waters of the sound. As it sank, he blew the bosun's whistle for the last time and tossed it into the waves to follow Captain Bill to the bottom.

Back at City Island, peregrine eyes behind mirrored sunglasses stared intently through the bay window of a nearby restaurant as the procession of mourners left the dock. The observer paid his bill, quietly left the restaurant, and carefully averted his face as he walked to his car in the parking lot. He drove onto City Island Avenue and pulled into a space a short distance away.

Before Lonnie got into his car, he slipped Steve a .38 Special in an ankle-holster. "I did the paperwork and just need your signature to register the piece in your name. You know how to use it?"

Steve nodded. "I qualified in the service. I just don't think it's necessary."

"I do. Take it, so I can sleep at night."

Steve signed the form.

"It's legal, now," Lonnie said. "Don't hesitate using it, if you have to."

Steve slid the pistol and holster into his wind-breaker and joined Nita. "I'll meet you at your apartment after I drop off Sam and Cleveland."

Nita hugged Steve, kissed him and caressed his cheek. "You'll be alright?"

"As long as I have you," Steve squeezed her hand.

Nita got into her car to return to Manhattan. She turned left and drove past the early model blue car parked on City Island Avenue. She didn't see the driver sit up, make a U-turn and follow her several car lengths behind.

During the ride to Westchester, Steve tried to explain to Sam the serious situation they were facing. "Dad, do you have to lecture me now? I'm too upset to concentrate."

"I'm sorry to alarm you, especially now, but the fact is, someone invaded my home and killed Captain Bill."

Sam grasped the roll bar turning her knuckles white. "Are you serious?"

"There's a psychopath on the loose. From now on, I want you to be extremely cautious away from home."

"What do you mean?" Sam turned pale.

"Promise me that you won't go outside unless you're accompanied by me, Cleveland, your mother, or Nick."

Sam stared at Steve, her mouth wide open.

"Cleveland, I'm counting on you to walk Sam to and from school every day. If you can't make it, call me."

"I will," Cleveland promised.

In the driveway, Steve held Sam for a long time, then kissed the tears off her cheeks. He watched Sam and Cleveland walk up the steps and waited in the car until they went inside.

Nita pulled up to the garage under her building and buzzed the door open. The massive door slowly lifted, and she drove in. The blue car that had remained three car lengths behind during the trip from City Island, stopped at the top of the driveway. She parked in her reserved spot, walked to the elevator, and pressed the button.

The garage door labored upward again. Nita turned to see one of her neighbors drive through in his Lincoln. As the door started to close, the elevator arrived, and Nita stepped in, but before the elevator doors closed, she glimpsed a man ducking under the edge of the descending garage door. Although she hadn't seen his face, she thought there was something vaguely familiar about him, as the elevator rose to her floor.

The man approached the elevator and watched the indicator stop at 19. When the elevator returned, both he and the driver of the Lincoln entered.

"What floor?" the driver asked.

"Nineteen, please."

The other tenant pushed the appropriate buttons before turning his attention to the Wall Street Journal. He never looked up to observe the stranger.

Twenty minutes later, Steve pulled into the public parking lot across from Nita's building. He greeted the doorman and entered the main lobby. He exited the elevator on the nineteenth floor as the emergency door to the stairway clicked shut. He walked down the hallway, past the emergency door with a feeling of unexplained uneasiness. He fumbled with the key Nita had given him, and then quickly let himself in.

"Nita, I'm home," he shouted. His voice reverberated off her paneled walls.

No answer. He surveyed the living room, noted Nita's leather jacket flung carelessly over the back of an arm chair and her open handbag on the cocktail table.

"Nita," he called again, a few decibels louder. He checked the bedroom and the bathroom, went back to the front door, and looked up and down the empty hallway before he closed the door. With sweaty palms, he removed the .38 from the ankle holster, checked the chamber and safety then slipped it into his pocket. He banged his knee on the cocktail table and cursed silently as he warily moved to the French doors leading to the terrace. He swept the curtains open and expelled a breath of relief when he saw Nita, looking out over the city. He slid the doors open. She jumped in surprise and ran into his arms. "Steve, I have that same awful feeling we had the night you took me home from my karate class."

"Me too, I hope we're not spooking ourselves with imaginary demons."

"Do you think we're being watched?"

"My eyes tell me, no, no, but my instincts say, *sí, sí*. Lonnie gave me this for extra protection," Steve showed Nita the pistol.

Nita flinched. "Those damn things make me more nervous."

"I'm not crazy about them either, but Lonnie insisted."

"Promise me you'll get rid of it after this is all over."

"Cross my heart..."

199

"Please don't say the rest of it."

Steve blanched. "Don't you think it's time to let Lonnie in on your patient's information, before Dracula strikes again?"

"He promised to tell me his decision in our next session."

"And what if it's 'No?' Damn it, Nita, Captain Bill might still be alive if he's our man."

"Don't you think I know that? It's eating my guts up." She walked inside and poured herself a glass of wine, sat down on the couch, and motioned Steve next to her. She sipped the wine and remained motionless for a while, before turning to Steve. "Please don't be angry with me. I'm between a rock and a hard place. Professional ethics have to be sacred, or patients would never open up to their analysts."

She took another sip. "If my patient chooses not to cooperate, I'll tell Lonnie everything I told you. But it'll be up to him to ferret out the details, and like he said, they don't call him *detective* for nothing. I'm sorry, but that's the best that I can do. Even that much is stretching my moral band to the breaking point."

Steve didn't realize how hard he had been clenching his fists until he relaxed and felt the indentation of his nails on his palms. "I didn't mean to be such a hard-ass, I guess I'm just beginning to mourn Captain Bill. The truth is, I admire your integrity." He kissed her and felt his frustration lower a few notches.

They were too depressed and tense to make love that night. They caressed and kissed lightly before they fell asleep, spooned tightly against each other.

24

The Terrorists

Waves higher than Impressions' mast crashed over the deck and swept down the length of the boat threatening to wash Steve into the boiling sea. He struggled to the bow to raise the storm jib, but the rain and sea spray choked and blinded him. He grasped the lifeline with all his strength but he couldn't make out who was steering Impressions. "Hold her into the wind," he screamed, but his words were lost in the maelstrom. He fought his way through the surge back to the cockpit. There he found Captain Bill at the helm. "Captain Bill! How the hell can you be here?"

"I came back to tell you who cut my throat."

"You can talk?"

"Just long enough to reveal my killer. It was..."

An insistent, reverberating ring drowned out Captain Bill's voice. Steve bolted upright, bathed in perspiration. Nita fumbled for the phone, but missed her first attempt. She finally picked it up, struggled out of her deep sleep to listen for a second, then thrust the receiver at Steve. "It's for you."

"Yes?" he whispered hoarsely.

"Dr. Landau this is Captain Chase, New York Fire Department, sorry I had to wake you. I got this number from the duty Sergeant at Police Plaza. We just extinguished a fire following an explosion at an all-night diner on the West Side Highway. Looks like a lot of people got caught inside. We're going to need your help identifying the victims."

Steve became instantly alert. "When are you starting your investigation?"

"It's in progress."

"If you can't find intact corpses, bag the heads or jaws, or even parts of jaws, with whatever you find around them until I get there. I'll be about a half hour." Steve copied the address, and the time, after he checked the red numbers four-ten on the clock.

Nita, fully awake said, "That sounds ghastly."

Steve quickly explained as he dressed. A hurried kiss, and he was out the door.

He drove through empty streets and arrived twenty-five minutes later to find the entire block cordoned off and surrounded by a half dozen fire trucks and police cruisers.

He wended his way through the confusion of kaleidoscopic whirling dome lights and the hundreds of feet of hoses crisscrossing the site. The familiar and unmistakable stench of charred meat mixed with burned plastic filled the air. "Going to be one ugly fucker," Steve said to himself.

Captain Chase, a tall man with sunken but piercing eyes and a heavy five o'clock shadow wore a red fire hat and a yellow slicker that accentuated his cadaverous features. He smiled grimly as he shook hands with Steve. "You're a man of your word, Doc. I appreciate that."

"Thanks, Captain. How'd you know where to find me?"

"Desk Sergeant at Police Plaza looked it up on the emergency duty roster."

Steve nodded. "Can you fill me in?"

"Since I spoke to you, our investigators found traces of plastique. I've called in NYPD's bomb squad. Evidence points to arson, possibly by terrorists."

"Terrorists? How the hell did you come up with that?"

"Twenty-five years' experience, good intelligence, and an educated guess. A Yugoslavian Croat family owned the diner. They had sponsored a political meeting with fellow expatriates tonight. Most of them had stayed to argue issues over coffee, when the bomb went off. We know plastique is the explosive of choice of Central European terrorists. The Serbs in particular, are known to have a large supply."

"If you're right, all hell could break loose in the city."

"Cops have a good description of three men in a van leaving the scene. Save us a hell of a lot of trouble if they make a quick collar."

Steve watched five men in carbon-stained white slickers inch their way through the smoking wreckage. Huge spotlights placed around the perimeter illuminated the wreaked site. Steve was reminded of the illustrations he had seen of Dante's Inferno.

Thirteen body bags lay lined up in a row on the sidewalk. Smoke-begrimed firemen carried out another victim. The stiff body was burned beyond recognition and, like most fire victims, in a pugilistic pose. Steve supervised the placement of the distorted form of the ebony boxer in the fourteenth bag.

At times like this, Steve tried to compartmentalize his mind to look at the disaster in a dispassionate manner. But bile still rose in his throat as he checked the remains in each of the fourteen bags. Three were filled with partial remains. He splashed through the flooded street to Chase who was sipping coffee from a steaming mug. "This is too big a job for me," Steve said. "I'm calling in reinforcements."

"Suit yourself Doc. Call in whoever you need."

Steve flipped his cellular phone open and woke Dick Marmor in Brooklyn and Al Fox in Queens. "Meet you at the Bellevue Morgue at seven," Steve told each forensic dentist, after he described the situation.

Steve remained for another two hours while investigators continued to sift through the destruction. He observed the discovery of one more intact body and the partial remains of another. "I'm outta here," he shouted to Chase. "If your men find any more remains send them to me at the morgue."

He accompanied the four ambulances with their mutilated cargo across town to the morgue on East 31st Street. They arrived the same time as Dick

Marmor, who helped Steve and the investigators unload the body bags. Al Fox arrived as the last body was wheeled up the ramp into a large room to join the other fifteen.

The forensic team removed each body from their zipped up cocoon and laid all of them out by following a diagram drawn by the Fire Department investigators. Steve supervised the placement of the twelve complete corpses in the approximate positions in which they had been found in the ruins of the diner. He stood back and surveyed what appeared to be the bizarre spectacle of twelve charred men preparing to box each other, before he took a wide-angle photo.

"Al, take one of the investigators," Steve said. "Chart the jewelry and any identifiable clothing or shoes that each victim wore. Dick and I will piece together the remaining three corpses."

The head of one of the upper torsos had been completely burnt, but was still intact, the mouth frozen in a silent 'O.' "We'll have to dissect the cheek and mouth muscles to examine the teeth," Dick said.

Steve nodded and made two anterior to posterior incision in the right cheek while Dick did the same on the left and they lifted the flaps of tissue on the upper and lower jaws.

"This guy's denture's in perfect condition," Dick said.

"The skin and muscles around the mouth must have insulated the acrylic. Hey, hey! Lookee here," Steve exclaimed. "The rugae on the palate's intact. Dick, take an impression and a photograph. I'll start on the next one."

"What good will that do?" one of the investigators asked.

"If we can locate the victim's dentist and he's retained the denture models, we can match the rugae or curvy raised lines on the roof of the mouth for a positive ID," Dick responded.

The second torso had only a section of skull remaining, but enough to make a comparative identification. Steve and Dick had to dissect the cheek muscles of this body also, then X-ray and chart the remaining teeth. The third victim was totally unrecognizable and would have to be identified by a DNA match up or by relatives and friends who would examine personal items found on or near the corpse. Steve wished he could spare the relatives the gruesome task, but it was unavoidable.

By the time Steve and his colleagues finished, the police had brought in the waitress who had gone off-duty shortly before the explosion. Grim-faced, she identified five of the victims. When she came to the sixth, she burst into tears. "That's my boyfriend, Armen. He's the cook. We just got engaged."

Dick gently led her away, while Steve motioned to the police officer who brought her. "You can take her home, now. No siren or flashers. She just had her whole world turned upside down."

The three forensic dentists worked non-stop for sixteen hours. It was dark by the time Steve left the morgue. Exhausted, he climbed into his car and drove back uptown. He was too tired to notice the funny looks he got from the parking lot attendant and Nita's doorman.

Nita was watching the evening news when he let himself into her apartment. After one look at him, she said, "I don't know whether to laugh or cry. You smell like a suckling pig and look like the charcoal they used to roast it."

Steve looked at the white eyes peering out of his blackened face in the hallway mirror and burst out laughing.

"Poor baby—you've had a rough time of it," Nita said. "Get out of those smelly clothes, while I run a hot bubble bath for you. You can tell me all about it while I wash your troubles away."

Ten minutes later, Steve lowered himself into the steaming tub, lay back, and let the hot water drain the tension from his body. Nita let him luxuriate in the bubbly heat for fifteen minutes, then came into the bathroom wearing only her bikini panties. She sat on the rim of the tub and kneaded his back and neck muscles until he was completely relaxed.

"This would be perfect, if I had a rubber ducky," he said.

Nita laughed, and started scrubbing the soot off his body. She never finished. Steve, with a lecherous grin, pulled her into the water.

"Enough with the relaxation," he said.

25

Art Powers

Steve and Nita met Lonnie for brunch at the Café Mozart. Steve planned to take Nita to a Dracula rehearsal afterwards.

"Steve, did you hear the one about the dentist and Speedy Gonzalez?" Lonnie asked.

"Don't tell me," Steve said. "You've taken the old Speedy Gonzalez joke and made a dentist the dupe."

Lonnie grimaced. "I think, I need a few sessions with Nita. I'm getting a complex."

"Save your money," Steve said. "Just learn some new material."

"Okay, okay. I know why we're here. Let's get down to business. Which sleaze do you want to discuss first?"

"Vincent," they said simultaneously.

Lonnie waited until the waiter served their eggs Benedict. "His alibis are as shaky as a thatched hut in a hurricane. Only one can be confirmed, but that's by his mother.

"Is he left handed?" Nita asked.

"Ambidextrous. Or so he claims. If it's true, he's mostly a southpaw.

"How'd you determine that?" Steve asked.

"Simple!" Lonnie tossed a rolled up napkin at Steve, who caught it with his left hand. "See which hand you used?"

"But I'm right-handed, Steve objected.

"That's the point. Anyone who played schoolyard softball or Little League would have automatically caught the napkin with his gloved hand, so that he could throw it back with his natural arm. Vincent caught the keys I tossed to him with his right hand."

"Elementary my dear Lonnie." Nita flipped a napkin at Lonnie. "And you're right handed."

Lonnie laughed. "And you're a good student. We're threatening to arrest Vincent, but we're open to letting him roam the streets a little longer, if he and his lawyer agree to a blood test."

"What if his DNA doesn't match our samples?" Nita asked.

"There's always Nagle. Although we still don't have enough hard evidence to charge him yet."

"Even after all the sick stuff we found at his house?" Steve said.

"That just makes him a pervert. Ain't no law yet, that stops him from cavorting with like-minded weirdoes. We got a make on one of the women in his photo album. She's a high-class porno model who gets a heavy fee for posing. We're still on wobbly ground, probable cause wise."

"Have you talked to the model yet?" Nita asked.

"She's coming in tomorrow for questioning."

"I guess that's it," Nita said.

Lonnie held his hand up. "Not quite. One of the waiters in the singles joint where our perp picked up Lydia, thinks he can ID the guy if he sees him again. He's agreed to go to Nagle for a dental exam. If he can finger the doc, we'll bring him in and let Perez and Stone put him through the wringer."

"Both suspects are such sweethearts, I can't say which one I'd rather see arrested," Steve said.

"Hold on Bro. We have a new entry in the field." Steve and Nita put down their forks and stared at Lonnie.

"Your friend, Norm Wagshul's hat is in the ring, now," Lonnie said.

Steve almost choked on his eggs. "Are you nuts? He's been my friend for years. There's no way he could be a serial killer. Maybe you *should* have a session with Nita."

"Not so fast, Steve," Lonnie said. "You've seen interviews on TV with neighbors of deranged killers, 'He was such a quiet gentleman. A model citizen.'"

"That's the most ludicrous logic I've ever heard," Steve said.

"Hear me out, boychick."

"I'm listening," Steve said.

Lonnie held up a forefinger. "Number one: He's an oral surgeon which means he's right at home cutting through flesh with sharp instruments."

"Give me a break. Any dentist can do the same."

"He recently bought a Vee Hee carver."

"So did the rest of the two hundred professionals on the list, including me. Am I a suspect too?"

"Not unless you're left-handed, have a blue car, and —"

"And?"

Lonnie sipped his coffee and looked over the top of the cup at Steve. "A record!"

Steve's mouth dropped open. "Norm?"

"Sexual harassment and stalking an employee. He settled out of court."

After a second's pause, Steve said, "That doesn't mean squat."

"It does, if you're Lieutenant Gagliardi and grasping at straws."

Steve slammed his fork on the table. "You boys call this bullshit evidence? You're leaving yourselves open to an extremely rancid bust," He turned to Nita, "Is there anything you want to add?"

Nita shook her head vigorously.

Lonnie stared hard at both of them. "What's going on with you two?"

Nita sighed. "I might have something for you in a couple of days."

"Why can't you tell me now?" Lonnie asked.

"I need more time," she said.

"Let me be the judge of that," Lonnie said.

"Sorry Lonnie. In this case, I have to be the adjudicator. Steve, aren't we late?"

Steve looked at his watch and jumped up. "We have to go. Talk to you later."

Lonnie reluctantly waved to them as they sped off in a cab.

The first act had already begun as they tiptoed down the dark aisle and sat a few rows behind the director and his entourage. With opening night only ten days away, the cast was fully made up and costumed. Technicians were still making final adjustments on the soundboard and in the lighting booth.

The complicated set was decorated in black, white, and gray. The effect was a compelling spectral mood. On stage, Count Dracula had just met Van Helsing and his niece, Susan. He had not yet changed into his blood-sucking vampire mode. Van Helsing sang a sentimental aria, about how much he loved his niece and how important she was in his life. After some dialogue, he left, and Count Dracula and Susan sang a duet about their attraction to each other. The last chord ended the first scene.

Steve and Nita were fascinated by the chaos on the stage as stagehands speedily rearranged the furnishings, so that the back of one piece became the front of another for the next scene.

The new set depicted the spooky web-filled room of the spider-eating Renfield, who lurched about, bouncing off the furniture while spouting an offbeat humorous monologue. He thrust his hand through a thick web, grabbed a spider, sang an up-tempo number to his victim and popped it into his mouth. He closed the scene with a hilarious, loose-jointed dance, chasing another spider, and finally catching it after running up a wall and somersaulting a la Donald O'Conner.

209

Steve recognized the next setup, as the four-poster bed with Susan on board was quickly rolled out. The flat with the window was lowered from the rafters and set upstage to the bed. Blue lights switched on, and a full moon shone through the window. The set was even more frightening than before.

"This is the scene I told you about," Steve whispered in Nita's ear.

He anxiously awaited Dracula's appearance to see how Art would handle the new fangs. A sinister figure with a black cape and extended collar appeared in the window blocking the moon. Nita dug her fingernails into Steve's arm when a screeching black bat flew in over Dracula's shoulder and out over the seats in the theater. The black-caped figure stealthily dropped into the room.

Susan said, "Who's there?"

"Count Dracula."

"What do you want?"

"To thuck your blood, Thuthan."

Nita broke up, but Steve was shocked. Not only did Art have a lisp, it was worse than ever. He had to admit the scene was hilarious, and in spite of his confusion, laughed along with Nita.

To close the act, Dracula sang a brilliant solo about how difficult it was to sing with his fangs. Steve and Nita howled. Tears streamed down their faces as the curtain came down. Steve grabbed Nita's hand. "Come on backstage, I want you to meet Art and find out what happened."

They threaded their way through the backstage bedlam, to Art's dressing room. Steve knocked on the door, Art opened it and grabbed him in a huge bear hug.

"Steve," he chortled. "You're a goddamn genius. You've single-handedly made us rewrite a major Broadway play."

"What the hell are you talking about?" Steve said, after introducing Nita.

"You're responsible for the remake of Dracula from a musical into a musical comedy." Art sat down at his dressing table to touch up his makeup. He spoke to them through the mirror. "We had a meeting after you left my first rehearsal with the teeth. The producer, director, and the author felt it was too good an opportunity to miss. We rewrote the serious scary parts, threw in a few different lyrics, and voila! We now have a play that would top anything the Marx Brothers ever did on Broadway."

Steve shook his head. "I should thank you for turning a dental failure into a theatrical success."

"That's good, very good," Art said, slapping Steve on the back. I'm going to ask Hal if we can add that to the dialogue."

"Curtain, Mr. Powers," the stage manager called.

"Keep opening night free. I want you all as my guests," Art whooshed out of his dressing room.

26

The Softball Game

"Tails!" Steve exclaimed. The call seemed appropriate for a man dressed in an ill-fitting black tuxedo, a stove top hat, and white sneakers.

Gagliardi, who wore the black robe and white wig of an English barrister, placed a coin on top of his coiled thumbnail, and prepared to flip it. They stood on the pitcher's mound of the Central Park ball field, preparing for the annual Labor Day softball game between the detectives of the homicide division and the civilian ancillary personnel.

Gagliardi won the umpire's role by mutual agreement and decided that any epithet or expletive could be used by either team, and especially by the umpire. Uniforms were up for grabs, anything that would distract the opposition.

"Losers pay for the beer," Gagliardi proclaimed, making his first call of the day. He pointed to the large keg of chilled beer on the sidelines, in case any of the participants expired from thirst before they could find it. The scrounge group milling around the pitcher's mound cheered.

A woman passing by announced loudly to her companion, "They ought to call the cops on this bunch of low-lifes."

"Lady, we are the cops," the group chorused.

"Okay, Paisans," Gagliardi addressed Steve and Lonnie, the opposing captains.

"Before I toss this coin, I want you fuckers to remember, no biting, gouging, kicking, or sticking fingers in eyes."

"Can we spit?" asked Steve.

"Can we scratch our balls?" inquired Lonnie.

"Absolutely — it's required. The women can also indulge, substituting whatever part of their anatomy they choose."

"How many gotchas are we allowed?" Lonnie asked.

"None," said the umpire, "it got too hairy last year."

Steve scratched his balls. "What's a gotcha?"

"That's when an opposing player is about to catch a ball, and you grab their crotch and yell 'gotcha,'" Gagliardi explained.

"Before the Loo flips the quarter, did I ever tell you guys about the three retired dentists in Florida?" Lonnie asked.

"No, but I bet you're going to try," replied Steve.

"No jokes on the playing field," Gagliardi yelled.

Steve gave a thumbs up, and the others cheered again. The umpire finally tossed the coin.

As the quarter turned end over end on the ball field, the bald man with the powerful arms and dead eyes gazed at his face in a mirror while he shaved in his downtown apartment. He nicked his upper lip and slowly licked the blood away. He stared at the oozing cut, and his thoughts drifted to the past.

He was thirteen and his mother's clients had just left. He lay bloodied and dazed on his bed, cursing the brutish lout who had just sodomized him. He was rebelling against the men his mother had sent into his room, while she entertained their friends in her boudoir. All he got for his resistance was a head ringing slap in the face, which bloodied his nose and led to a rougher than usual coupling. As soon as his mother heard about his attempts at refusal, she tongue-lashed him until she worked herself up to a hysteric pitch.

213

The bleeding over his lip stopped. "Fucking bitch," he muttered, "just like that whore I'm taking out tonight."

Naked, he walked into the bedroom and admired the way his body moved in the reflections of several full-length mirrors. He slid open the door of his room-sized walk-in closet, filled with designer suits, jackets, and slacks, all hung in a methodical pattern. He stood in the middle of the closet and pondered. What shall I wear tonight? He chuckled at his little joke, he always wore the same outfit for these dates. From the back of the rack, he removed a custom-made tan sports coat and a tailored pair of brown slacks—his work clothes.

"Heads it is," crowed Gagliardi. "You got the first pick Lonnie."

Lonnie, dressed in a voluminous African dashiki and turban, intoned in his booming baritone as if issuing an edict, "Little Lord Perez."

Perez, in a velvet jacket and knickers with a frilly white shirt and stockings, stepped forward and announced, "I'll play third base."

Steve spoke through his fake beard. "I'll take Nita."

Nita, dressed as Wonder Woman, in the shortest of shorts, whispered in his ear, "You already have." Then out loud, "Second base is mine."

Lonnie countered with "Karen."

Gagliardi raised an eyebrow. He looked dubiously at Steve. "I don't know if it's fair having you and Nita on the same team."

"Why not? Besides, Perez and Karen are a couple."

Gagliardi scratched his wig. "They are? I thought he was married."

Lonnie chimed in, "You better not go into matrimonial work when you hang up the badge Loo."

"You got the next pick, Doc." Gagliardi said in a mock angry tone.

The bald man placed the sports coat and slacks on his neatly made bed. He padded over to a chest of drawers on top of which sat two mannequin heads, each adorned with a different style wig. He favored the one with a modish style of dark, wavy hair for his dates with the blondes. He picked out a matching pair of socks from one drawer, then opened another to select a new pair of Japanese silk thong briefs. He stepped into them in front of the full-length mirror, but before he passed the pouch over his genitals, his thoughts drifted back again.

His mother stood in front of him, wearing only a pair of silk panties. "You should act like you're enjoying yourself with the men we entertain."

"They hurt me too much, Mama."

"It wouldn't hurt if you do the same as I do to them."

"But, Mama, you never showed me what to do."

She dropped to her knees, placed her painted red lips around his ten-year-old penis, and professionally gave him his first erection. He stared down at her blonde head bobbing up and down. She placed her hands on his buttocks and firmly drove him to his first orgasm. When it was over, he huddled in a corner of their tiny dilapidated apartment exhausted and confused.

The horrible truth was that he enjoyed it, but despised his mother with the sure knowledge, that what she had done, was wrong. He felt dirtier than he had when the men used him.

After her demonstration, it was a little easier with his mother's clients, but he hated it even more. By the time he ran away from her and worked his way to the United States, the consuming hatred was complete.

He came out of his trance, but found it difficult to pass the pouch over his engorged penis.

"My last pick is Len Frank," Steve pointed to the fingerprint expert who was dressed as an outrageous 9th Avenue hooker.

Gagliardi flipped the coin again. Steve won the toss and ordered his team onto the field. Steve, looking like Abe Lincoln, was at shortstop to join Wonder Woman for the keystone combination. O'Brien, the medical examiner, dressed in a clown version of a baseball uniform with the name Murder Inc. emblazoned on the back, was at first base. Brandi Villoldo, in a wedding gown with a pillow stuffed in her midsection, completed the infield. Sonny Klansky pitched in an oversized diaper, and Valerie Chen, in a kimono, held up her catcher's mitt. She rubbed her bustled rear end against the ump on close calls, and Gagliardi obliged her by vigorously yelling, "Strike!"

The players performed in deadly earnest, until the fifth inning, by which time a copious amount of beer had been imbibed. Lonnie belted a towering grand slam home run into the adjacent ball field, sending his team ahead, nineteen to sixteen. No one bothered to retrieve the ball. The spectators joined both teams in mobbing Lonnie at home plate in a manic version of a World Series seventh game celebration.

He waited for Eva at a corner table, watching her with a hawk-like intensity as she approached. He dutifully complimented her on her clinging, low-cut dress, while he thought how much he would enjoy ripping it off.

"Your hair is lighter than I remember," he said.

He finished his double dry martini and ordered another.

She raised her plucked eyebrows before telling the waitress, "White wine spritzer."

All these whores only drink white wine, he thought.

Eva chatted amiably, revealing the most intimate details of her life, and he asked the right one-line questions. He knew she would be impressed by a date who, listened so attentively. The only personal detail he volunteered was to tell her of the hardships he endured in dental school in Europe, and how difficult it was to emigrate to the U.S. By the time their marzipan bonbons and espresso coffee arrived, he knew by the look in her eyes that he had won her over.

The costumed teams left the ball field en masse and stopped traffic when they crossed Central Park West en route to a bar and restaurant on 72nd Street. Brandi Villoldo's brother-in-law owned the place and had closed it to the public for the private party.

"Holy Christ," he exclaimed as the players filed past him in their outrageous get-ups. "And look at these guys," he said, pointing to a group of Hasidic-looking Jews who came in with Lonnie. "They look like the real articles."

"They are," Lonnie said, and whipped out a clarinet. "They're my lantzmen. Hey, everyone, meet my Klezmer band."

Lonnie tapped his foot and counted off, "Einz, tzvei, drei, fier!" and led his musicians into a spirited rendition of *Hava Nagila*. In moments, a raucous hora, headed by Steve and Nita started. Everyone pounded around the room in circles several times before Lonnie and his group, The Klezmer Kool Katz, formed up at the beginning of the line and led the dancers into the outdoor garden, then out onto the street, before they all returned to the restaurant.

The owner's earlier premonitions were justified, as irate neighbors called in the local precinct cops twice. They only added to the confusion by joining the party after their tour.

After a few hours of revelry, the alcohol high began to fade for Perez, Karen, Stone, and Gagliardi, but Steve and Nita were having trouble keeping each other in focus.

"Your polka-dot shorts and high-heeled boots have been driving me crazy all day," Steve's grin was a lop-sided leer. "Let's go home and see if you really are Wonder Woman."

Nita ripped off Steve's false beard and was all over him during the cab ride back to her apartment. They raced in past the astonished doorman, and tried unsuccessfully not to burst out laughing as they rode up in the elevator with another tenant. Nita fumbled with the key in the lock and after finally getting the door open, they tumbled into the room in a passionate embrace.

"You're obviously a man of means. How come you drive around in this old heap?" Eva inquired as they got into his car.

Goddamn nosy bitch, he thought. "I need the large trunk, plus I don't have to worry about getting ripped off, when I park near my apartment. If car thieves knew I had a brand new V-8 engine under the hood, they'd steal it in a second."

"Where do you live?"

"I have a loft in Soho. Would you like to stop off before I take you home? I'm in the middle of a project. It will just take a few minutes."

"Only if I can have a night cap."

They took the creaky elevator up to the top floor, and after Eva walked into the loft he scissored the elevator door shut and quietly bolted the lock. She nodded appreciatively as she circled around the huge room, which had no demarcation other than furniture to segregate each area. On her left stood an overstuffed couch, a matching recliner, and a European rocking chair that faced a large projection screen. A library of videotapes was stacked underneath. An antique fireplace had been strategically placed on a blue slate hearth in the middle of the room. The black chimney extended twenty feet up to the skylight, where it vented. A round log holder, three quarters full, testified to its use. An immaculate kitchen and dining area dominated another section. A queen-size waterbed built on a platform, complimented by a French armoire sat on the left and four closets covered with mirrored sliding doors filled the right side.

"This is one majorly cool space," she marveled. "Did you have it professionally decorated?"

"I did it myself."

"A man of many talents. Does this door go to the little girl's room?" She pointed to her left.

"No, that's my work area." He opened the door next to it, which led to a black marble bathroom. "Be my guest."

"How about that drink?" she asked, when she returned. "Do you mind if I watch one of your movies while you finish your project?"

He drew the cork from a bottle of Chablis. "Only if you like X-rated movies."

"I'll pass."

He poured a generous amount into a delicate crystal goblet and, with his back to her, spilled white powder from a packet into the wine. He waited until it dissolved before bringing it to her.

"This should hold you until I finish," he said, "I'll be a few minutes."

"Take your time, I'll browse."

She sipped the wine while she inspected the sculptures and paintings displayed around the room. "This guy is hot," she murmured. "Every piece is totally erotic." She took out a tissue to wipe perspiration off her brow,

"God, it's so warm in here," she mumbled, unaware that her speech had become slurred. She stumbled to the raised waterbed, disoriented and dizzy. "Whoa, I only had two glasses of wine — why do I feel so weird?" she muttered incoherently. "Better lie down for a minute." She collapsed on the rolling waterbed, which increased her disorientation. She fingered the plastic sheets on the bed. Her brow wrinkled in query, before she passed out.

Steve threw his jacket on the floor and ripped all the buttons off his shirt in his frantic haste to remove it. He flung his trousers and shorts in the air without taking his eyes off Nita. He unzipped the back of Nita's red corselet, exposing her breasts and raised nipples. He gazed at them fondly before removing her brief shorts, which had driven him crazy all afternoon. She lay back on the bed, wearing only her gold tiara and calf-high blue boots, then seductively wrapped her legs around his waist and slowly pulled him into her.

The door from the workroom burst open, and the bald man, wigless and naked, exploded into the room. His previously expressionless eyes were wild, a mixture of passion and fury. His nostrils flared as he drew his lips up into a predatory sneer. He ripped Eve's clothes off so savagely that he cut and bruised her skin. She moaned and opened her eyes momentarily to see a glint of stainless steel, before the bald man slapped her as hard as he could, viciously turned her over, and pulled her buttocks up to him. He bellowed a primeval scream as he savagely rammed into her from behind. Her eyelids fluttered as she came out of her drugged stupor for a brief moment, but he savagely forced her head down into the pillow until his release. His lust abated, he yanked her head back, and with all the force he could muster, bit through her neck. Her cry of anguish echoed off the walls.

Nita cried out in ecstasy as their frenzied lovemaking reached its climax. Steve moaned moments later. Gasping, they remained intertwined in a sweaty embrace. After a long passionate kiss, they fell asleep in each other's arms.

The killer clamped his hand over Eva's neck wound and grasped it tightly to stem the flow of blood. Leaving a large pool of blood on the plastic bed sheet, he carried her limp body into his work area. He dumped her on a lab table with channels running down each side and wheeled over a medical suction machine. He inserted a catheter tube into her barely pulsating carotid artery, turned on the machine, and suctioned out almost a gallon of blood. Her body, vibrant pink and full of life only a half-hour before, became a sickly shade of dark blue.

He removed the stainless steel teeth from his mouth and washed them thoroughly. He smoked a cigarette before he scrubbed the table and floor and rolled up the plastic bed sheet with the clotted mass. He inspected the loft carefully, and once satisfied, wrapped the bloodless body in a blanket, walked down to the basement, and threw the blood-soaked rags into the roaring incinerator. After he returned, he took a long, almost unbearably hot shower and dressed quickly. He smiled for the first time that evening while he brushed his wig, then he slung the blanket-wrapped body over his shoulder and carried it down to his car, parked in front of the building.

Steve and Nita woke the next morning feeling so good about the night before they hardly noticed their hangovers. They showered and dressed in a hurry to make an eleven o'clock meeting with Sam and Cleveland at Grand Central Station.

Steve U-turned at the corner of 42nd Street and Vanderbilt Avenue. After the kids piled into the tiny back seat, he headed downtown to Greenwich Village.

"We're all having the brunch special," Steve said to the waitress in an outdoor cafe near Sheridan Square.

"How about a walk through Washington Square Park before we go to the art show?" Steve asked, midway through their meal.

"Yes!" Sam replied with such enthusiasm she almost choked on her bagel, cream cheese, and lox.

The group paused occasionally to watch the street musicians and jugglers perform before they passed under the arch and exited at Fifth Avenue.

They had just stopped to view the first artist's work, when Steve's cell phone went off.

"He dropped behind as the group continued on. Minutes later, he rejoined them as they were staring at a painting trying to decide if it was hung upside down.

"I'm sorry, kids — we have to call it a day. Nita and I must leave." Steve tossed Nita a grim look.

"Oh, no!" Sam protested. "You promised to spend the whole day with us."

"I swear, I'll make it up to you."

"What's so freaking important that you can't stay with us a little longer?" Sam demanded, the color rising in her cheeks.

"That was Lonnie on the phone. Nita and I are working on a case with him."

"What's it about?"

"I can't tell you. You know that."

Sam's face turned redder. "Dad, you promised to treat me like a grown-up. I think I have the right to know what you're doing, especially since it affects me."

Steve looked at Nita. She nodded reluctantly.

"There's a man going around town killing women in a sick way. Nita and I, have been consulting with the police about the murders. We think the killer knows who we are. The last three victims were found in areas close to where we live and work. I think the killer also murdered Captain Bill. Nita and I think he's sending us a personal message and stalking us. That's why I want you and Cleveland to use as much caution as possible. I have the New Rochelle police keeping an eye on you, but they can't be everywhere all the time."

"I thought I'd seen police cars everywhere I looked," Sam said in a shaky voice. "Is the case the same one that's been in the papers recently?"

"Yes, it is."

"Wow far out. Okay, Dad, you've got our attention. We'll be careful, I promise."

221

"Great, I have to stop off at my office to get my kit, it's on the way, then we'll drop you at Grand Central. Go right home, stay away from strangers, and for God's sake, stay together," Steve said with emphasis.

They watched the kids go through the doors of the train station, before Nita asked Steve, "What was that about, where the last three victims were found?"

"Early this morning, a cyclist found a body next to the Central Park ball fields."

"My God," said Nita, "Are you saying the murder near City Island, Agatha's friend, and this one in Central Park was for our benefit?"

"Exactly. As our beloved Lieutenant has proclaimed 'too many coincidences leaves a bad smell.' We both had the feeling we were being watched, and the incident with Captain Bill clinched it."

The East Drive of Central Park was closed to traffic. Steve and Nita displayed their ID's to the cop diverting traffic onto Fifth Avenue and he waved them through. A ring of TV trucks clogged the drive, and blocked Steve from approaching the crime scene.

Three-story antennas and satellite dishes competed for space amid the canopy of surrounding trees. Steve recognized a few newspaper reporters nosing around. Several chugging generators drowned out any thought of quiet conversation. Steve and Nita were stopped at three different checkpoints before they finally got through to Lonnie.

"You called it right, Nita," Lonnie said, wasting no time on small talk. "He took his time, but this time he did it with vengeance." Lonnie clenched his massive fists into tight balls. "M.O.'s closer to the one near City Island, than your friend in the meat-packing district, but even more brutal. O'Brien's still examining the body. He wants to talk to you, Steve."

Steve left Nita with Lonnie, ducked under the tape, and walked down the path, careful not to disturb the crime scene. Forensic investigators gathered around the corpse in the underbrush of a small gully. O'Brien was on his knees with a large magnifying glass checking the gaping neck wound. Steve took a deep breath and squatted down next to the medical examiner.

222

O'Brien turned to him. "Steve, I'm glad you're here. Fucker's changed his M.O. again. It looks like he bit her from behind. The damage is different, but the results are the same."

"She appears to be missing more blood than the last victim. How the hell does he do that?"

O'Brien ran his hand over his bald spot. "I'm not sure. It sounds crazy, but it looks as if she was hooked up to a heart-lung machine that ran amuck."

"Raped?"

"Yeah, except this time he sodomized her."

"Goddamn it! We have to find a way to stop this creep."

"Amen to that. I'm through here. You can take your photos and impressions now."

After Steve removed the set impressions, the latest blonde victim was placed in a body bag. The steep rocky incline prohibited the use of a gurney, so a couple of burly attendants carried her up to the idling morgue van.

Steve returned to Nita and Lonnie, as Gagliardi arrived out of breath. He looked more disheveled than usual, and appeared like a man with an obvious hangover. He spoke briefly to O'Brien, before joining his three colleagues.

"It's a fuckin zoo out there," Gagliardi grumbled. "We gotta jump on this one before they crucify us. O'Brien'll have the prelim post done by six. We'll meet in my office at six-thirty, and we'll be there a while. Let's hear what you got so far, Lonnie, I have to feed the vultures."

Steve poured up the models of his impressions, while Nita perched on one of the high stools in his lab. After he finished they walked along the river.

"I feel monumentally depressed thinking about those poor women," Nita said. "There must be something else we can do to stop this monster."

"Wish there was, hon. I don't remember ever feeling so useless."

Shark-fin soup and dim sum at Hung Fat didn't do much to lift their spirits.

They ate ice cream cones from the local Baskin & Robbins as they crossed the Bowery to One Police Plaza. Once inside, it was eerily quiet. They took the elevator to Gagliardi's floor and were not surprised to see the police commissioner nervously pacing the floor with his adjutant, Pete Christopher, close behind. The task force assigned to the case now numbered eighteen, and all were assembled in the large ante-room quietly talking in small groups. The commissioner, looking as if toothpicks were stuck under his fingernails, called the meeting to order.

"Ladies and gentlemen," he said. "Before this last homicide, we had a serious crisis on our hands. Now the proverbial dung has hit the fan. Our serial murderer, now dubbed the "Dracula Killer" by the media, chose as his most recent victim, Eva Haight. I'm sure most of you recognize the last name, but in case you don't, William Haight is one of the most respected justices on the New York Supreme Court. Eva was his only niece, and he loved her like a daughter. As you can imagine, he's distraught. He's in constant communication with our besieged mayor, who in turn calls your commissioner hourly about what we're doing to catch this madman. Careers and political futures are on the line, not to mention that female members of our city are once again afraid to go out on our streets. As in all chains of command, I now pass the gauntlet to you, Lieutenant Gagliardi."

He turned to Gagliardi. "I know you and your men have been working hard on this case, but I must insist you double your efforts." He waved the front page of the New York Post. "Our local rag has side-by-side photographs of your detectives in dresses and other outrageous outfits playing softball in Central Park next to Miss Haight's body being carried away in a body bag. Adding insult to injury, all three national networks have jumped on our departmental disgrace. The fact that your idiotic game took place a short distance from, and a few hours before, her brutal murder lowers the NYPD's image to a new depth. I know it was a cheap shot by the media, but once again the hounds are hungry, and your folly makes us prime beef."

The commissioner glared at everyone in the room, heaved an exasperated sigh, and continued. "As a last resort, I am assigning ten more detectives to the case. If you don't have anything concrete for me by the end of the week, I'll be forced by the mayor to call in the FBI. You all know what that would do to your promotion schedules.

"Your meeting Lieutenant." The commissioner stormed out with Pete Christopher in his wake.

Gagliardi looked even more hang-dogged than he had earlier that afternoon. He stared at the subdued group of detectives through basset hound eyes, and scratched his blue-black stubble of whiskers.

"In case you paisans didn't get the message, credit filters up, shit flows down. It's my ass and yours, if we don't come up with something fast."

Gagliardi rolled the blackboard to the front of the room, accompanied by groans from the old-timers on the case. He rapped it sharply with a pointer. "We'll go over this one more time," he said. "Maybe we'll come up with a new angle. This is what we know for sure. Our perp is around six feet, weighs about a hundred and eighty-five pounds, size eleven shoe, has brown wavy hair, is powerfully built and has an overlapping right eye tooth. He drives an old blue car and favors brown clothes, at least on the nights he does his thing. We also know he's left-handed, might have the clap, and meets his victims — always blondes — in singles bars.

"He's probably good-looking and has a weightlifter's physique. He's either a dentist or in the dental field, by reason of the dental instrument found at one of the sites and plaster of Paris on the backs of his last two victims.

Gagliardi gave one last rap with his pointer, and rolled the blackboard to the side. "Thanks to Doc Landau and Doc Lazar, we got a primary suspect who fits all the descriptions. Solid police work produced another good prospect. We've ruled out the third, Dr. Norman Wagshul, since he could prove he was in his Florida condominium at the times of two of the murders. That leaves Vincent and Nagle.

"Our case against Vincent's full of holes that are gonna be hard to plug, and his little old gray-haired Italian mama don't exactly fit Dr. Lazar's description of an abusive serial killer's mother."

"Sounds like she could be your grandmother, Loo," Stone quipped.

"My grandmother swears like a truck driver, smokes like a chimney, and plays poker with the girls three times a week."

"No shit," said Stone. "Maybe she'd like to meet my grandfather."

"Stone, eighty-six the matchmaking — we're talking careers here," Gagliardi said grimly. "So Vincent's still in contention, but drops down to

225

number two, which leaves our boy Nagle, who Lonnie and I, had always thought was the perp. Trouble is, since all the evidence we got on him is circumstantial, we decided to hold off bringing him in until we could build an iron-clad case. With this latest development, and the commissioner having a case of heebie-jeebies, we decided to take off the gloves, arrest him and get a DNA sample. Lonnie and Perez went to his office this afternoon to read him his rights, but he's skipped."

Steve looked at Nita and mouthed, "Shit!"

Nita nodded back.

"His secretary has no idea where he is, or so she says," Gagliardi continued, "but she expects him back next week. We checked his apartment in Soho, and the State Police searched his house upstate—no luck. His Forty-Seven blue Ford's missing from the garage. We got an all-points bulletin out for him and the vehicle. I'm assigning part of the task force to the search, and I want the rest of you to continue collecting evidence to build our case."

Gagliardi removed a handkerchief, mopped his brow, and went on. "Remember, the whole city knows what's going on, so you might get some unexpected leads. Do not discuss anything with the press. That's my job. Anyone got anything to add?"

Steve glanced at Nita, but she looked straight ahead.

"Okay, that's it for now. See me or Lonnie for individual assignments."

Steve and Nita joined Lonnie in the China town pastry shop. "Have you been holding out on us?" Steve asked Lonnie.

"No way. We've been going bonkers since Eva Haight was found. I had no time to bring you up to speed."

"What happened with Nagle?" Nita asked.

"Steve, your description of the formidable Ms. Rauscher was right on. After she told us Nagle wasn't in, she refused to let us look through the office and insisted on a search warrant. She wouldn't answer our questions until she spoke to her lawyer. Luckily, I had Perez with me. He laid one of his Zapata stares on her, and she finally caved."

Lonnie waited until Mrs. Chin served them with her delectable puff pastries. Before she scooted back behind the counter, she honored Lonnie and then Steve with a mischievous but toothless smile.

"Am I the last one to know?" Nita asked Steve.

"I'm just an innocent bystander. Her heart belongs to Lonnie."

Lonnie winked and twirled an imaginary mustache before continuing. "Nagle goes away every year for a week, starting with Labor Day weekend. She claims, she has no idea where he goes, and he never discusses where he's been, but looks very tanned and fit when he returns."

"Any change in his routine?" Nita asked.

"Interesting you should ask. Her veneer cracked when she told us he asked her not to book any patients until after he got back. By the way, Steve, he left your name to cover him for emergencies."

"Just like that arrogant bastard. He never called to check with me. You think he skipped?"

"We'll know in a week."

"What If the creep doesn't show?" Steve asked through a mouthful of Chinese pastry.

"We'll know we have our man. Any chance you can talk to his nurse from hell? I think she's still withholding information, and she spoke highly of you."

Nita formed a circle with her lips, "Oh?"

"She did?" Steve asked. "You'd never know it by the way she treats me. Anyhow, I'm tied up in court most of this week. I'll probably be on the stand for three or four days. If I get through early, I'll give it a shot."

"Nita, you ready to talk to me?" Lonnie asked.

Nita sighed. "I guess I have no choice. I have a patient, an ex-con, who claims he might know who the Dracula Killer is."

Lonnie's eyebrows shot up. "Why did you wait—"

"Hear me out, Lonnie," Nita interrupted. "His information is highly speculative and was told to me, in confidence, during a therapy session. He made it crystal clear he doesn't want to be involved. I'm walking an ethical tight rope, and I can only present it to you as a hypothetical case."

227

Lonnie took out his notebook. "I'll do everything I can to keep your name and his out of it. Let's have it."

After Nita related the same story she had told Steve, Lonnie folded his notebook. "I'm outta here," he said. "I'll talk to you guys later."

Steve put his arm around Nita's shoulders. She let out a pent up breath of relief.

27

Forensic Testimony

"Stow it, Steve. You must know by now that women need more time in the bathroom in the morning," Nita said.

Steve didn't stop drumming his fingernails on the kitchen counter. "Maybe I should move back to Impressions, until I finish my testimony."

"I know how hard it is on you to go back after Captain Bill's death, but as much as I love having you stay here, my apartment just isn't big enough for both of us. We both know you'd go bonkers if you spend more than one night at your office apartment."

"I realize I've been a pain in the butt, but I need one more favor," Steve said.

"Name it, big guy."

"I'll be spending the next few days downtown with the Greene trial and the Dracula case. Help me sail Impressions down to the North Cove Marina. It'll be easier on me, if I don't have to travel back to City Island every night."

"Of course my darling. But don't you want to talk to me? Maybe I can help you through this."

"I'll be all right. If it gets too much, I'll lie down on your couch. I promise."

Steve knew rush hour traffic would be total gridlock the first day after Labor Day, and already late, he took the subway down to the Criminal Court Building on Center Street. He was scheduled to testify in the murder trial of Morton Greene, charged with a double homicide

The prosecutor was Alice McGrath, the young A.D.A. that Steve had met at the jail while taking impressions of Pablo Simon and photographs of his murdered child. She gave him a warm smile as he passed her on the way to the witness stand. After he was sworn in, she asked, "Dr. Landau would you tell us how you became involved in this case?"

"I'm a forensic dental consultant to the NYPD. I was called in by Dr. Les Dahlen of the Medical Examiner's office to assist in identifying two bodies found in the trunk of a car parked in a long-term parking lot on West Houston Street."

"Why couldn't the M.E. do it?"

"The two bodies were fully decomposed down to skeletons, and the only way to make a positive identification was by matching their dental records."

"Tell us what methods you used."

"A forensic anthropologist had determined the sex and ages of the two corpses. The older female skeleton had no teeth in her jaws. An upper denture also found in the trunk covered her anatomical landmarks perfectly. A lower denture that had been found in the apartment of Irene Constantino had the same type of teeth and articulated exactly with the upper denture.

"The other skeleton, a younger female, had most of her teeth. The police located her earlier dental records, and although they were not a perfect match, there were enough characteristics to make a positive identification."

"What were your conclusions?"

"I was able to ascertain that the older women had been Irene Constantino, and the younger one was her daughter, Anita."

"Thank you, Doctor." Alice turned to the defense table. "Your witness." She walked back to her seat.

The testimony was damaging to Greene's case. He had claimed he had no idea there were bodies in the car he had stored in the lot and used the canceled checks of his monthly payments to the parking facility as proof of his innocence. He had also emphatically stated that he had no knowledge of their identity. The prosecution had established that Anita Constantino had been his ex-girlfriend, and their relationship had been stormy.

The defense attorney, aware that his case hinged on Steve's testimony, came out swinging. "Tell us what qualifies you as an expert witness." He demanded in a disdainful tone.

Steve had come up against Charles Case before. Case wore an ill-fitting black hairpiece made even more obvious by his sallow skin. He kept adjusting it which made both the judge and jury uncomfortable worrying about its security. His bulbous veined nose was a testament to many long nights of excess in neighborhood bars.

Steve considered him a sleaze ball. In a calm voice, he listed his academic qualifications, the extra courses he had taken in his specialty and the disasters he had worked on with a D-Mort team.

"Is it true that forensic dentistry is not an exact science?" Case asked.

"Not at all," parried Steve. "At times, when you can match the records perfectly, it is exact. At other times, it's a judgment call, based on scientific experience."

Case took the rest of the morning and the entire afternoon going over the minutest details of Steve's education. The defense attorney's attempts to discredit Steve and minimize the science of forensics was getting vacant stares over yawning mouths by the members of the jury. The judge finally banged his gavel. "We'll break for the day and start tomorrow at ten O'clock."

That evening, Steve, with Nita's help, sailed Impressions down to the North Cove Marina.

The following day Case changed his tack. "How could you be so sure that the lower denture, found in this woman's apartment, was the match to the upper, found in the trunk?"

Steve checked his notes. "The teeth in both dentures were thirty-degree porcelain Trubytes. The mould or shape of the front teeth matched, as did the shades—Bioblend number 106."

"Are these shades and moulds popular?"

"They're commonly used."

"So, if someone else had a lower denture made with the same moulds and shades, would it be possible that the teeth would line up correctly?"

"Possible, but more likely improbable."

Case let that one go. He walked back to his table, and with his back to Steve, he looked at his client and asked loudly, "Tell me, Doctor Forensic Dentist: What exactly did you mean when you said the younger victim's records were not a perfect match?"

Before Steve could answer, Case whirled around, strode up to the witness stand, and confronted Steve almost face-to-face. "Is this one of those cases where you identified the body with your so-called experienced judgment? Remember, a man's life hangs on the balance of your assessment."

"I'm well aware of that, Mr. Defense Attorney." Steve masked his anger at Case's blatant antics to bait him. "As far as we know, Anita Constantino did not have any regular dental care after the age of seventeen. The police located her dentist, Dr. Xavier Judge, who had treated her up to that point. He's now retired, but luckily, he still had her records and last X-rays."

"How convenient for you," Case spit out.

The jury members, aware the sparring between them was taking on a more combative tone, leaned forward in their seats.

"I wouldn't call it convenience. A lot of legwork and investigative hours went into finding Dr. Judge. The approximate age of the skeletonized body I examined was between twenty and twenty-five years old," Steve continued. "The difference in Dr. Judge's records and mine, was that one tooth, the upper left second molar, was missing, and the upper right lateral incisor was partially fractured and repaired."

Steve took a drink of water before continuing. "These procedures were probably done on an emergency basis, well after Dr. Judge had treated her. The dentist or dentists who performed them have not been located. However, Counselor, in my professional opinion, the remaining teeth of the victim matched those in Dr. Judge's files."

232

Unfazed, Case had Steve point out, one by one, the similarities between each tooth on Dr. Judge's charts and those of the cadaver. Steve fought to keep his voice level as he used slide projections of the X-rays he had taken next to the films of Dr. Judge to point out how little difference there was to the jury.

After three days of exhaustive questioning, Steve finally left the witness stand with a vein throbbing in his temple. He popped two Tylenols and called his office from the courthouse lobby. "Hi, Nance, any problems?"

"Eat a good breakfast, you have a busy morning tomorrow."

"I thought you booked a light day."

"It was, until Nagle's drill sergeant nurse called to send us his emergency patients."

"Oh!" Steve's interest perked up. "He never checked to see if I would cover."

"Sorry, Boss. Thought I'd have to do twenty push-ups, if I didn't comply."

"Did Commandant Rauscher happen to mention hearing from him?"

"Negative Señor Doctor. I told her you were in court. She said if he got in touch with her, she would have him call you later."

"Okay, prepare the implant kit, we're doing Mr. Snow tomorrow afternoon. Anything else?"

"Nope. Oh, wait! Hans Dieter, the lab tech, called. He wanted to deliver the extra Dracula teeth."

"Damn, I forgot all about them."

"No problemo. I told him you were testifying, and he said he'd get them to the theater for you."

"Thanks, Nance, see you in the morning."

"Have a good time tonight."

Steve hung up with a puzzled look as he mouthed, "Tonight?"

28

Opening Night

Steve dragged back to Impressions after the Greene trial, poured himself a heavy jolt of bourbon and went topside to unwind. He sipped his drink and watched the shadows of the Twin Towers and the surrounding lower Manhattan skyscrapers creep across the bow with the waning sun. The pain in his head eased, and he settled back to observe the mating game of Wall Street yuppies in adjacent singles' cafes.

The powerfully built man nursed a gin martini while he stared intently at Steve from a nearby outdoor table. His face was hidden by a low-slung summer fedora and mirrored sunglasses. Steve's gaze swiveled slowly from one outdoor cafe to another as he savored the atmosphere of Battery Park. An instant before his attention settled on the stranger with the reflecting glasses, his phone rang. It was Nita.

"Is my handsome date ready for the big night?"

"What big night?"

"It's the opening night of Dracula, and you want to know what night? Are you okay?"

Steve slapped his palm against his forehead and groaned. "That's what Nancy meant. I'm sorry, hon. I've just been put through the wringer by a smart-ass shyster."

"Poor baby. How'd it go?"

"Don't ask."

"Okay, I won't. What time is my Prince Charming picking me up? Remember, you have to meet Sam at Grand Central at seven-fifteen."

Steve kicked a bulkhead. "Goddamn trial's erased my memory. We'll be there at seven-thirty."

Steve raced around the boat like a beheaded roadrunner. He whipped his dinner jacket out of the closet, breathed a sigh of relief that it wasn't too bad and hung it on a hook while he showered to take out the few creases. After shaving and dressing quickly, he bolted out the hatchway, black tie in hand, and race-walked across the promenade to the American Express Building. Car-service limousines were lined up to whisk the masters of finance home to Park Avenue and Westchester in luxurious comfort.

Steve jumped into the backseat of a stretch Mercedes and startled the napping Filipino driver, "Grand Central, and an extra five bucks, if you get me there by seven-fifteen."

Sam was emerging from the station when the limo pulled up. "Cool, Dad, you really know how to do opening nights. I was expecting the Porsche."

"I left it on City Island. I thought it would look gauche if the three of us arrived in formal wear on the Harley." Steve studied his daughter. "You do me proud, Sam. You look beautiful tonight." He recited Nita's address to the driver.

Steve unfolded his gangly frame from the rear seat, when he spotted Nita coming through the lobby. Nita took his breath away again, moving like a dancer in a clinging sequin gown that rippled as she swept past the limo door held open by Steve and settled next to Sam in the back seat. The driver set off for the theater.

Steve proudly made his way down the aisle, squiring a glamorous beauty on each arm. His face-splitting grin, sabotaged his attempt at nonchalance, as they were shown to their house seats next to the two most important critics in New York.

235

Sam further ruined his charade with a loud, "Yes!" when she saw her father's name prominently displayed in the program. She fidgeted with excitement as the curtain went up.

The show went without a hitch, and was a howling success. Nita had to lend tissues to the New York Times critic to dry his tears from laughing so hard. The audience gave Art Powers a five-minute standing ovation.

Steve led Nita and Sam through Schubert Alley, to avoid the after theater crush. They crossed 44th Street to Sardi's for the opening night party. Hal spotted them as soon as they entered the restaurant. He introduced Steve to everyone as the unsung hero of the show. Art Powers arrived with his beautiful co-star, Elayna Holtz, shortly afterwards. Art made a beeline through the well wishers and kissed Steve smack on the lips.

"I love this guy," he projected loudly. "If it weren't for him, we couldn't have made Broadway history."

Nita smiled indulgently when glamorous Elayna also planted one on Steve's mouth and whispered in his ear, "Thanks, Doc, you turned a raving maniac into an almost normal person."

Later, Art stood on a chair in the middle of the room, raised his glass of champagne, and with a perceptible slur, announced, "I would like to toast our producer Mike Herrman, and, of course, our director, Hal, for having the faith to cast me as Dracula. I also want to thank all our backstage people and supporting cast members, with special kudos to my beautiful co-star and soon-to-be-Mrs. Art Powers, Elayna Holtz."

All the partygoers shouted congratulations. Art held his hand up for quiet. "A very special thanks to my new found friend, Dr. Steven Landau, for helping us make a hit. In appreciation, I have bought him and his guests these gifts."

A stagehand brought him a large wrapped box. The crowd parted for Steve and his women. Steve opened the box and took out three black satin jackets. Art held up the first one and displayed it to the crowd. Imprinted on the back was the show logo, a white set of Dracula teeth. Beneath that, in big red letters, was the caption, *Dracula's Dentist.* The second jacket read, *Dracula's Dentist's Doll* and the third, *Dracula's Dentist's Daughter.* Their names were sewn in longhand on the front of each jacket.

Steve gave Art a bear hug, and the first-nighters roared. "This is a beautiful gesture, Art. I promise never to take it off."

"Never?"

"Well, only if Nita takes hers off, first."

The three of them put on their jackets, and the party continued. The celebration grew more raucous as everyone waited for the reviews in the early edition of the Times. Steve took Nita aside. "This shindig's going on all night. I better get Sam to bed."

Nita nodded.

"She's sleeping aboard tonight, I'll take you home first."

"Rest up, my unsung hero. We have a lot of lost time to make up."

As the limo headed back downtown after Steve dropped Nita off, an old blue Ford followed three car lengths behind, unnoticed.

"Dad, I'm going to remember this night for the rest of my life," Sam yawned as Steve kissed her good night.

The stalker in the shadows of the American Express Building watched the light go out in the bow porthole and five minutes later in the aft stateroom.

Might be fun to do a young one. He lit a cigarette on the way back to his blue car.

29

The Intruder

Sam sat erect on the back seat of the motorcycle, her face pressed close to Steve's helmet, as he pulled out of the zoo parking lot. "That was so fun, Dad. Now, I know how cool it'll be to become a veterinarian."

"You got that right, kiddo. You have a sympathetic feel for animals," Steve shouted over the roar of the Harley as he headed north on the New England Thruway. A light drizzle began, clouding his visor, and with threatening clouds to the east, Steve detoured to the City Island Marina. He parked the bike, and they continued north to New Rochelle in the Porsche.

"Wouldn't it be super if I became famous, and we worked on the same cases?" Sam's projections for the future so charmed Steve that he didn't notice the old blue Ford weaving through traffic a few lengths behind them on the thruway. Nor did he spot the Ford pull off three cars behind them at the New Rochelle exit.

Steve stopped at the Dragons Delight restaurant, picked up a large container of shrimp in lobster sauce, Sam's favorite, and drove her home. He spread the feast over the picnic table on the front porch, while Sam brought a Coke and a Michelob from the refrigerator. Sam remained animated as she continued her discourse on the future, while deftly spearing shrimps with her chopsticks.

The rain stopped and daylight was starting to fade when Sam opened her fortune cookie. "Look, Dad, there's a tall, dark stranger in my future." She laughed and waved the slip of paper at Steve.

"When're your mother and Nick coming home from their weekend?" Steve asked. "I have to go soon, and I don't want to leave you alone."

"She said they'd be back between eight and nine. Don't worry, Cleveland will be here any minute."

"All right, but keep the porch light on, and double-lock the door. I'll call the New Rochelle police to check on you."

"Do you have to?"

Steve's look stopped her.

"Okay, I know. I'll call you tomorrow."

Steve left after Sam locked and chained the front door. From the Porsche, he called his buddy, Sergeant Joe Schaller at police headquarters, to request extra Surveillance, and headed back to the city.

An accident on the southbound Major Degan slowed traffic to a crawl. Steve used the stall time to go over a mental checklist of the Dracula Killer case. First on his to-do list was keeping his promise to Gagliardi and go to Nagle's office to question Frau Rauscher.

As the traffic started to move, his cell phone rang. "Dad! There's someone on the porch," Sam screamed in his ear.

"Did you see who it is?" Steve's heart raced.

"No. The light went out. I saw a shadow at the window."

"Is Cleveland with you?"

"No, he was supposed to be here fifteen minutes ago, and he's never late. Dad, I'm scared."

"Hang on, Sam, I'm coming back." Steve slammed the blue light on the roof and swerved sharply onto the grass divider. Spewing dirt and pebbles behind him, he fishtailed over to the northbound lanes and cut off two cars. He pressed his foot down on the gas pedal and picked up the phone again. "Sam?" The line was dead. Barely able to breathe, he punched in the number for the New Rochelle Police, but in his panic, dialed the wrong number. He weaved in and out of traffic at eighty-five miles an hour, and hit the operator button so hard he thought he broke his finger. "Emergency!" he yelled. "Get me the New Rochelle Police Department."

He cursed himself for the precious seconds lost while the operator finally connected him to police headquarters.

"Sergeant Schaller."

"Joe, it's Steve. Sam just called. Get a car there right away. Someone's on the front porch."

He hung up, and the phone rang immediately. "Dad!" Sam whispered hoarsely.

"What happened?" he cried. "We were cut off."

"I hung up when I heard a window break in the kitchen."

"Jesus! Where are you now?"

"I ran up to the room where you keep your extra boat stuff and locked myself in."

"Good girl! Don't hang up. Stay on the line, no matter what happens. The police are on their way. Do you know where I keep the flare gun?"

"I got it, and it's loaded."

Steve heaved a sigh of relief. "All right! Don't fire unless you're in immediate danger. If you have to shoot, aim for the middle of his chest."

"I don't think I can do that," she sobbed.

"Sam, listen to me. If it's the man we spoke about, you have to."

He heard her gasp. "Sam, what's wrong?"

"Someone's coming up the stairs," she whispered, terror stricken.

"Hold on, baby. I'm only minutes away, and the cops'll be there any second," Steve tried to keep the terror he felt out of his voice.

"There's footsteps outside the door," Sam whispered, barely audible.

Steve strained to hear any sounds beyond Sam's labored breathing.

"The door knob is turning," she whimpered.

Sweat ran freely into Steve's eyes, distorting his vision. He felt like he was breathing underwater, but he floored the pedal and revved the Porsche up to 120 on the Cross County Parkway. Images of the Dracula victims raced through his mind like a fast-forward movie. He could not erase the terrifying visions. He swerved onto the shoulder of the exit ramp, cutting around three cars, and just missed a Jeep driving in the opposite direction, then floored the accelerator again.

Still blocks away from the house, he heard through the earpiece, "Samantha Landau, this is Officer Elliot Blair. Are you in there?"

"Dad, what should I do?"

"Ask him the number of his badge and who dispatched him."

Steve almost pressed the phone through his ear to listen to Sam ask the questions in a tremulous voice. He breathed again when he heard, "Sergeant Joe Schaller sent us, and my number is 42765."

"Who's us?" Sam asked before Steve could instruct her.

"My partner, Olga Akpinar. She's downstairs, attending to a young man we found in the front bushes with a nasty bump on his head."

"It's all right, Sam," Steve said. "I just turned onto your block, and there's a police car in front. You can open the door."

Steve squealed to a stop and ran up the front steps. Cleveland sat on the top step, with his head in his hands, moaning. A policewoman was applying a bandage. Steve shot past them into the house.

Sam came flying down the hall stairway and leapt into Steve's arms. She let out a gasp when she saw Cleveland through the open front door and ran to console him. An ambulance roared into the driveway followed by Nick and Carol Ann's BMW. She jumped out wild-eyed.

Steve did his best to explain matters to Carol Ann, but she was too enraged to listen. He left her to lament with Nick, and called Sergeant Schaller aside. "I think this is related to a case I'm working in New York. Do you mind if I call in the NYPD?"

"Be my guest. Our blotter will only show an unidentified prowler."

Steve called Lonnie. Within forty-five minutes, a crime-scene team was combing the area. Steve remained until they were through, comforting Sam and Cleveland and reassuring Carol Ann.

He finally felt confident enough to leave after a back up New Rochelle patrol car, sent by Schaller, parked in the driveway for the night. Emotionally spent, he decided he needed the exhilaration of riding the bike back to Nita's and exchanged vehicles again on City Island. The one thought that kept running through his mind during the trip back to Manhattan was, *The next time I see Nagle, I'm going to rip his fucking heart out.*

30

Miss Rauscher

After a restless night, Steve was up early and on his way to Nagle's office. He parked the bike on the sidewalk, chained it to a light post, and entered the lobby of an art deco building on East 57th Street. He barely noticed the marble walls and gold-leaf-topped columns, as he strode across the lobby to scan the directory and note that most of the tenants were high-profile professionals. He took the elevator to the twentieth floor and entered Nagle's reception room. An attractive woman with ash blonde hair severely pulled back into a neat chignon sat demurely at a small teak reception desk. A tight-fitting uniform accentuated the curves of her voluptuous body. A short skirt and medium-heeled white shoes emphasized her shapely legs.

"May I help you?" she asked.

Steve tried to keep his jaw from dropping. This beauty was his nemesis; the dreaded, Nurse Rauscher.

"Yes, I'm Steve...Dr. Landau. So glad we're finally able to meet. You're not at all the way I pictured you, Miss Rauscher."

"Dr. Landau, of course—I recognize your voice. But what are you doing here? Dr. Nagle is away."

"That's too bad. I had something I wanted to discuss with him," Steve ad-libbed. "Since I was in the building, I thought I would ask him directly."

"May I give him a message?"

"Do you know how to get in touch with him?"

Tears welled in Nurse Rauscher's eyes. She turned away, took a tissue from her desk and discreetly blew her nose. When she had regained her composure, she replied, "He doesn't confide the destination of his trips to me."

"Do you know when he'll be back?" Steve thought her reaction odd, but said nothing.

"He's supposed to return on Monday."

Steve peeked at the appointment book. "Doesn't he have patients scheduled?"

"No, he told me to wait until he comes back before booking appointments."

"Strange."

"I know, he's never done that before."

Steve noted the reception room was furnished in the same style as Nagle's country home. "Your office is beautifully appointed,"

"Thank you." She displayed a weak smile. Her teeth were capped in the same dazzling white shade as Nagle's. "I decorated it myself."

Light bulbs went on in Steve's head, but he only nodded thoughtfully. "If you hear from him, could you have him call me? It's important."

"I won't. He never calls when he's away with one of his playmates of the year." She almost spat out the words.

"I don't understand."

"Dr. Nagle does the cosmetic dentistry for Playboy magazine–gratis. One of the models usually feels compelled to pay him back."

Steve softened, surprised at his compassion for the robot-like nurse. "I'm sorry to have burst in on you without notice."

Nurse Rauscher regained her professional demeanor. "That's quite all right, Dr. Landau, I'll have Dr. Nagle call you as soon as he returns."

Steve called Lonnie on his cell phone, from the lobby. "Nothing much to add to what she already told you, except she and Nagle are, or were, an item."

"No shit!"

"Yeah, she was pretty busted up about his being away, and vague about his return. She intimated he was with a Playboy bunny."

"Nurse Ratchet say anything about where he took her?"

"Not a word. What did Cleveland say? Did he see anything?"

"Last thing he remembered was walking up the front steps before his lights went out."

"The crime-scene crew, turn up anything?"

"Yeah, I've been reluctant to tell you. Threads on the bushes and foot-prints near your driveway match our perp. You guys were lucky."

Steve's blood ran cold. "Son of a bitch. What the hell am I going to do?"

"Why don't you have Sam stay with us until we get Nagle? Candy would love it, and my wife works at home. The kicker is my brother lives next door, and he's an ex-Marine"

"I'll discuss it with Sam and Carol Ann and let you know."

"Anytime, Brother."

"Anything on Nita's patient's lead?"

"Yeah, I sent out a bulletin to all the upstate prisons. The warden from Elmira thinks he was one of his guests. Last he heard his former inmate went back to wrestling in the Chicago area. I'm waiting to hear from the Chicago PD. They're checking to see if he had any bouts on the nights of our homicides."

"Has Gagliardi put him on the blackboard?"

"I haven't told him yet. In deference to Nita, I'm waiting until I get more confirmation."

"Thanks, Lonnie. I'm sure she'll appreciate that."

"Speaking of Gagliardi, I'm getting worried about him. I think he's los-ing it."

245

"How come?"

"The Lieutenant, our pillar of strength, looks more like Zombie City."

"Bring him out to the boat tomorrow. Brainstorming in the fresh air should make him feel better and it might give us a new perspective."

"Sounds great. We should be through around five."

"I'm docked at the North Cove Marina in Battery Park."

"I know where it is. We'll see you around five-thirty, if I have to hand-cuff Gagliardi and drag him there by his collar."

31

The Chase

Lonnie and Gagliardi arrived the next day as Steve was stowing the boat phone and answering machine in his dock locker. "I leave them hooked up and locked away so I can still get messages while we're out of range on the boat," Steve explained.

Gagliardi looked like a man possessed. His gray eyes were unfocused and crisscrossed in a road map of engorged blood vessels. Below the lids, purple pouches big enough to hide a quarter was evidence of sleepless nights. Disheveled hair, hoarse voice and three days stubble confirmed his distress.

Steve set out a cooler full of beer and a small buffet of cold cuts in the cockpit. The lieutenant munched on a ham and cheese sandwich in absent-minded isolation, as Steve backed Impressions out of her slip.

"Any more unannounced visitors?" Lonnie asked.

"Been quiet."

"You still carrying the piece I gave you?"

Steve smiled sardonically and showed Lonnie the snub-nosed revolver in his ankle holster. Steve steered through the entrance in the retaining wall around the marina, but a page of the marine operator broke his concentration. He handed the wheel to Lonnie and went below to pick up his VHF earphones.

Lonnie could hear Steve's half of the conversation. "Norm, how'd you find me?" There was a pause as Steve listened. "Yeah, Nancy's a brick. Norm, I'm underway, you'll have to make it quick." After a long pause, Steve said, "What? Are you sure? He was on board the entire week? Who was with him? You're breaking up, speak a little louder." Steve pressed the earphones hard against his ear. "I can barely hear you. I'll call you in a few days."

Steve removed his earphones and went topside, dejected. "Gentlemen, Nita's lead and Vincent have been bumped up to number one."

"What do you mean?" Lonnie echoed Gagliardi.

"That was my buddy, Norm Wagshul. He just returned from a dental seminar cruise to the Bahamas. Our friend Dr. H. Hugh Nagle was a guest lecturer—aesthetic dentistry. He was at sea screwing a Playboy bimbo when Eva Haight was murdered. Nagle was aboard until they arrived in Freeport on Wednesday, two days after Haight was killed."

"Goddamn it!" Lonnie bellowed. He slammed his beer can down, spilling foam all over the cockpit. "I drew a blank with the damn wrestler, too."

Gagliardi was stunned. "I was planning to tell you guys: Vincent's alibis are legit. He had theater ticket stubs and corroboration from two dates. We're batting a big fuckin' zero."

Steve thought he sounded like O'Brien, but after looking at Gagliardi's ashen complexion, said nothing. They sat quietly while Impressions drifted downstream.

"You got life preservers aboard this tub, Doc?" Gagliardi asked.

"Of course."

"Do me a favor, find the deepest part of this cruddy river and don't throw me one when I jump overboard."

"Not a good idea, Loo," Lonnie said. "Since Steve has to steer the boat, I'd have to go after you and I'm a shitty swimmer. How the hell would he explain that when he gets back to port?"

"Yeah, yeah!"

Steve looked at Lonnie and nodded as Gagliardi hunched into himself in a corner of the cockpit. They were quiet again as the boat continued to drift down stream.

Finally, Lonnie broke the silence. "We know the Dracula Killer's in the dental field. We checked out every dentist suspect, and none of the fuckers fit the profile. Maybe we were looking in the wrong area. Who else uses a Vee Hee carver and could make stainless steel teeth, Steve?"

"A lab technician makes all my replacements. Dentists don't have time to do lab work and see patients."

"Your guy make the Dracula teeth for you?" Lonnie asked.

"No, I used a specialist. Nagle recommended him."

"Nagle?" Lonnie looked at Steve over his sunglasses.

"Yeah, but those teeth are made out of acrylic. They're incapable of doing the damage we've been dealing with."

"Didn't you tell me Nagle made the steel teeth for the Iron jaw film?"

"He took the impressions and designed it, but his lab guy did the casting."

Gagliardi perked up, his blood shot eyes brightened with new life. "Let's get back and start working on it."

Steve whipped Impressions around and headed back to the marina. While cleating the stern line Steve spotted the reflection of the blinking light on his answering machine through the ventilation hole in his locker. He unlocked the door, reached inside and hit the playback button.

Nita's throaty voice sounded even deeper through the speaker, "Hi, darling. Nancy just called to tell you Hans Dieter, your lab tech, called to discuss a case with you. Since he also works for Nagle, I thought Dieter might have an idea where he is. I got his number from Nancy, and since you're out and about gallivanting with Lonnie and the Lieutenant, I'm going over to question him now. I'll speak to you later, love you."

"Who the hell is this guy?" Gagliardi demanded.

"What does he look like?" Lonnie asked.

"I don't know. I never met him, and I'm not working on a case with him now" Steve admitted.

249

Gagliardi, scratched his stubble. "That doesn't make sense. Isn't he your technician?"

"I've only dealt with him over the phone. I can tell you he has health club work out equipment in his loft, and uses it regularly. His voice is pleasant, but he's sarcastic as hell, and he did extremely good work for me. Oh, he also has a German accent."

"Like the masked guy in Nagle's film?" Lonnie said.

The three of them looked at each other.

"Son of a bitch! The goddamn answer was right in front of our noses all along," Gagliardi said.

"We have to get Nita out of there," Steve yelled as he unlocked the chain securing the Harley to a marina post. Lonnie and Gagliardi scrambled off the boat and sprinted toward their unmarked car that was parked two blocks from the marina.

"39 ½ Prince Street, Hans Dieter." Steve shouted as he roared past them, leaned sharply into a right turn and nearly did a wheelie as he fiercely twisted the accelerator handle.

Nita rang the bell under the nameplate, Hans Dieter Dental Laboratory. A window on the top floor flew open, and a man called out, "Be right down."

A few minutes later, the large freight elevator doors opened top to bottom and a handsome man with brown wavy hair, casually dressed in army fatigue jeans and a tan polo shirt stepped out to greet her. His crooked smile set in a square jaw was disarming, but his penetrating gaze produced a feeling of unease in Nita. She had trouble maintaining eye contact.

"Dr. Lazar, you look exactly as I had pictured you after our phone call. I'm Hans Dieter." He took her hand, gently brushed his dry lips over it, and gallantly ushered her into the elevator.

Nita studied his well developed shoulder and back muscles as he leaned on the handles to close the door.

The elevator laboriously inched up. "I'm sorry there are no stairs, and only the tenants can operate the lift."

Nita detected a slight German accent in Dieter's pleasant voice. The car came to a jarring halt, and Dieter pressed down on the horizontal lever to scissor the doors open. He locked the doors behind Nita and flipped the downstairs buzzer switch to the off position.

"This space is cavernous," she said. "Four of my apartments could fit into your one room."

He smiled, showing genuine amusement. "I'll give you the deluxe tour," he walked ahead of her, and with a gallant gesture motioned to the interior of the loft. "This leads to my laboratory," he said in front of a mirrored door.

Nita nodded. "I was in Dr. Landau's lab recently and found it very interesting. Would you mind showing me your work area, Mr. Dieter?"

"Please, call me Hans. Yes, of course." He opened the door to another, slightly smaller space.

Nita hesitated at the entranceway to take in the ambiance of the strange room. She didn't recognize any of the machines on one of the two large workbenches. "This is a lot more complicated than Steve's, I mean Dr. Landau's lab. What are these two science fiction devices?"

Dieter smiled condescendingly. "They are casting centrifuges," he said. "And these are the ovens I use to melt the gold for them and fuse porcelain."

"Isn't that a lathe next to the pressure cookers?" Nita asked.

"You have a good eye for equipment, Dr. Lazar. Are you familiar with this vibrating platform and water-cooled grinding machine?"

Nita shook her head. She didn't want to spoil Dieter's self-satisfied revelations. "And what is this strange apparatus under the bench, Hans?"

"Oh that—just a suction machine on wheels."

"Dr. Landau uses one for his work on animals."

Dieter's eyes narrowed, but he said nothing.

Nita ran her hand over the other workbench filled with artificial teeth set on wax rims, bins filled with plaster and stone, boxes of wax in all colors, and more than three dozen instruments, all arrayed in order of size. She stopped at the last one, picked it up, and examined it. "Vee Hee carver?" she asked.

251

"You know about Vee Hee carvers?" Dieter seemed amused.

"Quite a bit," she continued to stroll around the room. The walls and ceiling were painted a high gloss white, and large fluorescent lights hung over each workbench. "It's refreshing to see such a bright room in New York," she pointed to the twenty-foot-high skylight over their heads.

She circled two additional six-foot long tables in the center of the room. One had a butcher-block top, and the other was generously covered with a blue plastic sheet. An elaborate gym setup occupied the far corner. She walked around a stationary bike, a Stairmaster, an inclined board, and a half dozen Nautilus machines with weights. The work area and entire room was scrubbed scrupulously clean. "You could open a professional health club," she said to Dieter's reflection in a large mirror.

Dieter smiled indulgently. "Can I get you something? A soda, or per-haps coffee?"

"Coffee would be nice. Milk, one sugar."

Dieter walked to a coffee urn on a worktable. With his back to Nita, he filled a cup while she inspected the Nautilus machines. He brought the cup to her and elaborated on his equipment as Nita sipped her coffee.

"You look like you're in good shape, Hans," she said. "Do you exercise often?"

"Every day. It helps me work out my aggressions."

"That's an intelligent way to do it." She placed her cup on a stack of weights. "I wanted to talk to you about Dr. Nagle."

"Yes, of course, but first I have something to attend to next door. I'll only be a moment. You are welcome to try out the equipment. I'll be right back."

Nita finished her coffee and tried the Stairmaster, but the control was set too high, and she didn't want to alter the setting. She decided to have another cup of coffee. She filled her cup and added milk, but couldn't find the sugar. She opened the cabinet above the urn, and found it filled with various model formers and rubber bowls.

The cabinet below contained five large glass jars that smelled of for-maldehyde. She picked one up and observed what appeared to be an umbilical indentation surrounded by white mottled skin. The second jar contained a pale human nipple, complete with a milky-white areola.

She gasped and dropped the bottle, as the full realization hit her. The bottle burst on the floor, spilling foul smelling formaldehyde over her slacks. She stood up quickly, but immediately felt the room start to spin. Fighting to keep her balance, she stumbled to the table covered with the blue plastic sheet. She grasped the edge to steady herself but slipped and pulled the sheet off, which exposed a gray slate slab with two channels running down the sides. It's like the table in Nagle's movie, she thought, as she slumped to the floor.

Steve drove the Harley like a man possessed. There was an accident on Canal Street, a bus had run into an eighteen wheeler and the traffic was backed up all the way to the Manhattan Bridge. Steve put on his flashing blue light, but after a few hair-raising turns he was blocked in. With no options, he jumped the curb to the sidewalk, and created havoc in his wake, as pedestrians dived out of his way. He narrowly missed colliding with the door of a cab, when an unwitting passenger swung it open in his path. Defying gravity, he remained seated by sheer perseverance, while taking corners at impossible angles.

Two cops drinking coffee in their cruiser almost spilled some on themselves as Steve roared by, but by the time they got ready to give chase, their quarry was long gone.

Steve fishtailed to a halt in front of 39 ½ Prince Street, jumped off the smoking Harley, and streaked full speed to the front metal door. He located Dieter's name on the entrance register and frantically rang the doorbell. No answer.

Desperate, he searched for passage to a staircase, but could find none. "Nita!" he screamed and pounded on the elevator door in frustration. Passersby gave the wild-eyed man a wide berth.

He knew Lonnie and Gagliardi would be held up by the accident, so he ran next door to number 39 and found a stairway. He bounded up six flights, two steps at a time, only to find the roof door locked. Bent over, gasping for air, he looked around with dilated eyes for something to break the lock. He remembered the pistol Lonnie gave him and impatiently jerked it out of the ankle holster. He swung the butt against the lock, but the hasp remained stubbornly closed.

"Fuck this." He slipped the safety off, took careful aim, and pulled the trigger. The shot echoed like an explosion in the small space, and still reverberated in his ears as he body slammed the door open and ran across the roof to the edge. He stopped to catch his breath, and looked around frantically, until his eyes rested on the skylight on the next roof.

He swung over the ledge, dropped five feet, and rolled to a stop. His ears were still ringing while he stealthily crawled to the skylight. Cautiously, he got on his knees, and peered down to see a huge empty room, with one end filled with gym equipment and another with steel tables. A chimney pipe obscured his vision of the central section, so he worked his way around the skylight, looked down again and, gasped. Nita was tied down by straps across her chest and arms to an autopsy-like slate table in the middle of the room. She wore only her bikini panties and bra. Her slacks and blouse were lying in a heap at the end of the table. Her eyes were closed.

"Nita," he screamed and waved his arms frantically trying to get her attention. A terrible thought jolted him. He stopped abruptly and bent close to the skylight to see if she was breathing. He heaved a sigh of relief when he saw the rise and fall of her chest.

His attention was diverted to the far end of the room when a heavily muscled man with fevered eyes burst in. The fluorescent lighting reflected off the top of his completely bald head and he was naked. He stood stock still for a moment, staring hard at Nita, and then walked purposefully toward her prone body, fondling his very erect penis. Steve shouted his rage. The bald man could not hear him. He stood over Nita, breathing hard, and gloating. He threw his head back, and then savagely clawed at her panties. Panting with lust, he bared his teeth. It was the look of a madman, a psychotic killer, worse than anything Steve had ever seen or could imagine.

Fear gripped Steve's heart like a vise when he saw the glint of stainless steel. He fought to think and not panic. He had to do something to save Nita—he couldn't stay paralyzed on the roof. He gripped the pistol barrel and smashed the hand grip against the skylight with all his strength. The glass, reinforced by chicken wire, shattered and thundered down in shards behind the startled bald man. Steve couldn't risk a shot, Dieter was stand-

254

ing too close to Nita. He put his breathing on hold, picked a spot between Nita and Dieter and leaped through the opening and watched wide-eyed as the floor rushed up from twenty feet to meet him.

Dieter stared at him with blank astonishment as Steve landed on one of the larger pieces of skylight. He crashed to the floor as it slid out from under him. The crack of his fractured ankle sounded a split second before the searing pain shot up to his brain. The pistol clattered out of reach across the floor behind him. He pulled himself to his knees and rolled toward the gun, but before he could reach it, Dieter, whose features had transformed from shock to animal rage bolted with sickening speed to outflank Steve and grab the revolver.

Roaring in agony, Steve forced himself up and punched Dieter in the jaw with all the strength he could muster. The Dracula teeth flew out of Dieter's mouth and clattered away with the light reflecting off the stainless steel, while Dieter slid through the broken glass along the polished floor past the table where Nita was tied down. A new spasm of pain shot up Steve's arm to his shoulder.

Dieter rose, brushed the shards of broken glass off the cuts in his back, and circled around Steve, to the other end of the table, toward the gun. In his determination to reach the pistol, Dieter failed to notice Nita's eyes slit open. In a drugged stupor, she became aware that her legs were free, even if her chest and arms were not. Her mind still reeling, she called on her training and muscle memory to unleash a karate kick straight at Dieter's groin. His face registered the shock and pain, before he doubled over and bounced back four or five steps and screamed, "Bitch!" before he crumpled in a heap.

Dozens of prickling shards of glass dug into his arms and back as he rolled over.

Steve, hampered by his injured leg, dragged himself over the broken glass toward the revolver. With grim determination he wrapped his hand over the edge of a counter, and lifted himself to an unsteady stance, and then began a chaotic hopping run to the gun, five yards away.

Dieter hissing in agony forced himself up and lunged in a low tackle to fling his body against Steve that knocked both of them halfway across the floor. A lightning stab of white pain bolted up Steve's leg when his ankle struck the floor. Grunting, they rolled over and over, blood spurting from their glass cuts while they desperately sought an opening in the other's defense. Each man feinted left and right in an attempt to land a blow or gouge his opponent's eyes.

Steve finally freed his right arm and rammed his fist into Dieter's throat, and when his head jerked forward, Steve elbowed him across the bridge of his nose. Steve heard the satisfying crunch of cartilage. He grabbed the leg of a counter with both arms for leverage, raised his body, and kneed Dieter in the groin with his good leg.

Dieter blanched in agony at this second assault on his privates and doubled up moaning. He opened his eyes to see Steve reach for the gun. Panicked, Dieter struggled to his feet again and, in a desperate lunge, bolted for the door. Steve fired two hasty shots, which only hit the molding over the door. Splinters rained down on Dieter's head as he stumbled out, clutching his injury.

Once Dieter disappeared Steve dropped the gun, and turned his attention to Nita, who had lifted her head and smiled at him for a second before collapsing again. Steve crawled over to the table, raised himself on his good leg, and began to unbuckle the straps that held Nita a prisoner on the table.

In the next room, Dieter grabbed a towel, his fatigues and sneakers and staggered to the elevator, still cradling his bruised testicles. He unlocked the door, pressed the lever down, and cursed the lumbering car as it made a snail-like passage down to the street level. He wiped off as much blood as he could from his back and arms before he slipped into the jacket, zippered up his pants and tied his shoelaces. He lurched out onto the sidewalk without closing the doors. At the same moment, Lonnie and Gagliardi's Buick careened around the corner, tires shrieking as loud as their siren. Gagliardi jumped out with the agility of a rookie cop before Lonnie fully stopped the car. The car was still rocking on its suspension when Gagliardi shouted at Lonnie and pointed at the fleeing Dieter.

Lonnie caught sight of Dieter just before he ducked into a narrow cobble stoned alley that connected to Spring Street. Lonnie took off after him like a thoroughbred out of the starting gate, while Gagliardi scrambled into the open elevator.

The memory of one of his mother's brutal customers chasing Dieter through the ruins of his ravaged city flashed through his consciousness and spurred him on.

Dieter had made provisions for just such an emergency he just didn't think he would be implementing it so soon. He had taken advantage of a local bank anxious for credit card business, and obtained one under an alias. He had also bartered a full set of dentures for a counterfeit passport with a neighborhood printer; and he owned, under his alias, a small fully stocked cabin in Central Vermont where he could lay low until things quieted down. All of his documents plus twenty thousand dollars was secreted in the trunk of his car. All he had to do was get to his wheels, and he would be free.

Desperation drove Dieter down the alleyway and he never turned to see if he was followed, until he reached the end. Then he heard footsteps behind him, and glanced over his shoulder to see the huge black giant, only forty yards behind with his eyes focused onto Dieter. The lab tech called on his reserves, turned left and sprinted down Spring Street toward his garage, and freedom.

Lonnie tore out of the alley shortly afterwards, but slammed into a group of Japanese tourists. By the time he worked free from the bowing, disheveled crowd, Dieter had picked up an extra ten yards. In the confusion, Dieter realized he couldn't get enough of a lead on the black pursuer, and charged into a Rite Aid on the next corner, and then scrambled down the steps to the lower level.

After Lonnie disentangled himself from the tourists, he scanned Spring Street, but he couldn't see Dieter. His eyes zeroed in on a faint trail of blood at the entrance of the Rite Aid. He stepped back and spotted a sign on the edge of the store that read, 'Deliveries.' He had both exits of the store covered, so he backed across the street, yanked out his cell phone and called in for back-up.

Dieter waited until his breathing returned to normal while reevaluating his choices. He spotted a young male employee surrounded by the odor of nicotine burst through a pair of swinging doors, marked "Employee, only.'

Dieter waited until the boy disappeared into a nearby aisle, and then crashed through the swinging doors and found himself in a store room with a metal door at the other end. .He hustled over and tried it, but it was locked, he turned the handle below the knob, and the door began to open, just as the smoker returned to the store room, and yelled. "You aren't allowed in here."

"Where does this lead to?" Dieter yelled.

"It's just a passageway to the street, but you can't..."

Dieter gave him the finger, before he burst through to the passageway and ran to the street exit. He looked to the right and left, and saw the way was clear and took off toward the garage.

Lonnie spotted him immediately, and ducked behind a parked car. He waited until Dieter began to run down Spring Street. Then Lonnie broke into his famous hundred-yard sprint and quickly closed the gap. He knew he had his man just as he used to draw a bead on a NFL quarterback before he sacked him. If the crème de la crème of professional players. couldn't avoid him, Dieter didn't stand a chance. He could hear Dieter's labored breathing before he launched into a flying tackle that was fondly remembered by thousands of Giants fans. Dieter never knew what hit him. When he came to, he was only hazily aware of the giant black man cuffing his hands behind him.

He offered absolutely no resistance.

Epilogue

Five patrol cars with flashing lights were parked in front of the lab on Prince Street when Lonnie emerged from the alleyway dragging a dazed Hans Dieter. Lonnie handed the suspect over to one of the beat cops. "Book him. I'll get in later to do the paperwork. Make him as uncomfortable as possible."

A city ambulance, siren blaring, pulled up as the elevator doors opened. Gagliardi emerged carrying Nita over one shoulder and supporting Steve with his other arm.

Lonnie gently lifted Nita off the exhausted lieutenant's shoulder and carried her easily to an ambulance gurney. The paramedics checked Nita's vital signs, flashed an okay sign and eased her into the ambulance. They placed a temporary splint on Steve's ankle, helped him inside and made him comfortable on the other gurney. They attempted to pull out without Lonnie, but the look on his face convinced them that would be a mistake. He climbed into the rig, and the attendant slammed the doors shut. The driver turned on the siren and lights and burned rubber pulling out.

Lonnie sat between his two friends and said, "Steve, did I tell you the one about—"

"Are you kidding? I don't think we're—"

259

"About the stripper with the tooth in her navel and the dentist?"

Steve looked over at Nita, who smiled wanly.

"All right, go ahead."

"No, you're right. Maybe next time."

About the Author

Dr. Stanley Woods-Frankel is a member of the American Society of Forensic Odontology. He has worked closely with the New York Police Department, written articles for professional publications, testified as an expert witness, lectured extensively, and appeared on radio and TV.

Stanley completed the masters writing program at New York University, is a member of the Mystery Writers of America, and participates in a bi-monthly writer's group. He lives in New York City with his wife, Elayna.

Credits

This book is a work of art
produced by Zharmae, an imprint of
The Zharmae Publishing Press.

Concept Editor
ANNA MCDERMOTT

Cover Designer
SHERWIN SOY

Typesetter
SHAUGHNESSEY MARSHALL

Readers
SUZANNE GRUNDY & LEIGH FARINA

Publisher
TRAVIS ROBERT GRUNDY

TZPP
The Zharmae
Publishing Press

SPOKANE | MARCH 2012